BOOK TWO

Love Sick

International Bestselling Author

MONICA JAMES

Cover Model: Darcie Hamilton
Photographer: Michelle Lancaster
Editing: My Brother's Editor
Formatting: E.M. Tippetts Book Designs

Follow me on:

authormonicajames.com

Other Books By
MONICA JAMES

THE I SURRENDER SERIES
I Surrender
Surrender to Me
Surrendered
White

SOMETHING LIKE NORMAL SERIES
Something like Normal
Something like Redemption
Something like Love

A HARD LOVE ROMANCE
Dirty Dix
Wicked Dix
The Hunt

MEMORIES FROM YESTERDAY DUET
Forgetting You, Forgetting Me
Forgetting You, Remembering Me

SINS OF THE HEART DUET
Absinthe of the Heart
Defiance of the Heart

Author's Note

LOVE SICK is a **DARK ROMANCE** containing mature themes that might make some readers uncomfortable. It contains violence, attempted suicide, death, drug use, medical procedures, psychological treatments, misuse of a corpse, blood gore, and some dark and disturbing scenes. In no way, shape, or form is the author glorifying any of the situations or circumstances in this book.

There is no cruelty to animals.

You've been warned…

Dutch

Welcome to my hell.

"Here comes the airplane. Open up."

I once thought Alanna to be kind, caring. But as I look at her now, all I can envision is ramming that silver spoon she holds into the side of her throat.

My lips are pulled into a tight line because I would rather starve to death than eat her fucking pureed apple.

"Dutch, stop this. You need your strength. You're injured."

"Yeah, I'm injured because you broke my leg with a fucking hammer!" I retort, turning my cheek so she gets the memo that I am not going to be spoon-fed—now or ever.

Alanna sighs, but I'm not sure what she was expecting.

"You've already got the perfect patient over there." I gesture to good ole dead Jonathan with my chin. "He won't object to anything because he's, you know…dead."

Alanna knows who my Achilles' heel is. So it's only fair that I know hers.

She pulls back her shoulders and drops the spoon into the baby dish she holds. It's got blue bunny rabbits running laps around the lip.

"A gift for your nonexistent children? Makes sense you use it, I guess. Seems a waste otherwise."

Tears begin to well in her eyes, but she can blow me. I don't feel sorry for her. She chose the wrong person to fuck over because the moment I'm strong enough, I'm getting out of here. But not before burning this place to the ground.

"I should have let you die," she says, coming to an abrupt stand.

"Yeah, you should have," I counter, content she's pissed off. "Because there is no fucking way I'm helping you, and you want to know why? Because it's insane. You are insane! And I swear to God, the moment I'm free, you'll pay for what you've done."

Alanna's lower lip trembles. "I just wanted my happily ever after. Why is that so bad? Why does everyone else get to be happy but me?"

"Oh, grow the fuck up," I spit, not interested in her sob story. "Do you see me skipping off into the sunset, picking daisies? No. No one gets what they want. Did Misha?"

Alanna's tears stop when I mention the man whose heart gives me life—literally.

"Did Luna?"

Just saying her name makes my heart ache because it aches for the both of us. Me and Misha—her son.

This story doesn't need a rotting corpse or crazed scientist to add drama because it's a horror story within itself. This is the stuff you read about in Gothic horror books, it's not real life. But here I am, living this fucking nightmare.

I knew Luna was someone special the moment I laid eyes on her. It felt like I knew her, and that's because I did. Misha's heart is what drew us together. His heart gave me his memories and showed me who Luna was.

The odds of this happening are slim to none. Alanna said it's called heart memory transfer, and it's happened before. That it's not uncommon for the recipient of the donor heart to fall in love with the donor's family.

But what I feel for Luna, those feelings are mine alone; Misha's heart has nothing to do with it. Even without his heart, I would love Luna, and I do. I fucking love her with every beat of this heart. And I never got the chance to tell her that.

All because Alanna is hell-bent on using me as some science project to revive her very dead fiancé.

"I would rather cut out this heart than give you what you want."

In all honesty, I still can't wrap my head around what Alanna wants to do. It's that messed up. She believes she can give Jonathan Misha's heart and give me my old heart back, which she kept, just in case.

What I don't understand is why she didn't just do the damn transplant on Jonathan in the first place. Why did she go to the effort of giving me Misha's heart if she always intended it for Jonathan?

"I wish you wouldn't fight me," she says with a sigh, removing her glasses and massaging the bridge of her nose.

"Yeah, well, I want a unicorn, but I don't see that happening."

"Don't you see? We would be creating history. If this is a

3

success—"

"Alanna!" I cry, angered and confused she's still convinced this will work. "This will not be a success. I can guarantee it. All that you'll be creating is a huge fucking mess for yourself because you'll have two corpses to deal with."

"Why do you speak to me with such cruelty?"

I blink once, my mouth agape. "Are you serious? I'm your prisoner. I'm tied to a fucking bed in God knows where and the only person I ever gave a fuck about thinks I'm dead! How do you expect me to behave?"

The mere mention of Luna has my heart skipping a beat. I wonder why Misha has been so quiet. Once upon a time, the asshole couldn't shut up. Now it feels like he's taken a vow of silence. I know the reason is because he misses her as much as I do.

Luna was the tie that connected us, and now that she's gone, so is he. I've never felt more alone than I do right now.

To hear Misha, his heart had to be in danger, but something suddenly occurs to me. I thought it was his heart he cared about, but I'm beginning to suspect it was when my safety was in jeopardy that he spoke to me because he could see what Luna and I shared.

He loved Luna so much—I can feel how much with every beat of this heart. So it's no surprise he isn't speaking. He lost her too.

We'll find her. I promise.

This is what I think, hoping Misha can hear me. I got used to the annoying asshole.

"You will see reason soon enough," Alanna says like it's a premonition. I don't like it.

She exits the room, leaving me alone with Jonathan—the corpse.

His bandages are off. The macabre scene is too horrible to believe, but here I am, staring into the yellowed, decayed face of Alanna's true love. He's the key to all this. If his well-being was in danger, then I'm certain I could get Alanna to do anything.

I need to be creative, however, because I'll only have one shot at it.

Alanna may be crazy, but she isn't stupid. I have to be smart. But how, when I'm tied to this bed?

"Stay away from me! I don't know who you are! Your name is Jonathan?"

Luna's voice crashes into me, and it's a flood of emotion. Happiness. Sadness. But at the forefront is love. I miss her so much every part of me aches. I need to get out of here and find her.

I quash down the nostalgia and focus instead on why that particular sentence played over in my mind. Instead of Misha, do I now hear Luna? Doesn't seem so peculiar considering the shitshow I find myself in.

Luna asked if that was my name, meaning she must have heard Alanna call me that. So…

Alanna must have thought I was Jonathan at one time or another, which means the line between reality and fiction blurs. I need to catch her when it does and hopefully trick her somehow long enough to free myself.

My stomach drops at the thought, but I'm prepared to do anything.

Alanna returns with a large white ceramic bowl. The steam rising from it reveals it's time for a sponge bath. The pungent

5

stench of lavender fills the room, a smell which I will forever associate with death.

"It's time for your bath," Alanna says to me, but her pursed lips give away the fact that she'd rather me smell as bad as Jonathan. "Not that you deserve any kindness."

It's on the tip of my tongue to tell her to go fuck herself, but I remember Luna's words.

"You're right. Sorry. I was out of line."

Her surprise is clear, but I don't overdo it. I don't want her to grow suspicious.

She clears her throat and places the bowl on the bedside table. "Apology accepted."

She doesn't meet my eyes as she reaches behind my neck and unties the string of my hospital gown. My long hair is tied back, but Alanna brushes a stray strand behind my ear. There's tenderness to her touch.

"I'm going to unfasten one hand so I can get your gown off," she says. "Please don't make me regret that decision."

This is the first step toward gaining her trust, so I nod.

She unfastens the leather strap around my wrist with a small key, prepared for me to fight. But I simply stretch out my fingers. Truth be told, it does feel good to be freed.

Alanna wets her lips and slowly removes my gown. As one of my wrists is still tied, she maneuvers the gown so it gathers by my hand. I'm naked underneath the sheet which rests just below my navel. Alanna inhales sharply as her eyes descend my chest.

She reaches out and toys with the crucifix around my throat. The gesture is personal—too personal. "I didn't take you for the religious type."

"Why not?"

"I guess you seem more like the practical type," she settles for after mulling over my question. "You were hardly accepting of when I told you about the heart memory transfer theory. You looked at me like I had lost my mind."

Been there, done that, but I simply nod, remembering the greater good.

She releases the crucifix and reaches for the sponge in the bowl. The smell of lavender has me almost gagging as she wrings it out. She commences washing my chest. The warm water feels good against my skin.

We're quiet, the only thing filling the small space between us is her breathing which seems to heighten with each touch.

"She likes you."

Luna's voice is like a salve to a burn, and I can't help but soften and harden at the same time. Alanna, however, believes the reaction is because of her. Is that what Luna wanted?

"Tell me about Jonathan."

Alanna pauses. "What do you mean?"

"Tell me how you met."

Alanna's eyes narrow, as if attempting to decode whether there is some ulterior motive to my request. But in the end, her need to talk about her dead fiancé prevails.

"We met when I was in college," she says in a faraway voice. "He was playing at a recital. La Campanella. I fell in love the first moment I saw him. The moment we met, I knew I was going to marry him. Over the years, our love was tested. But no one was going to ruin what Jonathan and I shared."

A slanted grin plays on her lips and the image has me wondering what lengths Alanna went to, to ensure no one ruined her happily ever after.

"Jonathan's dream was playing music. He worked odd jobs, but his life was music. I wanted to do everything I could to support him, which is why I got into medicine. I had the brains and the stomach for it. I worked so hard for our future."

Being an artist isn't easy. I know firsthand how tough it can be. Making a career out of your passion almost always means you're struggling to pay the bills. Or skipping meals so you can make ends meet. I was one of the fortunate ones because Juilliard changed my life.

I was sought out to play at many events—weddings, funerals, and everything in between. Word spread about my playing, and I was making more than enough to live comfortably. But for me, being able to play music was the greatest reward of all, which is why not being able to play has been a death sentence for me.

"And Jonathan was okay with that?"

Alanna's lips instantly turn downward. "Why wouldn't he be?"

Most men are proud, alpha dickheads, that's why, and they want to be the main breadwinner in the family. Alanna's social standing and the money she makes might have made him feel less of a "man." And when that happens, some men have to prove their masculinity in another woman's arms.

I don't get it and it's as fucking stupid as it sounds, but it happens. I suddenly wonder how Jonathan died.

"You're a strong, independent woman," I casually reply. "Most men would be intimidated by someone as beautiful and smart as you."

"You think I'm beautiful?"

"Yes, I do." That may be the truth, but that doesn't mean I

intend to go easy on her when I get the fuck out of here.

She clears her throat before dipping the sponge into the water to continue bathing me. She lifts my arm and washes me thoroughly. When she descends to my ribs, I notice her fingers trembling. I hate what I have to do.

"I can't clean myself. I need you to do it for it me." I leave out the fact that I can't clean myself because I'm her prisoner. My hopes are if she feels needed, she'll eventually lower her guard and trust me.

She appears apprehensive.

"Please," I add, needing this to work.

She looks over her shoulder at Jonathan, and I wonder why. But she eventually concedes. She repositions the sheet so it covers just enough, but all I would have to do is shift slightly and she'd see it all.

She commences cleaning down my chest and works her way to my stomach. I don't work out, but thanks to running, I am lean yet muscled. Alanna's gaze lingers on my body for far too long.

"Do it." Luna's voice permits me to commit what feels like a betrayal because I soon understand why Alanna looked over her shoulder—she doesn't want Jonathan to see that she's attracted to me.

A horrible thought suddenly turns my stomach.

The way Alanna dotes on the very-dead-as-a-doornail-Jonathan as if he were alive, I wonder if she does all the things they would do if he were alive. This entire thing just gets more fucked up by the second.

"Don't be shy, Alanna. You've seen it all."

She bites her bottom lip, clearly grappling with her morals.

But in the end, the need for warm human skin wins out. She shifts the sheet, and when I'm exposed, her eyes widen. She likes what she sees.

At first, my sponge bath is purely professional, but professional isn't going to get me the fuck out of here.

"Do I make you nervous?"

Alanna shakes her head, but she's full of shit.

"I think you're lying," I counter smoothly. "How long has it been since you've been fucked, Alanna?"

The sponge drops into my lap, and a gasp escapes her. "I don't feel comfortable discussing that with you."

"I think we passed the line of comfortable a few chapters ago. Tell me."

When she reaches for the sponge, I quash down the urge to grip her throat and not let go, but grasp her wrist instead. Panic overcomes her as she tries to break free, but I make my intentions clear when I place her hand over my dick.

"I think it's been a very long time." I relax my grip but don't let her go. "A shame that. A beautiful woman like you has needs, needs which should be met."

"Dutch, no—" But her plea is weak.

Forgive me, Luna…

With eyes locked, I encourage Alanna to wrap her fingers around my shaft. My hand is still on hers. I don't move, however. If she wanted to break free, she could, but that's not what she wants. She makes clear what she wants when she begins to slowly pump my cock.

The fact that I hate Alanna more than I've ever hated anyone before leaves me with a limp dick, and no matter what she does, I would never be aroused by her. I'd rather cut off my dick and eat it. So I have to pretend she's someone else, someone who gets me hard just by hearing her name.

I can't close my eyes as Alanna will know I am visualizing someone other than her. To play music, I didn't just feel the music, I saw it. It's hard to explain, but I became an almost extension of the music. I was the notes. I was the melody. I was in everything I played.

So I decide to do the same with Alanna.

I focus on her face. The way her blonde hair flutters against her long neck as it catches the breeze from the fan. Her lips are a glossy pink. I see the hint of red beneath her fitted white shirt from the bra she wears.

I see Alanna and feel her touch in a way that feels good because I then think about Luna's hands and mouth on me. How she always fit perfectly in my life and in my arms.

I remember the first time I was lost inside of her. Jesus, she felt like heaven. I would happily die a thousand deaths just to feel that again. The stench of lavender is soon replaced with keynotes of vanilla and strawberries—Luna's unique fragrance.

And it's also the way she tastes when we kiss and when I'm buried between her legs. The noises she made when she exploded on my tongue punch me in the guts, and I begin moving my hips because my cock is rock hard.

Loving Luna isn't voluntary. It's ingrained in me. In this lifetime, you're lucky if you meet one human being you connect with so deeply that without that person, you can barely breathe, but I met her, and I will never let her go.

I will do anything I must to find her, and if that means fucking the antichrist, then send my soul to hell because I will do anything for the woman I love.

"Oh my god," Alanna whimpers, her strokes gaining speed and confidence. "You're so hard."

Her comment cements what I know to be true—I'm hard in comparison to the corpse she's fucking.

But that horror is quickly replaced with Luna's beautiful smile, her melodious laugh. Alanna's face flickers in and out of picture, like an old TV finding a station, and with that comes the white noise.

It resonates loudly, so loudly that the repetitive pattern transforms into music…

I hear it.

I feel it.

I am one again.

I see Luna.

I feel her.

She is in every breath I take.

She is in every beat of my heart because it's her heart too. It's made up of her blood, her body. It's because of her that I am alive. What we share stems so deep, deep enough that our connection is sealed with a bloodied kiss.

I see Luna, and I hear music…it's all around me.

I am home.

"No, no…I can't! I'm sorry."

And just like that, the needle drags across the record and the music is replaced with reality.

Alanna leaps off the bed, wiping her hands on her skirt in disgust. If I cared, I would be offended she appears to want to erase me away. But she can't. Her flustered cheeks and shortness of breath reveals her true feelings.

"I'm sorry, Jonathan. Forgive me." She begins pacing the

room, wringing her hands in front of her. "It didn't mean anything. He didn't even come."

I settle back against the pillows with a smirk. I shouldn't take great pleasure in seeing her upset, but call me a bastard because I do.

"No, of course not," she says, talking to Jonathan. "I don't love him more than you."

Jesus fucking Christ, this would be comical if I wasn't tied to a bed.

"Don't say that!" she cries, storming for his bed and dropping to her knees, hands interlaced. "I love you. I am doing all of this for you."

I look at Jonathan and wonder what he would say if he could talk. Maybe let me rot in peace?

"You want me to prove it? Okay, fine, I will."

She springs up and violently opens the drawer of the metal bedside table. She frantically hunts through it and when she grabs the container of Vaseline, I'm glad I declined eating because I would throw it up any second now.

It's like a car crash—I should look away, but I can't, and that's because there is no way Alanna is going to do what I think she's going to do.

She shimmies her red underwear down her legs before pulling up the hem of her dress. She yanks the sheet off Jonathan, and my mouth actually drops open when I see his wrinkled dick is erect. I don't want to know what's inside of it to keep it that way because it's just fucking...gross.

She scoops a blob of Vaseline on two fingers and begins rubbing it onto his shriveled cock.

I dry retch because no, just fucking no...

13

When it's shinier than Rudolph's nose, she climbs onto the bed and hikes up her dress, exposing her ass, before sliding down onto his dead dick.

A moan leaves her before she begins to move.

I suddenly wish I was dead because I can never unsee Alanna fucking a corpse.

"I love you. No one but you," she says between moans.

At this point, Jonathan would probably be more verbal than me because I am speechless.

She continues riding him wildly, unbothered that she's the one doing all the work. I suppose she's used to it.

A small pang of sadness swells inside my heart because I feel sorry for Alanna. She is sick and needs help, which is ironic, considering she was the one I once looked to for answers. But this proves that she is unstable and very dangerous.

I need to tread with caution because she is far worse than I thought.

She suddenly lifts her hips and just when I think the horror show is over, she turns around to face me and slowly sits back down onto Jonathan's dick. She begins riding him reverse cowgirl, eyes locked with mine.

I don't know where to look. I want to look away, but that would show weakness. So, I watch Alanna fuck her corpse fiancé, wondering where we go from here.

She lifts her hips, exposing her pussy to me, before slamming back down onto Jonathan's dick. Her movements become faster and frantic, and I wonder if she's turned on by me watching. She cups her breasts through her shirt and arches backward.

Is she trying to prove a point? That she's stellar in the sack? The fact that she's a necrophiliac is not sexy…in any way, shape, or form.

She continues riding Jonathan until she shudders and comes with a sated moan. The entire time, her eyes never leave mine.

When she's done, she slowly climbs off Jonathan and rearranges her clothes like nothing just happened. She places the sheet over him while I wish I could wash my eyeballs out with bleach.

"You will never do that again," she warns me. "I love Jonathan."

Her saying this is more for herself than it is for me.

I know what I have to do.

My competition is stiff, and I mean that in every literal sense there is.

It won't take long to break Alanna down, and when I do, she'll regret ever saving me because doesn't she know...I'm beyond saving.

Dutch

Since being here, I've slept with one eye open, so to speak, which makes me tired as fuck, but I can't let my guard down. So I feel Alanna before I hear her.

Gathering my wits, I open my eyes slowly, unsure what to expect because after yesterday, nothing shocks me anymore.

"Good morning," Alanna says, changing my IV bag.

She's in her doctor's coat, so I wonder what's going on.

"Have you heard his voice since being here?" she asks, purposely refusing to use Misha's name.

"Whose?"

She pauses from attaching the tube to the bag, lips pursed. "Don't act coy. You know who."

It takes all my willpower not to reply with a smart-ass response because that isn't going to do me any favors. "Why do you ask?"

"Because I need to know everything before the surgery. I need to know what Misha says to you." She reaches into her pocket and when she produces a vial and syringe, I know this can't be good.

"What's that?" I crane my neck to watch her load the syringe with the clear fluid before injecting it into my IV.

I try to struggle, but I'm helpless, and the drugs...they're quick.

"I need to know what's ahead for Jonathan," she explains calmly while my heart begins to slow down and race at the same time. "If he's going to experience what you do, then I want to make sure I understand it so I can help him through it."

"Alanna!" I say, but it's slurred. "This is...fuck."

The world begins to spin, and I surrender to the madness because it's peaceful. And then...it's not.

"Run!"

I'm no longer in bed but rather on a football field. Peering down at the football in my hands, I see that they're not my hands. They're Misha's.

This skin isn't mine. But the memories are, so I do what I was born to do—I run.

No one can stop me as I dodge my opponents and when I score a touchdown with ease, my teammates holler loudly in excitement because I won them the game. They throw me onto their shoulders—I'm the hometown hero.

I look into the cheering crowd and see Luna who claps happily. She's always been so proud. Standing next to her is Joy. My happiness is soon replaced with shame. Joy is Luna's best friend and I've been fucking her since I was sixteen years old.

Vomit rises, and I don't know whose it is—mine or Misha's.

But I sink deeper into this memory, hoping it reveals the answers I'll need to help Luna.

"Baby, I'm so proud of you!" says a pretty girl I don't recognize.

"Her name is Trista."

And just like that, in this drug-induced state, I hear Misha again.

"Welcome back, motherfucker."

Misha chuckles in response.

I can feel Joy watching Misha closely. I now know that Joy was the one who ran him off the road that night, but he still doesn't know why.

He wished he never did what he did with her. But she promised she would tell him who his father was.

Misha had asked Luna many times, but she said it was better he didn't know. He didn't understand what that meant, but as Misha got older, the voices he heard got louder.

He didn't tell Luna because he didn't want to worry her. But he was also ashamed. She thought he was perfect, and he couldn't break her heart by telling her the truth. So Misha got into drugs as self-medication to help block out the voices. He then realized he had an addictive personality which led to harder drugs, which then led to dealing to feed his habit.

Football coaches turned a blind eye to his abuse because he was a fucking god on the field.

Joy groomed Misha for a reason. She has the answers I need.

I don't know why she lied to me. I'm ashamed I believed her. But she and Alanna are in cahoots for a reason. Alanna confirmed what Joy told me when I confronted her.

She was living in Luna's house, for fuck's sake. And Alanna had the paperwork to corroborate the lies Joy spewed.

"You know her better than anyone, Misha. Why is Joy doing this?"

He lifts his shoulders in response, as frustrated as me.

The victims here are Luna and Misha. They trusted the wrong person. I don't understand why Joy would do that to Luna. What does she have to gain?

Just as I feel myself losing grip on this reality, I'm sucked back in. No doubt, Alanna has pumped more drugs into my IV. But the drugs are nothing compared to the line of cocaine I just snorted off Joy's chest.

"That's right, baby boy, it's just us," she says to Misha, shoving him onto his back as she climbs onto his lap. "Tell me you want me."

Misha doesn't have a chance to reply before she's riding his cock wildly.

Those feelings of disgust and shame swarm in my belly, but Misha wants me to see it all.

"You look just like him. Handsome, just like him." Joy is giving Misha what he wants, but she's also showing him who's in charge. "She is cruel not to tell you who he is."

I want to vomit. This is beyond repulsive.

"It can be like this always. But I'm about to lose everything. That bastard took everything in the divorce. There's a way we can be together. But—"

But what?

Why does that "but" have to do with Luna?

"Why is she doing this?"

Misha shakes his head. He has an idea why, however.

"Tell me!"

The drugs make talking to Misha easier because they allow me to straddle the line between his world and mine.

"This is my fault."

"Well, stop being a pussy and make it right. Tell me what you know! Why did she kill you?"

Misha looks up at Joy as she fucks him into next week. Her obsession with him is unhealthy. There's a reason she preyed on him so young.

"I don't think it was me she wanted dead. It was…Mom. I was driving Mom's car. I think Joy thought it was my mom."

Time stands still as Misha's revelation winds me.

I can feel his uncertainty, but I believe him.

The love Joy felt for Misha was strong. Even though he tried to end it because he was seeing Trista, she wouldn't hurt him. But she would Luna. She hurt Luna the moment she fucked her underage son.

But why? What does she stand to gain by Luna's death?

Tears leak from Misha's eyes as he wraps the belt around his upper arm, syringe between his teeth. As he finds a vein, he injects heroin into his body, wishing he could stop, but it feels too good. It helps numb the pain.

He falls back onto the dirty floor, syringe still embedded in his vein as his pupils dilate and our heartbeat slows.

"Everything," he whispers, eyes slipping shut as the sound of absolute nothingness drags him under.

Everything? What the hell is that supposed to mean?

No, motherfucker, no!

Wake up!

But soon, I too am dragged back into reality as my eyes are

pried open and a bright light is shone into them.

"Welcome back," Alanna says with a smile on her demonic face.

When I focus, she turns off the penlight and places it into her pocket. "That was so fascinating to watch."

"I'm glad you take pleasure in my pain," I spit, eyeing her something wicked.

"What did you see? He spoke to you, didn't he?"

There's no point in being evasive. She's going to poke and prod until I give her the answers she seeks.

"Yes. It was the first time since being here. What drugs did you give me?"

"Just some very mild, mind-altering medication. The effects will wear off very quickly."

And just like that, I have an idea.

"It's not long enough. What can you give me for it to last longer?"

She mulls over my question, not at all suspicious as she thinks aloud, listing the drugs…drugs which will come in handy when I get the fuck out of here. I keep a mental note of the names.

"I'm so pleased we're finally seeing eye to eye," she says happily. "And because of that, I've decided to reward you."

Now my interest is piqued.

She leaves the room, and I always wonder where she's going. I hear wheels turning against the floor, but know it's not a wheelchair. We're not there yet. But what she pushes into the room is second best.

"I know you'd appreciate listening to music this way."

And she's right.

21

This gramophone looks vintage. I like it. But the moment Mozart sounds, I forget about everything and surrender to the music. It's been so long; I've almost forgotten the impact music has on me. But it doesn't take long for my heart, and for my body, to remember.

Closing my eyes, I focus on the melody and am transported to another world where none of this madness is real. It's just me and the music.

Usually, I would progress so far before I hit a wall, and it's radio silence. But today is different. Today, I hear music—my own.

Even though my wrists are bound, my fingers move on invisible keys as I compose a song in my head. I can see it.

Hear it.

Feel it.

The music is my breath, animating me to be alive.

I wish I were sitting at my piano because I want, no, I need, to write. The notes resonate louder and louder until all I can hear is the music. This is the first time it's happened since I woke up from surgery. Yes, I've heard music and been able to write here and there, but this is the first time I hear it loud and clear, like how it once was.

Nothing else exists but the melody.

I'm dragged under and spat back out on the other side and where I sit, I have to rub my eyes to ensure I'm really seeing this.

I'm back home, my piano in front of me. The shine from it instantly gets me hard. I know I'm not really here, but this is my happy place, and for so long, the door has been slammed shut.

But here I am.

I wonder what happened for me to be able to experience it again. I assume it's the drugs Alanna gave me. But this isn't a hallucination. This is something different.

Just like always, the moment my fingers touch the keys, it's an adrenaline rush and I inhale sharply. I never want to leave this place. I run my pointer along them, almost salivating at the music I'm about to create.

My mind is a blank slate. It's peaceful. But then I see it…I see the music and I begin to play. Every single emotion I feel spills out of me and into the piano. It's a rainbow of notes.

I've missed this so much. I finally feel like me again.

I don't know how long I stay here for because when lost in this place of nothing but melody, it can feel like a second. But when I play the final note, I slump forward, hair shrouding me from a world I don't want to return to.

But I can't stay here.

This is a premonition of what's to come…

The fact that I can play again means I'm getting stronger; strong enough to find Luna. And she's the only reason I wade through the light, only to return to the darkness where the devil awaits.

"You're amazing," Alanna says in awe.

I've been told watching me play is a godly experience. I don't get it. But if it's going to get me the fuck out of here, then I am Jesus fucking Christ.

"It's all coming back? The music?" she clarifies.

I nod.

She writes something down in her notebook. A how-to on making a monster, perhaps?

"I knew it would. Your mind was clouded before. But here,

you have clarity. I need the music to return. It'll help Jonathan."

He is beyond saving, but I've given up on Alanna seeing reason on that.

"Today was progress, Dutch. If you continue this way, I'll bring in a piano. I think Jonathan would love that too." She claps once happily before walking over to her fiancé. "I told you we would be together forever. I never break my promises."

"What happened to him?"

Alanna's happiness soon turns sour. "Nothing happened. He's resting."

Yeah, resting forever...but again, my bad. I need to rein in the sarcasm because I know she'll read it all over my face. So, I decide to rephrase.

"What happened for him to be so...tired?"

Alanna watches me for any signs of deceit.

I simply smile sweetly in response.

"He worked so hard. He would bend over backward for anyone...even for people who didn't deserve it."

And there it is—jealousy. And from the bite to her tone, I dare say it was a woman.

This house of horrors sits on a throne of lies, lies which I need to uncover to get out of here.

"How old was...is he?"

"What does that matter?" she snaps, which means he was either a lot older or younger than her.

I can't gauge an age just by looking at Jonathan because he's a dried-out piece of jerky, so I will assume older than Alanna. Was he married? Was Alanna the "other woman?" It would explain why she is going above and beyond to prove her love for him.

The possibilities are endless.

"I just want to know him better, that's all. I already know he has good taste in music…and women." My pause is intentional and works like a charm when Alanna's cheeks turn crimson.

No wonder she hates Luna—she sees her as competition. But this is a race Alanna will never win.

A phone vibrates in her jacket pocket, interrupting the moment. She retrieves it, and when she peers down at the screen, her lips pull into a thin line. I dare say whoever the caller is, is not someone Alanna wishes to speak to.

"I told you I would call you," she snarls at the caller, not bothering with hellos. "What? No. Absolutely not."

Panic sets in, and I watch with interest as Alanna throws a sheet over Jonathan and quickly releases the bed brakes, and frantically wheels him out of the room, her white doctor's coat chasing her as she continues talking to whoever it is on the phone.

I crane my neck, hoping to catch a glimpse outside the door, but I can't see anything. Frustrated, I slump back down onto the pillows, cataloging over everything I've learned.

The undying love Alanna has for Jonathan is unhealthy, which has me guessing she did something when he was alive that she is trying to make amends for in death.

But what?

I suddenly hear voices—real ones this time.

"Where is he? I want to see him! You promised me you would take care of him! I've waited long enough!"

"No…" I hear Misha say loudly.

They are animated and the closer they get, I recognize one as Alanna and the other…no fucking way. No wonder I heard

Misha.

Joy bursts through the doorway with Alanna hot on her heels, but the moment Joy sees me, she stops dead in her tracks, eyes wide. She doesn't speak. She just looks at me in utter shock.

"Alanna, what is this?" she gasps, placing a wavering hand over her mouth. "I never agreed to this!"

Alanna is unmoved by Joy's hysterics. "I'm cleaning up your mess, Joy."

"My mess?" she snaps, spinning around to face Alanna. "We agreed that it was always going to end with Luna. He was never part of the deal."

"What did she ever do to you?" I question Joy, unable to keep the contempt from my voice.

Rage runs through me, and I know it's not just mine—but Misha's as well.

When I first met Joy, Misha didn't say a word. I could feel his disgust—I just didn't understand why. But now I do.

"She spoke about you with nothing but love and you thank her by throwing her ass into an asylum and betraying her. Oh, I forgot to add, and killing her son."

The color from Joy's face drains and she wavers on her feet. "It was supposed to be her!"

So Misha was right. Joy did think Luna was the one driving the car. The guilt she must feel for that oversight which killed her lover.

"Joy, enough," Alanna warns, shaking her head.

She knows I'm taking this all in and making sense of a fucked-up situation which she wishes me to remain in the dark about.

"Why?" I ask Joy, needing answers. I need to know why

she'd work with Alanna when she can see she is clearly insane.

"Don't you dare," Alanna cautions Joy, but it's apparent by the tears streaming down Joy's cheeks that she can no longer live with what she's done.

"I needed the m-money," she confesses, her lower lip trembling. "I was going to lose my house. I was going to lose everything. But Luna…she's always had it all. The perfect looks. The perfect life. She's worth a lot of money and if anything were to happen to her…then that money would be mine. She left everything to me…after Misha, that is. I didn't want him dead. You have to believe me! I wanted to share everything with him! I wanted to be with him. I loved him! Please, believe me!"

Misha's pain and betrayal lingers on my tongue—it tastes of bitter lemons.

Alanna sighs, annoyed by Joy's weakness, it seems.

"So all of this was for money? You destroyed your best friend because you're a greedy bitch?" I scream, suddenly thankful I'm restrained because I would have no qualms killing Joy with my bare hands.

But the plot…it thickens when she shakes her head slowly, her mouth downturned.

"The money wasn't for me…it was for him. So we could be one big happy family. He loved me!"

"Misha?" I ask, but that makes no sense. He was the one who would inherit it all if Luna died. Was Joy worried she wouldn't see a dime of it?

I don't understand.

Joy slumps into the seat and begins to sob. "For Jonathan."

I open but soon close my mouth because I have no idea what to say.

"He needed it."

"How do you know Alanna?" I ask, but I think I already know.

"She is his doctor. She said she can save his life with a new heart."

Oh my motherfucking...fuck!

Before I know what's happening, Joy blinks once, before a trickle of blood seeps down her forehead and into her eye, before slithering into her parted mouth. She looks like a fish starved for oxygen, and that's all thanks to Alanna hitting her in the head with a hammer.

Joy loses consciousness and slides onto the floor with Alanna standing above her, specks of Joy's blood coating her face.

"She talks too much," she simply says with a carefree shrug.

I watch in horror as she places the hammer onto the table, before gripping Joy by the ankles and dragging her from the room. She whistles a tune as she does so, leaving a trail of smudged blood on the white tiles.

I wouldn't believe it if I didn't see it with my own eyes. I still don't. But I heard Joy loud and clear. She knows Jonathan and there's no doubt it's the same Jonathan Alanna rode like a pony into next week.

I don't know what's going on because although I've been given answers, I am left with more questions.

Alanna returns, and when I see the syringe and bottle in her hand, I shrink back, shaking my head violently.

"What is she talking about?" I demand, needing Alanna to explain.

"She could never shut up," she says coolly as she approaches my bedside. "No wonder he hated her. He loved me, not her."

Alanna quickly bites her bottom lip, aware that she's shared too much.

"Jonathan was Joy's...husband? Lover?" I have pieces to a puzzle, but I don't know what the picture is.

"No more talking!" Alanna screams, her hands shaking as she loads up the syringe with whatever drug she's about to give me. "He loves me. He loves me. He loves me."

Alanna is stuck on repeat as she injects my IV with the needle.

With my last coherent thought, I piece together what I know—Jonathan was Alanna's patient; whether they were a "couple" remains to be seen.

Joy betrayed Luna because she needed money. So this was done out of greed. But that greed was done out of love for Jonathan.

And Jonathan is who?

Both of the women's lover? Husband? Fiancé?

I'm not sure how Jonathan died. Alanna said he loved her so much his heart stopped working. Now I have my suspicions that that's the case because she drove a fucking knife through it when she found him in bed with Joy.

Jesus Christ, this shitshow just gets worse.

Misha and Luna were just innocent victims caught up in the madness of two psychotic evil bitches. Although I know Misha wouldn't want it, I feel sorry for the kid. He didn't deserve any of this. And neither does Luna.

As I'm dragged under into a drug-induced coma, Misha comes out of hiding and whispers what we both know to be true.

"This is only the beginning..."

Three

Luna

"That's Big Bird. He's from a TV show called Sesame Street."

The sunlight streaming in from the barred window catches the yellow fur of the stuffed toy in my lap. I wish I could feel it beneath my fingertips. I think it would be soft. But I can't because my wrists are bound by brown leather straps.

So are my ankles to the wheelchair I sit in.

I don't remember my name.

But I don't remember much of anything.

I don't know who I was before. I don't know who I am now.

What I do know, however, is a name which I can never forget.

Misha.

I don't know why that name holds so much significance. It

just does.

I want to ask so many questions, but I don't remember the words. So I just sit here, silent, never speaking. It feels wrong to and on cue, my heart begins to ache. It aches for a loss I can't remember. I just know the loss was of someone I loved deeply.

Was it Misha?

I don't think so.

This feels like a different sort of love.

The orderly leaves me alone, not that I can blame him. I'm hardly any company. I wonder if I was before.

Big Bird stares back at me, and I wonder why his golden fur sings to me. It reminds me of dirty blond hair and…music.

My heart begins beating faster and colors swirl before my eyes. It feels as if I've stared at the sun for too long and suddenly looked away. I can see images I don't recognize through a veil, but no matter how hard I try and remember, I just can't.

A frustrated sigh leaves me.

Every part of me begs I fight, but I'm so tired. I don't have anything to fight for.

A whistling interrupts my pity party for one. I hear it often, but never bother to pay attention to it. But today is different. I wonder why that is. As the whistling gets louder, I focus on the tune…it feels familiar.

Lifting my chin, I peer at the man a few feet away from under my lashes. My long hair shrouds my face, so I feel confident he can't see me staring at him.

He's an older gentleman and appears quite content sweeping the floor. I look at his hands. Each wrinkle represents a second lived. A breath taken. I like measuring life that way.

But a sudden sadness drags me under because life was

robbed from someone…no, from two people I loved very much.

But who?

"Dry those tears, pretty one."

My ruse is up, so I don't bother with pretenses and meet his stare. I wait for recognition.

For something.

Anything…

All I'm confronted with is a big fat nothing.

I don't even realize I'm crying until the man says that I am. The thing is, he couldn't see my tears. But somehow, he knew.

He sweeps toward me, looking from left to right. I think he's ensuring we're out of earshot. We're in the clear for now.

"What did she do to you?"

I continue staring at him, hoping a spark of recognition hits.

"Do you remember me?"

The theme song of The Brady Bunch in the background conceals his question from prying ears.

This is the first time I've wanted to answer someone. I get asked endless questions in therapy in hopes that one day, I'll answer. But I never do.

So I shake my head.

I know that I should remember, but I don't.

"Do you remember…him?"

Him?

I'm suddenly robbed of air and I squeeze my eyes shut, afraid I'm about to be sick. This is a bittersweet memory I don't want to remember because I know that it ends in tears.

"Do you want me to tell you?"

Tears slip into my lips as I nod slowly.

"There's the fighter I know," he says, which makes my heart swell. It's nice to know that I once was. "You almost beat her. You both did. My name's Old Timer. It's what he called me."

"Let's just say we have come to an understanding. He helps me. I help him. And he's the best help I've had in a while. He calls me Old Timer, by the way."

The memory catches me off guard and I stare at Old Timer; not the present, but the past tense.

It's so surreal—I can see it. And I welcome it…

He retrieves a pair of keys from his pocket, muting the jingling by cupping them into his palm. We turn corner after corner, and before long, the lights grow dimmer and the atmosphere colder—in every sense of the word.

Above the doorway are the words, Acta, non verba, which is Latin for 'deeds, not words.' In plain English, actions speak louder than words.

He leads the way, clearly knowing his way through this dark, dank corridor. It's deadly quiet—the only sound I hear is a drip…drip…drip from a leaking pipe somewhere. The buzzing fluorescents flicker on and off, the strobe effect hurting my eyes.

I venture deeper and deeper into this vision which is sure to be a nightmare.

This place is hell.

It's stimulation overload, so much so, I think I'm about to be sick. But I quash down my fear—I've had enough of being afraid.

A single white tub sits in the middle of the room, and unlike the other rooms, this one is immaculate. It's so damn white, it actually hurts my eyes. But the white is overruled by black writing, scribbled all over the walls.

It appears like someone was punished and forced to write a single line a hundred times.

That line reads: Cleanliness is next to godliness.

My heart begins to beat frantically…just like his. But who is he?

"Get him out of here!" I tug at the leather straps securing him down, but they won't budge because they're locked with a gold padlock.

"It's called hydrotherapy," Old Timer explains calmly. "It's a continuous bath. The cold water is used to treat manic depression and agitated behavior."

"I don't give a fuck what it's called!" I scream, cupping his beautiful face in my palms. "Help me! Oh, god, what have they done to you?"

"You want me to go?" I ask him, clutching his cheeks, and when he blinks once, a sob gets caught in my throat.

Even stuck in a medicated nightmare, he's trying to save me. And this is the only way I can save him.

And his name…it's Bowie. No, it was Bowie…but his real name…his name is Dutch…and I love him.

I get sucked back into the present, eyes locked with Old Timer, who grins. "You remember?"

Nodding slowly, I lick my dry lips. "…Yes."

Who would have thought my first word spoken after so long would hold such power. But it does. It's the first step toward uncovering why the fuck I'm in here and finding the man whose name has the ability to bring me to my knees.

"Do you remember?"

I shake my head. "Will you help me?"

My voice startles me because I can't remember what it

sounds like. Has it always sounded this…indignant? But I soon realize it's a reflection of how I'm feeling inside.

I may not remember everything, but I know something awful was done to me and the people I love.

Old Timer nods, but I can see his help comes with a price. "I'll be in touch. But in the meantime, don't take the blue pills."

Before I have a chance to ask why not, an orderly comes over, eyeing us closely. His name is Noah and I want to pluck out his eyeballs. I don't know why, but I know I hate him. The fading bruises on his face hints someone else felt the same way I do.

Old Timer continues on his way, sweeping like nothing happened.

"How you feeling today, darlin'?" he asks me, bending low to make eye contact with me.

I simply stare at him.

"I know you probably don't remember me, but I used to look after you. I've been away, but I'm back now."

I don't sense any maliciousness to his words, but I still don't trust him. And I still want him dead.

"Time for your meds." He comes to a stand and wheels me toward the nurses' station where they administer our drugs.

I make quick eye contact with Old Timer, who nods discreetly. I have no idea how I'm supposed to not take my pills seeing as the nurses give my mouth a strip search to ensure I've swallowed them. But I have to try.

My fellow roommates are in line, waiting for the drugs which sedate us so we don't cause any problems. It's common practice for us now and we're like farm animals who come because we know when it's time to be fed.

It's disgusting.

I can't believe I used to welcome this time of the day. I once preferred to be numb, but not anymore. Now I need to get the hell out of here.

I don't fail to feel Noah's fingers stroke my back. The touch may seem innocent if anyone were to see because he's pushing my wheelchair. But I can feel it's done with intent...and I don't like it.

Nurse Belinda is on duty. She's like the drug police, but instead of saying no to drugs, she's force-feeding them down our throats.

I need to think fast because I'm next in line.

I notice Belinda eyeing Noah in a completely unprofessional manner. No wonder she wants us drugged and tucked into bed by seven p.m. God knows what happens once the lights are out.

When Teddy in front of me takes his meds, I watch closely in the way Belinda examines Teddy's mouth.

She asks him to open wide and to lift his tongue. When satisfied, she gestures with her chin that it's our turn.

Noah wheels me over while I ensure not to draw any attention to myself. I can only hope she's too enamored by Noah to notice me.

"I missed you," she says, retrieving the clear medicine cup containing my pills.

"I missed you too," Noah replies, but his enthusiasm lacks. "Have you seen her?"

Her?

Belinda shakes her head quickly, as if too afraid to say her name. She places the cup under my bottom lip and tosses the white pills into my mouth. Old Timer didn't say anything about these, so I swallow and open my mouth before she can ask.

She uses a penlight to ensure I've swallowed and when satisfied, reaches the medicine cup with the two blue pills.

"Have you seen her since—" Belinda soon pauses, however, paling. I can only assume that's because Noah has given her a facial cue not to continue.

Her fingers tremble as she places the cup to my mouth and tosses the pills into my mouth.

"She wants to check your cheeks, move it under your tongue. She asks to look under your tongue, you push it to the back of your throat."

I jolt when I hear a voice I don't remember, but it feels familiar.

I don't think twice when I do what the voice inside my head told me to do.

Pretending to swallow, I use my tongue to push the pills into my cheek and open my mouth so Belinda can look into the back of my throat.

"Tongue," she says apathetically, and I quickly do as the stranger said and use my tongue to push the pills to the back of my throat. "I wonder where she's gone. No one has seen her."

Belinda checks my mouth without care, as she's too occupied talking about whoever she is.

"Do you think—"

"Shh," Noah warns, and before she can ask him any more questions, he's wheeling me away.

Old Timer is sweeping under a table, but when I pass him by, he winks discreetly. "Help an old man out and lift this table for me?"

Noah sighs, but I'm surprised he does as Old Timer asks.

I know why he did it. What a crafty bastard he is.

With my head lowered and hair shielding my face, I wait for the right moment and when Noah turns his back, I spit out the pills. Old Timer quickly conceals them with the bristles of his broom before anyone sees. Once Noah is done, he wheels me out of the sunroom.

I can sense Noah's annoyance which makes me wonder just who this woman Belinda asked about is. He leads me down the corridor, the wheels squeaking over the polished linoleum. I know from experience the drugs take about ten minutes before they kick in.

Noah wheels me into my room and the thud of the door closing has me panicking. But I can't let it show.

He begins unfastening my restraints in belief I am about to succumb to a drug-induced coma.

My heart is racing and memories of him being in my room sit on the surface, dipping in their toes and teasing me to remember.

"I think I preferred it when you were calling me a son of a bitch," he says, unfastening the final strap around my wrist. "Now, you're so…boring."

I wait, however, and be smart. If I run now, I don't know where I'm running to.

Noah lifts me into his arms and places me into bed. It takes all my willpower not to bite off his nose. Once settled against the pillows, I wait for him to leave. But he doesn't. He does something which creeps me the fuck out.

He lies down beside me.

There's hardly any space, which has him dragging me into his arms. He doesn't speak. He simply strokes over my hair and face, watching me closely. I don't mistake this gesture as one filled with love.

It's obsession.

"I wish you remembered...I liked the way you smelled when scared." On cue, he bends low and smells along the side of my throat.

I remain passive because I can't let him know I'm alert. This is the only advantage in this place, and I can't blow it now.

When I feel his fingers caress my breasts, I hold my breath. The thin hospital gown does nothing to conceal his touch.

"I know a secret," he whispers into my ear which turns my blood cold. "I wonder if I should tell you? I know lots of secrets about you."

His touch gets rougher and all I want to do is break every single bone in his hand. But I can't. I need to know what this secret is.

He licks a slow, deliberate path from my neck up to my mouth, where he then begins to kiss my slack lips.

I dare not move.

I dare not breathe.

All I can do is helplessly lie there, plotting my revenge.

I am going to kill this asshole and it's going to be messy.

He kisses with me passion and if I were insane, I would suspect this kiss is done with love. But the fact that I am supposed to be comatose erases out that thought. The kiss grows more intense and when Noah begins rubbing himself against my leg, I can feel he is hard.

But I'm used to some men being vile creatures. I've dealt with them in the past—well, I think I have.

A stripper pole and red monster heels flash before my eyes

as I see a woman dance in front of hungry eyes.

That woman is me.

My heart threatens to burst from my chest, but I will it to calm because I can't let on to Noah that I am alert. So, instead, I think of long elegant fingers playing over piano keys. The lights overhead catch the silver from the rings he wears.

His long dirty blond hair falls over his face, but I know his eyes are the deepest blue. So blue, it appears as if one is peering into the bluest waters where nothing exists but the ability of the sea to wash away one's pain.

And that's what he did.

He took away my pain.

He made me feel safe.

He made me feel loved.

But who is he?

I force myself to focus on this memory because it's the key to solving all of this.

He's tall. Slender, but muscled. He's younger than me, but age doesn't matter because when we kiss…

Splashes of color blind me and I wade through the confusion because I can taste him on my tongue. It's the sweetest of flavors—I think I'm addicted because he's my own personal brand of drug.

"Sleep, baby. I'm not going anywhere."

"Promise?"

"With all my heart."

His heart…why do I want to reach out and hold it in my hands?

Why do I feel like his heart is mine?

"I like the way your heart beats. Is that weird?"

"No, because it always seems to beat faster whenever you're near."

So much love is passed between this man and I, but then suddenly…the colors are replaced with black.

"It's true? Your heart…his heart, it's true, isn't it?"

"I hate you."

"You should. But you're about to hate me even more."

I'm blinded by rain and headlights.

"That's right, you son of a bitch! Talk! Tell me what to do! You want me to save her? Tell me how!"

I am so frightened…not for me, however…I am frightened for him.

"No! Please d-don't do this."

"You want her to die? Then fucking fine! You want to be a chickenshit little pussy when she needs you the most? No wonder she fucking killed you!"

Who is he talking to?

His body seizes around mind, protecting me in his own way, which is an oxymoron considering he's about to kill us both.

Who is this man he seeks the answers of? This man is important to us both. I feel nothing but love for both men…but one love is that of a mother. The other, a lover.

"Talk! If you ever loved her, tell me what you could never do. Tell me how to save her!"

The breath is knocked from me, and all I see is white.

I'm ripped from my mind and spiral back to the present where I feel my leg is wet from Noah's cum. He dry humped me like the dog that he is.

I disassociated myself so easily from something so vile and

was immersed in beauty, no matter how tragic it was because I remember him.

I remember them.

No matter what was done to me, my mind refuses to forget the love I feel for them. And I'll be damned if I don't get out of this place to find him.

But I can't…

"He's dead, Luna. He died because of the voices inside his head. He was very sick. He had hallucinations, just like you. What he was claiming, to hear the voice of his donor, it's not real. His mental illness took his life in the end. But I won't let that happen to you."

That voice is like a thousand fingernails scraping down a blackboard. I want to silence her…forever, just as she tried to do to me.

"He's not dead!"

"He is dead. I am so sorry. But if it gives you any solace, his last act was to save you. The love you shared wasn't conventional, but it made sense to you both. A unique love."

"Stop it! You're lying! He wouldn't leave me."

My world is suddenly shrouded in darkness because the man I loved…is dead?

They're both dead?

Once Noah rearranges himself back into his pants, he kisses me one final time. "Thanks, baby. That was amazing."

He stands and before he leaves, he makes a mistake which lights a scorching fire inside my belly. "He's not dead. He's alive…and she has him."

And with those words, he animates me back to life because my son…his name is Misha.

And the man I love with all my heart…his name is Dutch.

Misha is dead.

And I believed Dutch to be too…but he's not.

That has given me more reason to get out of this fucking hellhole…but not before burning it to the motherfucking ground.

Four

Dutch

I force my eyes to open even though my body protests that I remain in this drug-induced sleep where there's no pain.

But I can't.

An unlikely ally has now been brought into the game.

Joy can explain what the fuck is going on because once I know who exactly Jonathan is and how we're all connected, I can outsmart Alanna.

Blinking a few times, my vision adjusts and I see Joy is in a bed beside me. She too is strapped in. A white bandage is wrapped around her forehead. Where Alanna smashes a hammer into the side of it is stained red.

Unlike me, she isn't connected to an IV.

It appears Alanna doesn't care whether she lives or dies. Time is of the essence then.

This is a fucking nightmare.

"Joy!" I whisper, hoping by some miracle she's alive.

When I hear a pained moan, I sigh in relief.

It takes her a moment, but she finally stirs awake and when her eyes open and she takes in the horror before her, she opens her mouth, ready to scream.

"Don't scream," I quickly warn her.

Thankfully, she listens.

Turning her cheek, she looks at me with tears in her eyes. "She's mad. I didn't think she would do this. We have to get out of here."

Joy tugs at the leather restraints around her wrists, but they're done up tight.

"I didn't mean to hurt him," she says, and I know she means Misha.

"What about her?" I spit, disgusted she's playing the sympathy card.

"If I could take it back, I would." She bursts into sobs. "Alanna promised me he would be okay. I didn't want to do it, but he stopped talking to me. I thought if I did it, he'd come back to me."

"Jonathan?" I ask because I need to know just who this asshole is.

She nods.

He stopped talking because he's dead…but I leave out that minor detail for now.

"Who is he?"

Joy sniffs back her tears. "I can't—"

"If you want to get out of here, then you need to trust me because I have no doubt Alanna will kill you."

Joy senses the seriousness of my tone, and her lower lip

trembles. I would feel sorry for her if she didn't betray Luna in the worst possible way, but as far as I'm concerned, if Alanna doesn't kill her, then I will.

"Jonathan is my lover," she confesses sadly. "He has been for many years."

I know next to nothing about Joy other than she is a lying bitch. But in this circumstance, I believe her.

"Then why were you fucking around with Misha for so long?"

She lowers her eyes, ashamed. "I loved him. I loved them both."

That isn't love.

That is greed. And obsession.

My heart begins to ache and I know that's because Misha is listening.

"Do you know who Misha's father is?" I ask the question which killed Misha because he believed Joy knew.

All he wanted was answers which he hoped would help him identify what was "wrong" with him. He didn't understand why Luna never told him. He was forever angry at her for the fact.

Joy nods once again.

"Who is it?"

She never has the chance to answer because Alanna enters the room humming, wheeling in the man of the hour. Horror overtakes Joy when she sees the very dead corpse in the hospital bed.

While me? I'm annoyed my answer remains unanswered.

Alanna positions Jonathan across from Joy and I know this is done with intent.

"W-who is that?" The terror in Joy's voice only feeds a sicko like Alanna.

Alanna smiles, but doesn't reply. Instead, she walks over the partition which conceals her wedding dress. She wheels it away, unveiling it with pride.

"That is my fiancé," she finally reveals, stroking over the beads on her dress.

"Is?" Joy questions, confused why Alanna is speaking about him in the present tense.

Alanna doesn't bother entertaining her with a reply. "I don't know what to do with you, Joy. You've seen too much."

"What?" Joy gasps, shaking her head in fear. "I won't tell a soul. Just let me go."

"I can't do that. We both know that."

Joy desperately looks at me for help.

I simply yawn in response.

"It does seem a waste, however. I could use you."

"Yes, you could. I'll do whatever you want."

Famous last words because when Alanna walks over to the silver table and pulls back the white paper cloth, revealing sharp medical tools, it's apparent Alanna doesn't want to sit around a campfire singing Kumbaya with Joy.

"No!" Misha screams, which surprises me.

He cares what happens to her?

But he soon clarifies.

"I need to know why."

Of course he does.

Don't we all?

Is this Misha's closure? Once he finally uncovers the whys, can he finally be at peace?

The crucifix around my throat reveals my faith, even

though I've questioned it more than once. But I can't help but feel our connection speaks to me beyond this world.

"Please…I need to know it all."

This is the least I can do for Misha. It's because of him that I'm alive. I owe him this.

"My heart hurts," I say to Alanna, as I know this is the only thing she cares about. If my heart is a risk, so is her reunion with Jonathan.

Immediately, she rushes over to my bedside, ensuring the IV is still attached to me. "What's wrong with it?"

"It aches."

She retrieves the stethoscope from around her neck and places the drum to my chest, listening closely.

"It's beating normally. What other symptoms do you have?"

"Nausea and light-headedness."

Alanna sighs, her worry clear.

"Maybe if you didn't break my knee, this could have been over with by now and you'd have your fairy-tale ending?" I can't help but twist in the knife.

She ignores my jab. "I'll give you some vitamins. We need you strong."

I know Joy is hanging onto every word, but she would never guess what Alanna has planned because it's that farfetched.

The moment Alanna leaves the room, I whisper to Joy, "If you want me to help you, then you need to tell me everything."

Joy nods quickly, understanding the dire circumstances we find ourselves in. "I was married, but Jonathan wasn't my husband."

"Whose husband was he then?" I ask because I don't understand how he fits in this.

"No one's," Joy replies. "Jonathan wouldn't commit to anyone. He didn't have to because he had women who were willing to do anything for him. He strung us all along without any promises because we wanted to be the one who 'fixed' him. Alanna and I are the perfect example of this."

What she adds next brings me one step closer to solving this mystery.

"All but one woman, that is."

"Who?"

Joy's sadness turns to scorn. "You know who."

Misha's gasp resonates loudly in my mind.

Not much shocks me anymore, but this, this just gets worse. "Luna?"

"…Yes."

She was always the final piece to this puzzle.

So the three women are connected because of Jonathan, and he is dead because I assume of Alanna.

"How is he connected to Luna?" I question and now, my heart really begins to ache.

"Oh my god…no."

I feel every shred of Misha's pain.

"Tell me!" I demand Joy when she has the audacity to cry.

"Jonathan is…he is Misha's father," she whispers, tears spilling onto her trembling lips.

Clearer than day, I see Misha slump onto the floor, head hung in shame. He's finally got the answers he sought out his entire life. But now that he does, can he really move on?

It takes me a minute to process over what Joy just shared. I don't think there is a filthier act than what she committed. She had sex with Luna's ex, who is Misha's dad, and then proceeded to have sex with Misha and Jonathan because it seems she likes to keep it in the family.

Now I totally understand her comment.

"The money wasn't for me…it was for him. So we could be one big happy family."

No doubt, Jonathan thought he was entitled to Luna's money. Were they all working together? Is that why Misha is dead? Did he convince Joy to run Luna off the road that night, but unbeknownst to him, he killed his son instead?

But by the looks of Jonathan, I think he's been dead for a while.

"When did you last see him?"

Joy shrugs. "Over a year ago. But he texted me throughout that time."

No, he didn't.

The messages may have come from his phone, but he didn't send them. No guessing who did.

"Jonathan got sick. His heart," she shares sadly, which explains the tie to Alanna. "He promised me he was coming back to marry me, but had to take care of a few things. He was in debt for his gambling and other…addictions. He didn't have any money, but—"

"But if you could get it for him, you could live happily ever after?" I fill in the blanks sarcastically as everything is starting to make sense.

"Yes. I met him when he was trying to see Misha when he was a baby, but Luna refused."

"She was trying to protect me. That's all she ever wanted to do." Misha realizes why Luna never wanted him to meet his father.

She was trying to protect him from a man who would prove to cause him nothing but pain.

"We fell in love. He was my true love. Then he just disappeared without a trace. My car wrapped around a tree the only clue he left behind."

Oh, bull-fucking-shit. He used her as a pawn to get what he wanted and when it failed, he moved on to the next victim until he met Alanna and got his karma once and for all.

I suddenly don't blame Alanna for taking this son of a bitch's life. He deserves to die over and over again for what he's done.

"I just wish I knew where he was. I have the money now. He can come back and we can be a family. That's all he ever wanted."

Things are starting to come together, but I know there is more—there always is.

Not bothering to sugarcoat anything, I casually gesture with my chin to Jonathan. "Well, you got your wish."

Joy has no idea what I mean until she looks over at the bed, which contains the wrinkled, decaying corpse of her "true love."

"What? No," she gasps, shaking her head violently. "You're l-lying!"

"I'm really not. Jonathan is right there. Dead as a doornail, and I'm pretty sure the cause of death is one Dr. Alanna Norton."

"No!" she sobs, spittle running down her chin. "This can't have been for nothing. Alanna told me where Luna was that night, but it was Misha. Why did she do that? Did she know it was him all along?"

"Why the fuck would you listen to Alanna?" I ask, confused.

"Because she said she would provide the heart…if I were to provide the money; Luna's money she would leave Misha in her will. I thought with Luna gone, Misha would share the money with me and then I could pay Alanna to do the operation for Jonathan. And he would come back to me. I was going to tell Misha who Jonathan was. I swear I was. I just needed Luna gone."

This doesn't make sense.

Alanna didn't want money…there is something far more valuable to her…Misha's heart, which would be a perfect match for Jonathan seeing as Misha is his son. Same blood. Same tissue. Jonathan's DNA made up Misha's heart.

He was the perfect match.

So why the fuck did she give it to me?

The similarities between Jonathan and I are a little uncanny—he needed a heart and was a musician. No wonder reality and fiction blurred for Alanna.

What a twist of fate.

"Oh, Jonathan," Joy sobs hysterically. "Please tell me this is all a bad dream."

"No, you fucking bitch, it's a fucking reality which you created. You killed your best friend's son, but not before fucking him because if you couldn't have his dad, he was a consolation prize? You make me sick."

Jonathan got what he deserved and I suddenly don't hate Alanna as much. She's a lover scorned and Jonathan was nothing but a walking red flag and instead of licking her wounds and learning from her mistakes, she took matters into her own hands and those hands killed him.

Kudos to her.

"Do you hate Luna that much? She never wanted Jonathan! Why did you do that do her?"

"She's the reason he's like this!" she screams, refusing to take blame. "He tried to get to know Misha, but she refused. He only wanted to love his son!"

"Don't you dare blame her!" I cry, tugging at the restraints because I want to kill her myself. "He is hardly a suitable role model. She was trying to protect her son from turning into that motherfucker."

Jonathan was clearly a predator who preyed on weak-willed women. He took what he could and then moved on to the next. Until he met Alanna…

"I loved him. And he loved me." Joy continues to sob while I want to break her neck. "I did all of this for him. For us."

"Wake up, sweetheart, there is no us because you killed his only son."

Alanna enters the room, clapping slowly, and it's apparent she's heard it all.

She claps one final time. "Oh, Joy, you're such a fucking idiot."

Looking between Alanna and Joy, I don't know who I hate more.

"Is that really Jonathan?" Joy asks, appearing hopeful I'm lying.

Alanna shatters that dream, however, when she nods. "Yes, it is. He's looking well, don't you think?"

I hysterical laugh spills from me because, what the fuck is going on? I'm ignored by both women, however.

"Did you kill him?" Joy cries, eyes wide.

Alanna simply grins sweetly. I don't want to be rooting for anyone in this fight, but I'm in Alanna's corner and I can't wait for her to dish out what Joy deserves.

"Why?" Joy shouts, her cheeks turning red in anger. "I had the money. Why did you do this?"

Alanna is cool, composed, how you'd expect any sociopath to be, I suppose. "Because he never loved you...he loved me. You were nothing but a two-dollar whore he called when he was desperate. The cheap motels he took you to is proof of that."

Joy gasps, offended, or surprised Alanna is in on her secret affair, I'm still unsure.

"There never was a heart, was there?"

Alanna looks at her French manicure, bored. "Of course, there was."

"So you knew it was Misha driving that night and not Luna?"

Alanna's smirk says it all.

"Why?" Joy screams hysterically.

Misha is also listening. I can feel him closer to me than I ever have before.

"Because I needed a perfect match, and what better match than Jonathan's own son."

"You set me up," Joy sneers, sniffing back her tears.

"You set yourself up the moment you took what was mine."

"He was never yours!"

Joy is poking an already irate bear, a bear which had no qualms killing the "love of her life" because he was a philandering lowlife.

I now understand Alanna's hatred toward Luna. Luna was the only woman Jonathan ever loved; she was able to achieve what none of these women could, no matter how hard they tried. No wonder her hatred for Luna was so personal.

She knew who she was this entire time.

"That money, it's mine. It's ours," Alanna states without fault. "I am his fiancée, after all."

"And that's why you've been entertaining Joy this entire time? You kept her on your side with promises that Jonathan was under your care?" I say, knowing the answer but needing to say it out loud. "But once Luna signed everything over to Joy, you were going to…"

I leave the sentence unfinished because Joy can connect the dots.

Joy did all of Alanna's dirty work. What a true mastermind she is.

Joy is simply a means to an end for Alanna and no doubt, uncovering their affair was motivation for Alanna to enforce her plans of revenge.

I wonder if what she told me about Jonathan was true.

I do believe he was seeing Joy before he ever met Alanna, so in reality, Alanna is the "other woman." I dare not tell her that, though, because they are both seeing Luna as the one he always wanted.

"Kill her."

Misha's words echo loudly inside my head. I can taste his anger once again. Poor kid, he never stood a chance.

These women are delirious if they believe Jonathan loved either of them. He only loved himself, and as far as I'm concerned, he got what he deserved.

It's hard to wrap my head around, but I think I understand it all. But there is still one glaring question—why did Alanna give me Misha's heart? I don't buy her caring doctor act at all.

Alanna hated Joy and possibly Misha as well because she wanted to be the only person in his life. She saw them as people that could take away his love. And Alanna clearly doesn't like to share.

I wonder why she killed him then? Or could her story of his heart giving out be true? Is she just a broken-hearted woman who would do anything to revive her dead lover?

"So what happens now?" Joy asks, her trembling voice giving way to her fears.

Alanna mulls over her comment. "Do you promise to not tell anyone about this?"

Joy nods frantically, while I wonder what the hell Alanna is up to now. There's no way she's letting her go.

"Very well." Alanna reaches into her doctor's jacket and produces a piece of paper.

She walks over to Joy and holds it up for her, allowing her to read over the content. I wonder what it is.

"I sign this and you let me go?"

Alanna nods with a smile.

"Okay, fine. I'll sign it. I have no use for it now."

"It appears you're not a complete idiot, after all," Alanna says, unfastening the tie around Joy's wrist.

Joy knows better than to try and take Alanna down and signs along the dotted line. Once the deal is done, Alanna looks at the paper, smiling broadly.

"We did it," she says, and talking in the plural sense, she somehow thinks Jonathan was somehow involved. But this crazy is all her. "The hospital thanks you for your very kind donation, Joy."

I shake my head, actually impressed with Alanna's deviousness. She has devised a ploy that the money Joy signed away is for the hospital, but in fact, Alanna will take it. She's got it all mapped out.

I wonder what happens now.

"I did what you wanted. Now let me go."

I sigh because there is no happily ever after for Joy.

She looks at me, her eyes wide in fear when she soon realizes this too. "No, you promised!"

Alanna folds the paper and places it into her white jacket pocket, ignoring Joy's pleas as she walks over to the table of torture.

"Help me!" Joy begs, but how can I—my hands are literally tied. "Alanna, no! Jonathan wouldn't want this."

The moment Jonathan's name passes Joy's lips, Alanna growls and lunges for the scalpel. She slashes it across Joy's cheek, instantly drawing blood.

"Don't you dare say his name!"

Joy begins to scream and rightly so, seeing as her cheek is now a dangly flap of skin. This is only going to get worse.

"You're cr-crazy," Joy sobs, her heavy tears mixing with the blood pouring down her face.

"Am I?" Alanna questions, tapping her chin with the bloody scalpel, deep in thought. "I don't think that I am. If I were a man, would this be more acceptable? Or what if I gave you some childhood sob story as to why I am like this? Would that be easier for you to accept?"

I listen intently because this is information I could use.

"I do this because I like it. There is no mystical reason behind it."

Some people are just born bad...and fucking crazy, and Alanna is both.

"You, Joy, are a fucking idiot. And as I see it, you're about to get what you deserve. You betrayed your best friend...but not before fucking her son."

"You killed Misha!" Joy screams, violently tugging at the restraints.

"No, you did," Alanna counters with a shrug. "I wasn't the one behind the wheel that night."

"What happened to Jonathan? What did you do to him?"

I think Joy senses her demise is around the corner, so she's not holding back.

"I didn't do anything."

But Alanna is lying.

The more this fucked-up story unravels, the more convinced I am that Alanna killed Jonathan.

Is that why she's so intent on "saving" him? Does she feel bad?

Then another thought occurs.

Could it be the reason Alanna gave me Misha's heart is because deep down, she knows what she's proposing is impossible, and that she wants me to take Jonathan's place?

This is the only advantage I have, the one which makes the most sense, not that any of this does.

"I have an idea...Dutch, you decide."

I arch a brow, not liking where this is going.

"You decide if Joy deserves to live...or if she deserves to die."

Joy looks at me, her eyes pleading I spare her life. But this is a test and if I fail, I fail Luna. But how can I do this? Can I live with this on my conscience?

"Ticktock," Alanna singsongs.

All I can think, however, is if I do this, my heart will always pulse with a sickened beat, echoing the choice I make.

Tick…tick…the sound of my heart suddenly pulsates with a new beat.

Sick…sick…

And that's what I'll be if I condemn Joy to death.

Alanna can see me grappling with this choice. My pain equates to weakness and to someone like Alanna, she will use that against me. This will cost Luna, and I just cannot risk that. I would kill anyone to protect her.

I failed her once before…I will not again.

Forgive me, Father…

"Please, god, no!" Joy cries, tears streaming down her face as she can read what I've decided.

Alanna appears shocked, which is what I wanted.

"Every action has a consequence, Joy, and Alanna is yours," I blankly say, barely keeping it together.

Vomit rises, but I swallow it down because I too have to live with the consequences of my choice.

"Well, it seems Dutch has decided," Alanna says with intent as she wishes me to know that Joy's death will be on my head. She is merely the messenger; the angel of death.

I watch as Alanna walks over to her medical table and examines the tools before her. Joy is screaming hysterically, while me, I just want to close my eyes and wish for this nightmare to end.

"Help!" Joy screams over and over again.

But we're beyond that.

"What would you do to save Jonathan?"

Alanna's question ceases Joy's screams. "An-anything."

"Anything?"

"Yes! You heard me! Anything!"

What game is Alanna playing?

Alanna smirks, and the sight sends a chill through me.

I want to tell Joy to shut her mouth because there is no saving either her or Jonathan. But I can't. All I can do is watch as Alanna tears Joy's white blouse down the middle, exposing her chest.

Before Joy has a chance to breathe her next breath, Alanna stabs the scalpel into Joy's chest and begins to slice downward. Joy gasps, her eyes parted wide, appearing to be in disbelief at the fact that Alanna is hacking through her flesh and muscle with a fucking scalpel.

The sound of Alanna cutting through Joy's flesh turns my stomach and I want to be sick. But I do all I can in this circumstance—I keep eye contact with Joy as I owe her that; I was the one who decided her fate, after all.

Once Alanna reaches Joy's navel, the scalpel clangs against the floor as she drops it, only to retrieve a small surgical hammer. She then peels away Joy's flesh with her fingers, exposing her rib cage. This macabre sight is so surreal, I wonder if maybe I'm still wrapped in a drug-induced reverie, but my imagination would never be this creative.

Alanna begins to tap away at Joy's ribs and my mind focuses on the rhythm, constructing a gruesome song in my head. It's entrenched in blood and gore, but the notes grow stronger, the melody clearer. It's becoming easier to hear the music, but what have I sacrificed to hear it again?

The squelching of blood and tissue morphs into notes, and although my wrists are bound, my fingers move against invisible keys, playing the music I hear and feel. I wonder if this is how I cope with situations I don't want to deal with.

Music has always been my salvation, and I need redemption now more than ever.

Joy's breathing is a rattle and I realize that's because her chest is now an open cavity, her lungs on the outside instead of on the inside.

"The heart is the epicenter of us all. One thinks they are broken-hearted when they lose the love that made their heart worth beating. They can literally feel their heart break. It feels as though someone has reached inside of them…and ripped it from their chest."

And that's exactly what Alanna does.

She cracks Joy open like a walnut and reaches into her chest, removing her beating heart. This sounds implausible to most, but not for Dr. Norton.

I can heart Joy's heart beating…

Thump…thump, thump…

And then silence as Alanna squashes it in her hands.

Joy's eyes are still wide open, but her face is one of serenity. It's the most puzzling thing I've ever seen. Was she relieved that the pain finally stopped?

The last thing she would have seen was her bloody, beating heart in Alanna's hands. There is no peace in that. Only a fucking horror story.

Her chest cavity is one gaping, bloodied wound, but it's not messy. There is precision to the dissection because it was done with a surgeon's hand.

Joy is simply an empty shell now, a reflection of how I feel for condemning her fate.

So this is what we're all made up of? Blood. Tissue. And

bones.

At the end of the day, no matter our circumstances, we are all the same. And we all come with an expiration date. Some premature. Others, if fortunate enough, can experience life until they're old and gray.

Joy, however, isn't one of those fortunate ones.

"You're fascinated, aren't you?" Alanna says, and I only just realize she is watching me. "Most would recoil in horror, but not you. What do you see?"

"It's not what I see, but rather, what I hear."

With Joy's warm heart still in hand, Alanna walks forward, offering it to me with an outstretched hand. "What do you hear?"

Closing my eyes, I hear the steady echo of Joy's heart and the cadence it once followed. I hear the blood pulsating through the veins and arteries, giving her life. But that is no more.

The change in music comes, a dramatic twist and turn as the melody becomes darker, the notes heavier, so heavy you feel them in the dark depths of your belly. To be able to hear this is something I never believed I would experience again.

But here I am; in the face of blood and gore, I can hear it and it's…beautiful.

"Don't be ashamed," Alanna wisely says, reading my dilemma. "All's fair in love and war."

"Is that why you killed her?" I ask, opening my eyes and looking at a blood-splattered Alanna. "Because Jonathan loved her too?"

This is a risky game I play, but to get out of here, I need to ask questions which will help me understand.

"He never loved her," she spits, blood staining the white

floor as it drips from her hand. "He was using her to get to Luna and his son."

I don't need to ask if he loved Luna, because the answer is clear.

"Why did you give me Misha's heart then?"

Alanna's fingers making a squelching noise as they clench Joy's heart. "Because you remind me so much of him."

"Was he—" I search for the right word, not wanting to anger her. "Like that before you got Misha's heart?" I gesture with my chin to Jonathan wrapped snug as a bug in his bed.

"Yes."

This is the first time I see clarity behind Alanna's eyes, and I realize that's because she knows this won't work...but if she can't have Jonathan, then she'll take everyone down with her. But the way she looks at me, I know the reason she saved me was because she wants me to be her happily ever after.

She gave me Misha's heart in hopes I would see her as the hero of this story and what...fall in love with her? She just never factored in Luna and the instant connection we would form.

Alanna is in need of some serious help as reality and fiction blur. For her to do all this she feels guilt, and I am certain that guilt stems from her taking Jonathan's life.

"What will you do with it?" I ask, meaning Joy's heart.

"I was going to give it to Jonathan, but I don't want that bitch inside of him. Each breath he takes will be a reminder that that is possible because of her. Besides, if you're anything to go by, I want her and her memories far away from him."

Something suddenly clicks.

I was Alanna's lab rat in more ways than one. No wonder she showed such interest in me. She was studying me in more ways than one.

Trying to reason with Alanna is out of the question, so I need to play along with her insanity. "Yes, I am starting to understand that now. What I feel for Luna…I can't help but wonder if maybe it's because of Misha."

Alanna's attention is piqued. "How do you think you'd ever know if it was?"

I take my time, appearing to mull over her question before finally replying, "If I saw her again."

Alanna watches me closely for any signs of deception, but she won't see any.

"That's why she's still alive, isn't it? You need her as part of your research. You need to know what makes a heart…love, in hopes that you can find love again."

Alanna wets her lips. "You're a very smart man, Dutch."

Finally, I'm making headway with her. But I can't push. "Will you let me play? You're the reason I'm still alive."

"I'll think about it."

That's not a no.

Alanna tosses Joy's heart onto her cooling corpse and wheels her from the room, humming happily, while I wonder what I will have to sacrifice to get the fuck out of here.

Five

Luna

I think I would enjoy Casablanca if not for the fact that I am held prisoner in this fucking wheelchair.

I need to get out of here, and the only person who can help me is Old Timer. I just need to find something I can bribe him with.

Fragments of my memory are returning piece by piece. It's so surreal to relearn what you were like, to relive what you once lived. There are still black holes I cannot remember, like who the fuck did this to me?

I know it's a woman, however.

I just don't know who.

Or why.

Misha and Dutch, I remember. I may not recall every detail, but I remember I loved them deeply. And that's all I need to know.

Subtly peering around the theater, I look for a way out. There's a memory scratching at the surface, but I can't remember what it is.

Frustrated, I slump into my chair, wishing I could move.

Noah places his hand onto my leg, rubbing gently, but in that touch is nothing but satisfaction that he has me where he wants me and I can't do a damn thing about it.

"Do you want to go back to your room?" he whispers into my ear.

That is the last thing I want. I need to find Old Timer.

Before I have a chance to object, Noah unlocks the brakes and wheels me away.

Helplessly, I look from left to right, desperate for someone to help me. But there's no one. I hate being vulnerable this way.

I peer at the crucifix above the doorway and pray for some sort of miracle because that is what I need.

I want to scream out for help, but I know that won't achieve a thing.

When we pass a young woman with a cat finger puppet, the cat hisses at Noah. He merely chuckles in response. But when a slanted grin twists on her face, I realize the joke is on him.

One moment the room is lit up with the moving pictures on the screen and then the next, we're shrouded in darkness, thanks to the power going off. There is a deadly silence before the room erupts into pandemonium.

The panicked screams of my fellow friends pierce through the air, disliking the darkness while me, I see this as my out.

Orders are barked over Noah's walkie-talkie to get the flashlights from storage. The longer we remain with no light, the more frantic things will become. I can hear the soles of his shoes squeak on the floor as he retreats, leaving me unmanned.

This is my chance…but I can't move, thanks to the leather straps tied around my waist and chest. I'm about to cry out for someone to untie me, but I smell cigarette smoke and it calms me.

"I gotcha, darlin.'"

Old Timer is the hero in my story as he quickly unfastens the straps. The moment I'm free, I spring up, ready to flee.

"Go to the projection booth. Open the door and follow the tunnel, which veers to the far right. I think he is there. Don'tcha ever come back here unless it's to burn this place to the ground."

Although that's not the best endorsement, I'm willing to take the risk. I'm not sure if I will see Old Timer again, so I plant a quick kiss on his cheek.

"Why are you helping him?"

"Because he risked his life to save my daughter."

"Who is your daughter?" I ask with a gasp.

"They call her Kitty."

I put two and two together and realize the girl with the cat finger puppet is Kitty.

From the anger in Old Timer's tone, it's clear he wants his revenge on Noah too. I wonder why he hasn't acted sooner. Maybe he just found out what happened? Or maybe he is biding his time like we all are?

"Thank you."

If I've ever run faster, I don't remember because I get to the booth in seconds. Yanking open the door, I see a man inside who stands by the open door. I grip his shoulder in gratitude and do as Old Timer says and run into the darkness.

It takes a while for my eyes to adjust, but when they do, I

take off into a dead sprint. I extend my arm out so my fingertips can touch the wall and when I feel the unmissable scratch marks carved into the cement walls, a shiver rocks me from head to toe.

My bare feet splash in the puddles of water, and I wonder what these tunnels are used for. Nothing good, clearly. When I see the two tunnels, I take the one on the right, as Old Timer suggested.

I keep on running blindly, hoping I find what I'm looking for.

My raspy breath bounces off the walls and the urgency to this situation is almost suffocating. I am putting my faith in a stranger and I don't know what I'm running toward. But when I see an old wooden door a few yards away, there's no turning back now.

The large brass handle is as antique-looking as the door, so I have no idea where this leads to. Any sensible person would stop and think rationally about this, but I don't think twice as I turn the handle, sighing in relief when it whines open.

There are no lights, so I assume the power is also out wherever and whatever this is. I walk into what I assume is a basement from the cold, hard floor. The only source of light I have is from the full moon which shines through the small window.

It's enough for me to see a wooden staircase ahead.

This is how every horror movie starts or ends.

I take the stairs quietly, pausing when the wood protests under my weight. I don't know where this leads, so I need to be careful. This may be my only chance. Once I reach the top of the stairs, I grip the door handle and suck in a deep breath.

I exhale when it turns and carefully open the door. I brace myself for anything, but what I see leaves me confused. I expected to be confronted with some horror scene, but instead, I see tapestries on the wall and a collection of spoons from all over the world.

The unmistakable smell of lavender and bleach hits my nostrils and I cover my mouth, attempting not to gag.

Closing the door behind me, I wonder which way I should go. I'm in the middle of a corridor, however, half is carpeted, while the other is linoleum. This was done with intent. I trust my gut, and follow the linoleum path that winds around a wall.

The hallway is long, but I can see a doorway at the end of it. There isn't a door, which strikes me as odd. And that's the reason I walk toward it.

I mask my footsteps as best I can, but a sheen of perspiration coats every inch of my skin. I'm scared. For the first time in my life, I'm fearful to see what's behind door number one.

I focus on the doorway, straining my eyes in hopes I can make out something which will hint at what's inside.

The smell of lavender only gets stronger. I've smelled this before…I just can't remember when.

Steps away from the doorway, I take a quivering breath before walking inside. It's dark, but I think I can see two single beds and the reason I think that is because these images are ingrained in my mind—the beds are similar to the ones in Parkfields.

Now the question is, who's inside of them?

"Who's there?"

And just like that, two words have the ability to render me to my knees.

Even in the darkness, Dutch is my beacon of hope, and like a ship coming home, he is my guiding light.

"Luna?"

Tears instantly tumble down my cheeks because he knows it's me. He may not be able to see me, but our connection runs so deep, it's enough for him to know that I'm here.

"It's me."

Composing myself, I sniff back my tears and race toward where his voice came from. I still can't see anything, but the moment I reach his bedside, I am overcome by his unique fragrance and without thought, I throw myself into his arms.

However, he cannot reciprocate because I realize he is bound.

"How are you?" He nuzzles into me, the warmth of his flesh like a comforting embrace.

I can't help but laugh. "I've had better days. But I feel better now. They said you were dead."

He kisses the top of my head. "I'm right here, baby."

"I really missed you." Hardly eloquent, but it's the truth.

"And I really missed you too. I'm so sorry they've done this to you. Where are we?"

"I followed the tunnels under the hospital. Who did this to you?" I ask as I wrap my arms around his thick neck. His long hair tickles my nose as I inhale his scent deeply.

He smells like home.

"You don't remember?"

"Things are starting to come back slowly, but it's still so foggy," I confess, unable to help myself as I press my lips to the side of his throat.

He hums low and a fire burns within me. I need him more

than I need air to breathe. But first, I need to untie him.

Fumbling with the leather straps around his wrists, I feel they are locked with a key and not a buckle. Without a key, I don't think I can free him.

"She has the key," he says, reading my frustration.

"Who does?"

"Dr. Norton, the same woman who made you forget."

"Why is she doing this to us?"

Dutch sighs, revealing there is so much more than I thought.

"There should be some surgical tools on a table near the other bed."

He doesn't need to say any more as I jump up and blindly feel around the room for something that resembles a table. I find it when I bump into it, making a loud clanging noise as instruments clatter onto the floor.

"Shit!" I curse, dropping to my hands and knees and scrambling for the tools.

A hiss leaves me as I cut my thumb on something sharp, but that something sharp is exactly what I need. I suck on my thumb as I grab the scalpel in my other hand and race back to Dutch. I still can't see well, so I carefully feel where the leather cuff sits on his wrist as I don't want to cut him.

It's a thick piece of leather, but the tool is sharp, so it won't take long to cut through it. Just as I press the tip into the strap, the lights flicker on with a buzz, and the darkness subsides. The harsh light burns my eyes, but that pales in comparison to when I focus on Dutch's face which is inches away from mine.

It's the most surreal feeling—I remember him, but I don't.

It suddenly feels like I've been brought back to life and,

forgetting the task at hand, I lift a trembling finger and gently brush back a strand of soft blond hair from his forehead. I trace the slope of his strong nose, running a finger to the apple of his cheek, and then back to his nose.

His Cupid's bow just accents his luscious full lips, lips which I remember kissing and forgetting the world exists.

But it's the blueness of his eyes which render me speechless, because it's like I can see inside of his soul. And what I see…he takes my breath away.

He is so beautiful, angels weep, but I know beneath that beauty lays a warrior who would fight for me until death. He has before…

Placing my hand to his cheek, he leans into it, watching me as closely as I watch him. It's like we're seeing one another for the first time.

"Are you…hurt?" he asks, his Adam's apple bobbing with a deep swallow.

"I'm okay," I assure him. "I just need to remember."

Sadness overcomes him, and I wonder why. Doesn't he want me to?

"You don't remember me?"

"Bits and pieces," I confess, caressing the hair at his temples. "There are holes in my memory, but it's coming back."

Unable to stop myself, I press a splayed palm on his chest. "I remember your heart. It sings to me."

"You always said that. It's because my heart is your son's."

"Misha," I whisper, because I remember him. I knew he was dead, but I didn't remember how or that he donated his heart to Dutch.

Tears gather because this feels like an old wound which will never close.

"I'm sorry, baby. I hate seeing you cry. But you need to know it all."

"There's more?"

With a heavy sigh, Dutch nods. "So much more, but now...I need you to get me the fuck out of here."

His words jar me into action because time is of the essence. I forgot anything existed outside of this room because everything is so...calm with Dutch nearby.

"Is it always like this between us?"

I am drowning in a sea of blue as Dutch's eyes soften. "Yes."

I don't need to explain what I mean because he gets it; he gets me, and that has nothing to do with the heart beating inside his chest. Misha's heart may give him life, but that isn't the reason I...love him.

I love him because he completes me in ways I don't understand.

I suddenly hear music and when I look at the musical inspired tattoos on his body, I know that music comes from Dutch. I feel like I'm falling in love with him all over again and nothing has felt more beautiful.

Falling in love is a magical experience. So to be able to do it twice—I won't waste a single second.

The leather whines under the blade as I hack at it quickly, but it just doesn't seem to want to budge.

Dutch suddenly stiffens as his astute eyes focus on the doorway. "You've got to go!" he says on a rushed breath.

I have no idea why, until I hear it...

Click...click...click.

And just like that, I'm transported back in time...

Suddenly, I hear the click...click...click of heels echoing down the corridor. The sound sends chills down my spine.

A beautiful blonde woman appears, wheeling a chair, her spotless white doctor's coat hinting who she is. But I've never seen her before.

She enters the bathroom and stops beside the bathtub. She exhales when she peers down at Dutch. I don't know what it is about her, but I instantly don't like her. Even though she wears a doctor's uniform, I don't think she's here to help.

"I'm sorry, but you gave me no choice," she scolds, arms folded. "I can't show special preference because of who you are."

What does that mean? Just who is he, then?

"You can't behave that way," she continues, talking to him like a child. "I'm trying to help you. I'm trying to make you better so you can play music again. I know that if you can do that again, everything will be all right. We'll be all right again. I love you, Jonathan. Please come back to me."

Reality winds me as I focus on the truth and time stands still as I turn over my shoulder, only remembering there are two beds in here.

What I see has me gasping in horror.

A wrinkled corpse is propped in bed like a living, breathing being. A blanket covers its legs. I don't know what gender it once was, but I think it was a man. His yellowed eyes almost appear glass-like, staring a hole straight through me.

His mouth is slightly ajar, as if the last words he ever uttered were ones of pain.

"Luna!" Dutch whispers with urgency. "Please, go. At the end of one of the tunnels there is a ladder which brings you outside the fences of Parkfields. Free yourself."

But I can't.

"Who is t-that?"

"Luna—"

"Tell me!"

The clicky clack of heels along the linoleum only gets louder and louder, but I don't care. I'm not going anywhere until I know what's going on.

"It's Alanna's fiancé…who was Misha's dad. His name was Jonathan."

"Misha's father," I say, shaking my head because this means…

The faceless corpse soon morphs into a person, a person I once knew. Memories flash so quickly before my eyes, my stomach rolls and I want to be sick. But I push past the nausea to remember the man who I once loved.

I use that term lightly because I didn't know what love was. I was just a child when I fell head over heels for Jonathan Stand. He was the epitome of a bad boy who had the gift of bullshitting anyone who would listen—me included.

He was tall, older, and handsome. If I had my time over, would I have declined the offer of him giving me a ride home? The answer is no because I will never regret Misha; the only good thing to ever come from Jonathan.

Memory after memory assaults me and it feels like now that it's started, it won't stop. It's come full circle and I realize none of this was a coincidence. We're here because Dr. Norton is a fucking psycho.

"Does she have something to do with Misha's death?"

The despair on Dutch's face says it all.

"I'm going to fucking kill her."

"Luna, no!"

But Dutch's warning falls on deaf ears because there is no way I am letting this bitch live.

I jump down from the bed and desperately scour the room for a place to hide to catch Alanna unawares. I have the scalpel in hand, ready to end this once and for all.

"I can't help you if something happens."

"What's going to happen is that I plan on jamming this scalpel into Alanna's throat," I counter, anger surging through me.

There is no way she's getting away with what she did to Misha.

"Please, we have to be smart. We finally have the upper hand. If this place is connected to the hospital, not only do we have Alanna to deal with, but the others she has working with her too. You manage to overpower her. What then? We go on the run again?

"She has too much power. She will just manipulate the situation. She has in the past. She has the ability to make everyone believe they're the crazy one.

"Please, go. I can't protect you now. But when I can, that's when we go. I can't walk…because she broke my fucking knee."

I am torn with what to do and time isn't on our side. "What if she kills you?"

"She won't."

"How can you be so sure?"

However, he doesn't need to reply; the look on his face says it all.

I suddenly feel sick for another reason. This is an advantage he has over Alanna, but what will Dutch have to sacrifice to play her at her own game?

"It doesn't mean anything," he says softly. "I'll do what I have to, to make sure you're safe."

Tears sting my eyes because I don't want to be here. I don't want to be wrapped up in this mess…and that's the reason I am going to kill this fucking bitch.

"Luna, no!"

But my mind is made up. It's a risk I'm willing to take because I am sick to death of being helpless. Why do the monsters get to win?

No.

I refuse to surrender.

You reap what you sow, and Alanna is about to reap her karma—tenfold.

Dutch's blue eyes plead with me one final time, but my mind is made up. This ends now. An eye for an eye, and as I see it, Alanna has destroyed my life in every possible way, so I plan on bugging out her fucking eyeballs before shoving them down her throat.

There's no place to hide, so I decide I only have the element of surprise on my side.

I quickly place all the fallen medical tools back onto the table and arrange the room how Alanna left it. I race toward the doorway and press my back up to the wall, planning on striking the moment Alanna walks through.

My heart beats uncontrollably and I realize this entire nightmare begun because of the one thing we all have, the one thing which makes us do some fucked-up things all in the name of love. And now is no exception because in the name of love for my son, for Dutch, and for myself, I am going to take what

Alanna took from me—her heart.

The sound of her heels announces her arrival and the moment she enters, I raise my arm, ready to drive the scalpel into her throat, but what I see has me retreating quickly because I did not factor in the possibility that she wouldn't be alone.

But whose hand she holds has me realizing that Dutch is right—this intricate web has the ability to trap us all, making us Alanna's prey.

"It's okay, Bobby," she says sweetly to the young boy with hair rivaling the sun. "This is Dutch. He's sick, but I'm making him better."

Dutch has the perfect poker face, but I know he's just as shocked as me.

Who is this child who looks no older than five years old? And more importantly, where are his parents?

An image of a little boy riding his bike without training wheels careers into me and it's so lucid, I'm certain it's happening right in front of my eyes. "You're doing it all by yourself. Good boy, Misha."

My memory is coming back and instead of being frightened, I use it as fuel to avenge what was taken from me.

"Dutch is a very talented pianist. Would you like to hear him play?"

Bobby turns into Alanna, afraid.

"What is this?" Dutch asks, keeping his tone calm.

"This is Bobby," Alanna replies smartly. "He's going to stay with us for a while."

Dutch doesn't want to scare Bobby, so he's keeping calm. "Why?"

Alanna runs her fingers through the young child's hair. I

have no idea what her motives are until Dutch shakes his head, clearly disgusted.

"Cover your ears, Bobby."

He does as Dutch says.

"You think he's going to keep you safe?" Dutch spits. "That keeping him a prisoner too will somehow win over his love? You can't make people love you, Alanna! That's not how love works!"

I now understand what Bobby's role is in all of this.

Alanna believes Dutch won't hurt her because he won't want Bobby to witness such violence. She clearly doesn't trust Dutch. It's a smart plan only a psychopath can conjure up because it will work. As long as Bobby is here, Dutch won't hurt Alanna, which means she is afraid of Dutch.

She knows if he managed to break free, he would have no qualms killing her.

Looking at Bobby, I now have an obligation to both him and Dutch. I want to save them both, but how? If I go, I may never have this chance again. But if I make myself known, I take the risk of Alanna killing me, leaving Dutch and Bobby at her mercy, and my Misha's death will never be avenged.

There is no way I'm returning to Parkfields because I can't help Dutch being locked away in there. But Noah will notice my disappearance soon. If not already.

I am running out of time.

I stay here, they'll sound the alarm. I go back, I will be subjected to Noah's perversions and who knows when my luck will run out with Alanna.

But if I escape, they'll look for me—I'll be a fugitive.

I'm faced with so many scenarios—I wish I knew how this

story ends so I can make the right choice. But there is no right in this circumstance. I do know, however, that when this does end, I'll be slathered in Alanna's blood as I eat her fucking heart.

Going back to Parkfields isn't an option. Neither was slitting Alanna's throat. So as much as it pains me, there seems to be only one choice.

"Come here," Dutch orders Alanna. "I'll show you what real love tastes like."

I close my eyes, swallowing down my horror because I know what comes next.

Her heels resonating on the linoleum is a sound which is forever burned into my memory, but when I hear her moan softly, that sound replaces all others and is the incentive I need to open my eyes and sneak out of the room undetected as Dutch sacrifices his self-worth by bedding the devil.

We needed her distracted and what better way than by Dutch giving himself to Alanna.

My body trembles in anger, demanding I go back, but I know that's not the smart thing to do. Running isn't the right thing to do; but it's the smartest thing to do because I'm Dutch's only hope, and I won't fail him.

I make my way through this house of horrors silently, memorizing every step because when I come back, I'll come prepared, prepared with a fucking shotgun.

Once I'm back in the tunnel, I take a moment to gather my bearings and once I know where I am, I take off into a dead sprint.

My heart beats frantically, it echoing in my ears so loudly, it leaves me dizzy. But I persevere because I know the window for escape grows smaller and smaller. Once I reach the crossroad, I

turn and venture down the tunnel farthest to the right as Dutch said.

And that's when I hear it…the barking of dogs and the frenzied voices of men.

I am now the hunted.

Every muscle in my body protests that I stop as I can't take in breath quick enough, but I focus on nothing but getting to the ladder.

"This way!" I hear a man scream, followed by the snarls of what sounds like the beasts of hell.

The tunnel is suddenly illuminated in flashing red as an alarm is in sync with the strobing red lights. The strobe effect only adds to my hysteria, testing my already frail sanity. I trip over a crack in the ground, falling face-first onto the cement.

I taste blood…

Without delay, I pick myself up, ignoring the blood pouring from my nose because the metallic taste is what I need to run faster than I've ever run before. This scene is pure bedlam, but I realize as a maniacal laughter spills from me that I am now one with the darkness.

All that was done to me comes bursting from the seams and I won't rest until every single person who has wronged me pays.

The snarling of dogs and the feverish catcalls of men echo from the walls, hinting they're getting closer. But the chase excites me. It only cements that I won't come out of this a victim—no, I am a survivor.

And when the silver of the ladder is illuminated red, I realize surviving is literally a step away.

"I know you're down here," Noah singsongs, excited by the

game of cat and mouse. "And when I find you, I am going to have so much fun with you."

His lewd comment gives me an idea.

I grip onto the rungs of the ladder and scramble up the steps so quickly, I lose my footing and trip down. But I yank myself up and the moment I reach the manhole, I attempt to shift it, but it's stuck firmly in place.

"Come on!" I curse under my breath as I use all my strength to move it.

There aren't any handles, so I place my palms flat against the metal and shift it to the left.

Nothing.

"Lunnaaaaa…" Noah calls, sending chills down my spine.

His voice is the motivation I need to contort my body and use the top of my shoulder and hands and push with all my strength.

It still doesn't budge.

I wipe my sweaty hands on my clothes and try again.

I use the anger, the sadness, every emotion I can tap into, and use it to fight for my freedom. And it works because inch by inch, I see it. First, a new moon faces me, which then slips to a crescent, and then to a quarter moon.

I need to catch my breath and the cool air gives my lungs the life I need to inhale deeply and finish what I started. I hear the chirping of crickets and the hoot of an owl. It's like the animals are spurring me on, cheering in support that I'm almost there.

With a roar, I grip the edge of manhole and shove it with all my might until finally, it's a full moon and I am free.

I boost myself up, not able to appreciate my freedom just yet because I'm not done.

I don't cover the manhole, but grip the metal disc in my hand and the moment I hear frantic footsteps climb the rungs, I prepare myself. Noah's face appears like a mole emerging from the dirt and when we lock eyes, I smile.

"Hello, darlin."

Before he has a chance to speak, I use the manhole covering as a baseball bat and strike him in the face with it.

He is stunned, his eyes wide, so I strike him again and again, until he tumbles back down the hole with a thud. I wish I could admire my handiwork, but I don't have time.

I quickly place the cover back onto the manhole and jump onto it, hoping it'll wedge it into places so Noah's friends have a hard time reopening it.

Dutch was right—I am standing outside the steel fences of Parkfields.

Taking one last look at the place which is hell on earth, I vow to return and save the man I love.

But now…now, I run.

Six

Dutch

Bobby uses the yellow crayon to color in the sun in the coloring book Alanna gave him. He sits on the floor quietly, almost afraid to look up from the picture on the page.

Alanna left some time ago. No word on where she went. I can only hope she doesn't return with another child.

I do know she's up to something, however, because she wheeled Jonathan away, and I doubt it's to his final resting place, because that ship has sailed.

This plan is smart on her part because she knows I would never hurt her with Bobby here. This means she doesn't trust me. And it also means she fears me.

I wish I knew if Luna made it out of here safely. If she did, I would almost be happy to give up. But until I know she's safe, I have to fight.

Seeing her was the most bittersweet feeling, because I knew I'd have to let her go. I also know that if and when we meet again, I will have to tell her I'm the reason she was back at Parkfields—all because I trusted Alanna when I should have trusted my heart.

I have no doubt, however, that Luna will remember it all soon, and when she does, I wouldn't hold it against her if she left me here to rot.

Alanna made sure I'm an invalid by breaking my knee, there's no need for her to tie me to this bed. But she's done so to ensure I know she's the one in control of my future. And I can honestly say I have no idea what's coming.

"Bobby?" I say, realizing my only ally is a kid. "Do you have any brothers or sisters?"

At first, he doesn't reply, but eventually, he shakes his head.

"What's your mommy's name?"

His small hand stills from coloring.

Oh my fucking god…what has Alanna done?

"It's okay, Bobby. I'm your friend. It'll be our secret."

He is afraid and I hate that Alanna has dragged yet another person into her vile games.

"Do you have a mommy?" I ask because Alanna has connections all over, and it wouldn't surprise me if Bobby is a child who's been in the system. She would use her status to win over the authorities, promising Bobby a better life, but in reality, he is just another pawn for her to use.

He shakes his head once again, confirming my fears.

I don't have time to ask him anything further because something happens, which confirms the stage is set for the next scene.

Alanna comes rushing into the room with a man I've never seen before. He is wearing blue scrubs, a surgical face mask, and tying the cord of some ridiculous mesh hat thing around the back of his head. They're muttering to one another, but the sense of urgency is apparent in their actions.

There's no point crying out for help because it's obvious this man is aiding Alanna. So all I can do is watch and prepare for what comes next.

"Come, Bobby," Alanna gently orders.

Bobby looks at me, panic in his blue eyes.

"It's okay. I'll see you real soon."

Bobby hesitates, but eventually takes Alanna's hand.

The man is looking over the surgical tools and the fact that he's in scrubs can only mean one thing. I doubt he will be performing any Frankenstein procedures on me today because Jonathan appears to be on sabbatical, but I am curious what he has planned.

I'm not afraid. I know I should be. But my heart is steady as he snaps on gloves and injects a needle with a clear fluid.

"This won't take long."

"I hope you don't start every conversation that way," I quip because at this point, humor is the only way I can cope with the crazy.

Mr. Personality ignores me and injects the syringe into my IV. It doesn't take long until the noise drags me into nothingness…and I let go.

It's the most surreal feeling waking from a drug-induced coma.

It's like your mind is tricking you into believing you're still lost in a world where there is no pain. But the moment your conscious kicks in, you're dragged back into the last thing you remembered…

For me, that was wondering if I would ever wake again. But alas, it seems I survived another day.

Opening my eyes, things are foggy, a white veil clouding my vision. I blink a few times and when my sight clears, I see I'm no longer in the room of horrors.

The room has definitely seen better days, however. The faded floral wallpaper hangs in tatters from the walls, revealing white brick beneath. There's a massive hole in the ceiling where birds nest their eggs in the rafters.

The floor is littered with rubble from the caved-in roof and all I can smell is mold and cat piss.

The bed I'm lying in is an old Victorian style with a matching dresser. The single window has steel bars over it, so it goes without saying, getting fresh air is out of the question.

The place is a fucking squalor pit and I wonder where the fuck I am.

I try to move and am surprised to see I'm not bound, and that's when I realize my leg is bandaged—the one Alanna was hammer crazy with when she broke my knee.

Did the dude in scrubs operate on me to mend my broken knee? All signs point to that. It doesn't feel like I'm missing a kidney, so that means Alanna called on a favor from a friend to help me.

Why?

Turning to the left, I chuckle when I see my ole pal, Jonathan, sitting in a wooden rocking chair. A colorful crocheted blanket is placed over his knees in case he catches a chill.

I am so desensitized to all of this, I shrug off the fact that a corpse sits in my room and focus on finding out where I am.

Alanna moved me because no doubt, she found out that Luna has escaped and she's afraid Luna will come back and wreak havoc.

I exhale in relief.

But that's short-lived because now I have no idea where Luna is, or where I am. I also have no idea what Alanna has up her sleeve.

"You're awake," the devil says happily as she enters my room.

I don't reply and watch as she retrieves a syringe from her pocket. Again, I'm completely desensitized to her jabbing me with shit, I don't even flinch when she injects the needle into my IV.

"It's antibiotics. I want you better as soon as possible."

"Why? So you can try and revive Jonathan? Pretty sure that ship has sailed."

"I want you to finish your masterpiece."

"Excuse me?"

She smiles happily, brushing the hair from my brow. I turn my cheek, but she clearly doesn't read the room. "I know you want that too. There's a piano in the other room. I got it just for you."

What in the ever-living fuck is going on?

"So, you want me to finish my song and then what? Cut out my heart to say thanks?"

Alanna sighs, taking a seat in the ragged chair near my bed. A puff of dust, and probably asbestos, fills the room. "I'm not sure what I want to do yet."

Well, this is…progress? Has she finally come to her senses?

"This will be your greatest concert to date."

"Concert?"

Alanna nods. "I want all my colleagues to know I was the muse behind your work of art."

"Colleagues? What is going on?"

Alanna crosses her legs, flashing her black stilettos. "There's been some interest among the medical board about the success of your transplant and when they found out who you were, they were adamant you were to play for them at the Medical Annual Gala."

I look at her, waiting for the punch line. But that's it.

She's fucking serious.

That's the reason for the surgery. She can't parade me around like a prized poodle if I look as bad as Jonathan. What would the medical board think if she wheeled me out and sat me behind the piano with a broken leg and oh, a missing fucking heart?

I have a sneaking suspicion her reputation has been questioned, which is why the change of heart. I suddenly hate that phrase.

She probably didn't take that into consideration when she did a transplant on someone whose name you can find on Google 'cause I'm "famous."

"And your parents will be there."

I honestly hadn't given much thought about them because they're the reason I was committed in the first place. No doubt, Alanna has liaised with them and assured my safety and they believed her, because why wouldn't they?

This tale is so fucked up, I wouldn't believe it if I wasn't living it.

There's a giant elephant in the room, which is not Jonathan the corpse, but rather Luna. I thought Alanna moved location because she learned of Luna's escape, but maybe I was wrong.

This has definitely changed the course of direction because playing in front of people means I have the chance to tell them what Alanna did, and the atrocities that take place at Parkfields.

Alanna surely knows I won't remain quiet, so the question is, what does she have as collateral?

There's only one person…

Until I know where Luna is, Alanna knows I will do whatever I need to, to keep her safe.

"Fine. When is it?"

She smiles, clapping happily. "Four weeks' time. Your leg will be healed by then."

That's what she's worried about? That her professional conduct will be questioned if I hobble into a room filled with people. She really believes I won't tell a soul about what happened, and this is troubling.

"Where's Bobby?"

Her face lights up. "He's sleeping in his bedroom."

I want to ask where we are, but there's no point.

"Do you want to see the piano?"

This is like asking a junkie if they want their next fix. My heart begins to beat faster, an excited rhythm which betrays my composure.

"I'll get the wheelchair."

Alanna rises from her seat, a spring to her step, while I attempt to construct some sort of plan of escape. I can't go now, but I can map out the layout of wherever the fuck we are so when I can walk, I can burn this place to the ground—ensuring Alanna is inside when I do.

She re-enters with the shining wheelchair. Seems she went all out for the occasion. "Don't make me regret this," she warns sternly.

As much as I would love to run her over numerous times with the wheelchair, I know I'm not strong enough to overpower her. And I also have no idea what faces me beyond these dilapidated walls. There will only be one chance at escape.

There's no room for error.

She positions the chair near the bed and unhooks the bag from the IV stand. I remove the white blanket and shift my body, but my arms are weak from being tied for so long. I also haven't eaten for God knows how many days—weeks?

Alanna smiles, arms behind her back.

She wants me to ask for help as this is just another power play on her behalf. She gets off on being needed and as much as I hate it, I need her help.

Thinking of the greater good, I smile as sweetly as I can without telling her to go fuck herself. "Can you please help me?"

"Of course I can." She comes rushing to my aid, looping her arms under my armpits and slides me into the chair as I try my best to move.

Once strapped in, she places the IV bag into my lap and hums under her breath as she wheels me from the room. The moment we enter the hallway, I see the rest of this house is just as run-down as the bedroom.

In its prime, this house would have been the envy of many. The three faded golden archways of the hallway which face the main entrance would have gleamed in the sunlight. But now, it's just an abandoned mansion which sets the perfect backdrop for every Gothic horror.

There is a spiral staircase with rusted intricate balusters extending both sides from the corridor which leads down to the lower level. The carpet was once red, but most of it is now pulled up, so Alanna has no issues wheeling me down the stairs.

I take in everything I can, and when we get to a checkered flooring, Alanna stops so I can see the foyer ahead.

The large white doors are at the end of the entrance, but they are roped with heavy chains and a padlock.

The walls look to be a green marble and I wonder what secrets they house.

"Where are we?" I ask as Alanna wheels me down the center stairs.

"It's called Pennington Villa. It was built in eighteen ninety-two for Richard Pennington, a very famous surgeon. But as bad luck had it, he died of a heart attack his first night in the home. And his wife sadly passed a month later…of a broken heart. Such a tragedy. They could never enjoy what was supposed to be their happily ever after."

This tale is too close to Alanna's.

I don't believe a word, but I nod nonetheless.

When we descend the last step, I count four entryways extending from the foyer. Alanna heads for the first door to the left of which has red curtains draped over it and we enter what I guess may have been a sitting room.

Two red marbled columns frame three bay windows which has a settee underneath.

Lifting my chin, I see the ceiling is high and painted on

them are cherubs playing harps and other musical instruments as they sit among the clouds. The cracks in the plaster only make this sight even more beautiful as I feel like I've stepped back in time.

There's a fire crackling in the fireplace, the smell comforting me and replacing the anger with calm. There are hundreds of candles, burned down to almost the wick. This is what provides the light as there isn't any electricity.

But what I see in the middle of the room is the true beauty.

A black piano calls my name and the popping of the fire soon transports into notes I can see those tiny cherubs play. Music fills my body and I close my eyes, helpless to the sounds.

I hear it again; the only thing before Luna which made life worth living—music. How I've missed her.

A temptress to my soul, the music pulsates in time to the beating of my heart; the one thing that once stopped the flow. But now, in this forsaken mansion, it doesn't stop. It rushes from every pore of my body and I see it—it's white light.

However, that is soon replaced with darkness because I suddenly feel guilty for experiencing such a rush when it was delivered by the hand of the devil. But is that why I can feel it again? Every artist uses their pain, their sorrow, to express themselves, to expel the demons which are feeding on their souls.

Is Alanna in fact a muse of darkness? While Luna is the light?

I don't want to accept this as truth because what does that say about me if I use Alanna as anything other than a piñata?

The wheels of my chair crunch over rubble and the sound almost winds me because I hear it as musical notes; I can taste the music on my tongue. This hasn't happened in a very long time. It did with Luna, but this with Alanna is different…and it scares me.

I've been chasing this feeling since the moment I awoke, and to feel it here, now, I question what I must sacrifice to silence the monsters lingering in the dark. The music is their forage, and now, they are ravenous after being starved for so long.

I don't have to open my eyes as Alanna puts me in front of the piano. Touch is enough as I place my fingers onto the keys. An electrical shock renders me breathless. It's like coming home to a lover; your first love whose curves you've memorized with your tongue.

I take a moment to remember this moment because I need to revisit it if I ever get dragged to the abyss again.

I don't even think twice as my fingers work over the keys without sound. I want to take my time. I need to relish the touch which is akin to none. Music has always been my mistress and when I met Luna, she filled the void, but now that I am here, I realize no one can ever comfort me how music does.

The only song which seems to be the soundtrack of my life fills the room—Moonlight Sonata. But this rendition is different because I play it how I've never played it before.

The same feelings I felt when I watched Alanna rip out Joy's heart overwhelm me and animate me in ways I am ashamed for.

Once again, I hear the blood pulsating through Joy's veins and arteries, giving her life, a life which was snuffed out by Alanna…and by me.

Does bloodshed and violence now feed me? Is that why I can play?

Luna was the angel dust I needed, but with her gone, Alanna's venom seems to nourish me in ways I don't understand.

Ashamed, I pry open my eyes and yank my hands from the keys. I will not be that person.

But as I lock eyes with Alanna who sits on the settee with tears streaming down her cheeks, I realize a part of me will sacrifice anything and everything to feel the music again.

Alanna's nipples are straining against the thin material of her white cotton T-shirt and when she licks a fallen tear from her pink mouth, my dicks stirs—and I want to cut it off for doing so.

I'm disgusted with myself because I don't know who this man is. How can I react to her this way after everything she's done? Feelings of shame and guilt swarm in my belly and the only response I can make sense of is that I want to play.

The more sordid I feel, the louder the music. I fight it, but as Alanna flicks her long hair over her shoulder, notes crash into me and I am a prisoner to the blackened melody which will consume me whole.

I've never felt this before.

I don't understand.

I hate it.

But I don't.

The slope of Alanna's elongated neck catches my attention and I punish the keys as I look at her with not disgust, but interest. Her chest rises and falls quickly. She's excited.

And I hate that I am too.

Not excited in a sexual manner, but music has always gotten me hard.

The fact that Alanna is the inspiration for that arousal has me questioning what the fuck is wrong with me. I want it to stop. But I can't. I am a slave to the music, and just like before the operation, it is the only language I need.

The only love language I understand.

But that's abruptly replaced with laughter, with the smell of strawberries on a hot summer's day.

"I remember your heart. It sings to me."

Light cracks through the darkness and reminds me of who I am, of who I love…I love Luna. Whatever this is with Alanna needs to stop, regardless of the whispers the music speaks to me.

I cease playing and stare Alanna down. "I'm tired."

She wets her lips, my words breaking her from a trancelike state. "Of course. I'll take you back to your room to rest. Tomorrow, you could try eating. And maybe when you're better, I'll show you around our new home."

She rises and takes a hold of the handles of my chair, humming happily as she wheels me from the room, while I don't fail to take note of the horrifying words she just said—our new home.

Home sweet home…

Seven

Luna

I want to sleep for a hundred years, but I can't.

Opening my eyes, I see that it's still dark out. This motel is a real shithole, but it's the only place I could afford with the fifty bucks I stole from the trucker who was nice enough to give me a ride.

I never stopped running from Parkfields. I didn't look back. Just forward as I ran for my life. Each turn I took, I expected to be greeted by the police, ready to be dragged back to the hospital and dreading the worst.

But when I saw the red brake lights of the logging truck which stopped ahead, I knew I had made it.

I didn't think twice as I jumped into his truck and told him I didn't care where we went, I just needed to be far away from Parkfields. He seemed nice enough, happy for the company. He didn't ask any questions, not that he had to. My dirty hospital gown and scrappy appearance was explanation enough.

He chatted about his wife and two kids. How they were high school sweethearts and he was working the strenuous hours that he was to support them all. His name was Ray, and I did a dirty on Ray when I stole fifty dollars out of his wallet when he stopped to use the restroom.

Again, I didn't look back as I ran through the thick forest, heart in my throat, because I didn't have any idea where I was. Only when I was crippled with fatigue did I give in. I was happy to sleep under the skies, but the buzzing neon motel sign caught my eye from across the road.

I stumbled to the small window and the elderly women took pity on me clearly as she took my crumpled note and told me to stay for as long as I needed. I landed face-first on the smelly mattress and slept like the dead.

I'm not sure how long I've been out of it for, but I am rested enough to conjure up a plan.

First things first, I need to find out where I am.

Sitting upright, I switch on the lamp, open the bedside dresser drawer, and see a Bible and what looks to be a tourist map. Reaching for the map, I open it and spread it across my lap. I trace my finger over names and places I don't recognize.

"Remember," I berate myself because this is beyond frustrating.

I focus on town names and landmarks, determined to recall something. My eye keeps going back to one place. Somerton University.

I don't know why, but I trust my gut and decide to check out why this place out of all places stands out to me.

My body aches as I rise to shower off the filth from the

past few days. The light flickers above the basin as I stare at my deathly complexion in the mirror. My hair is a combination of faded black with my blonde roots coming through.

I look a mess.

There is a sadness imprinted all over me. I use two fingers to lift the corners of my mouth into a forced smile, but the gesture looks foreign. I don't want to smile. I just want my life, and the memories that go with it, back.

Standing under the shower spray, I wash away the sins of my past and wish I could emerge reborn. But I won't rest until I find Dutch and Alanna pays for everything she's done.

I remember the way I responded to him, like my mind and body knew he was meant for me in every possible way.

Drying off, I am now faced with the dilemma of finding clothes to wear. I look at the adolescent's bunny print robe hanging on the back of the door. Someone left it behind, no doubt.

Without a choice, I slip it on. I have no belongings to gather, so I slither into the darkness, faced with the first day of a life I won't forget.

I'm crouched on a bench, under a tree, trying to avoid getting wet from the rain.

Thankfully, on my journey, I passed a home which had some clothes hanging on a line and some men's boots by the door. Everything I wear is about two sizes too big, but fashion is the least of my concerns as I scour the university for something that looks familiar.

So far, nothing. But I won't give up.

Students run past me to get out of the pouring rain, paying no attention to me which is what I want. I need to blend in and be smart, how a predator should be.

Frustrated, I sink farther under the hood of my sweater, eyes peeled to anyone who passes me in hopes they spark a memory.

Everyone looks so…normal. I wonder what it feels like.

Two boys with broad shoulders run toward the doors, their varsity jackets pulled over their heads to shield themselves from the rain. I don't look twice until the yellow number eight on the back of one of their jackets leaves me with a dry throat.

I clear it, but it only becomes harder and harder to swallow.

"Mom, I did it! I'm playing college football. Can you believe it?"

"I never doubted it for a minute. I am so proud of you, Misha."

Tears are streaming down my face when a young man approaches me. "Luna?"

I quickly wipe away from tears. "Yes?"

The man with brown hair and kind green eyes quickly offers his jacket as coverage so we can get out of the rain to talk. I don't know who he is, but he knows me, which is enough for me to jump down from the bench and follow as he runs us toward cover under the walkway.

He waits for fellow pupils to pass us by before he speaks. "You don't remember me?" he asks, even though he knows the answer.

I shake my head.

He brushes the rain from his wet hair, as if needing a moment to divulge what he's about to say. "My name is Kyle.

I am Joy's son. Joy is your best friend. And I was Misha's best friend. We are neighbors. And my mom…she's missing."

I take a moment to process this because it's a lot. I try and remember him, but I know that's not how things seem to work. My memories return when I least expect them to. But if what Kyle says is true, then he knows where I live and if any place is going to help me remember, it'll be the house in which I lived.

"Here," he says, gesturing with his head for me to follow.

We enter the hallway and I peer at the high ceilings, overwhelmed at the open space. Being confined to my bed and tiny room for months has scarred me in ways I never imagined. The world is a big place and I am relearning how to walk in it.

Kyle stops when we reach a trophy case and a silence soon follows. I peer into the glass cabinet and see all the typical things you'd expect to see inside—trophies, ribbons, medals… but when I see a photo of a handsome young man leaning on one knee, football in hand as he smiles proudly at the camera, I realize this is also a shrine to my son.

Misha's name is engraved onto a gold plate with the year he was born and the year he died. The words etched beneath has a sob catching in my throat.

Gone but never forgotten. Fly high, Jack. Until we meet again…

Kyle consoles me as I weep because this is like losing Misha over and over again.

I remember that smile when I first saw it the day he was born. I remember it when we sang together in the kitchen to David Bowie. I remember it so clearly because it once reflected mine, which is why I cannot smile any longer.

My reason to smile was taken away from me and then I was

put into Parkfields by…

"It was Joy," I whisper against Kyle's chest. "Joy was the one who had me committed."

Kyle hugs me tighter. "Yes, but she was only trying to help. Let's go back to your house so we can talk."

As Kyle prepares us some coffee, I stand in the kitchen doorway, unable to move as I take everything in.

Again, things feel familiar, but then they don't at the same time.

If I focus hard enough, sparks of light, or flickers of a memory will flash before my eyes, but nothing solid—yet.

However, just being here, I know it won't be long until I remember.

Kyle can sense this is all a little too much for me, so he hasn't bombarded me with information, which I am thankful for. He places a cup of coffee on the kitchen counter and smiles.

I enter slowly, my boots pounding against the spotless floor. "Was I well off?" I ask because this house is gorgeous and in what seems to be a very expensive neighborhood.

"I guess both our families did all right for themselves."

"What did I do for work?"

"You worked for a men's magazine…one you used to model for," he replies, his cheeks turning red. "You were a centerfold girl. A very popular one."

I suddenly remember glitter and high heels. "Before that, though, I used to be a stripper, wasn't I?"

Kyle nods.

"Can you tell me who I was?"

Kyle takes a sip of his coffee. "Where do I start?"

"From the beginning?"

So for the next hour, Kyle details my life from when he can remember—who I was to him, his mom, and to Misha. He tells me how I helped Joy financially and how I helped pay for his college tuition so he could attend school with Misha.

He tells me how he watched Misha change before his eyes—once his best friend who slowly became a stranger. He says this is because he believes Misha was messed up with a bad crowd. I can read between the lines, however, because it's what he doesn't say that matters.

"How could I not see this?" I ask, shaking my head.

"Misha was very good at keeping secrets, Luna. Don't beat yourself up over this."

"Was he involved in drugs?"

Kyle sighs, only interlacing our fingers as he reaches for my hand over the counter. "You were the best mom to him. He loved you so much and I know whatever he was messed up in, he didn't want to worry you.

"He pretended like everything was okay because he wanted to protect you."

"It was my job to protect him," I reply, my lower lip trembling.

"And you did. His whole life, that's all you did. He told me this all the time. Accidents happen. And it sucks, but Misha would hate to see you this way because of him."

"It wasn't an accident…" a voice suddenly whispers into my left ear.

It's Misha.

The moment I saw Dutch in that room, I knew something

103

sinister lurked and it all had to do with Alanna.

Dutch told me there was more.

He knows what happened and he's the only one I trust to tell me the truth, no matter how badly it'll hurt.

"So I signed everything over to Joy?"

"Yes. She was taking care of your affairs until you were better. But she has been acting…strange for a long time now. I thought it was the stress of what happened to Misha and you, but there's something else. I know there is."

"You said she was missing?"

The worry is all over Kyle's face. "Yes. And this isn't like her at all. We've never gone this long without talking."

"Have you tried her cell?"

"Yes, many times. It keeps going straight to voice mail. We even have an app on our phones which allows us to track one another. It was her idea," he explains with half a smile. "Her last trackable movements were ten days ago at a supermarket parking lot. Then it's like she just vanished."

The mystery just continues to grow and I can't help but think Alanna is responsible for all of it.

"I don't mean to pry, Kyle, but where's your father?"

It's apparent Kyle isn't close to his dad. "Last I checked, he was living a happy life with his new wife, who was once his secretary. He cheated on my mom," he explains angrily. "I don't have much to do with him."

I mull over his words. "Would he know where Joy is?"

"I doubt it. But at this point, I'm willing to talk to anyone. The cops won't help because there aren't signs of any foul play. But this isn't like her."

Kyle places his head into his hands, his shoulders trembling as he begins to cry.

Without thought, I walk around the counter and hug him. "We'll find her."

I allow him all the time he needs to grieve because I understand firsthand how losing a loved one feels.

As he seeks solace in my arms, I think over everything he shared and something keeps niggling at the back of my mind— Joy isn't innocent in any of this.

When I think about her, only bad memories linger. I can't help but feel betrayal. Kyle said she did what she did to help me, but nothing about Parkfields has helped.

"Can I stay here tonight?"

"Of course." I rub his back softly.

He sniffs back his tears and pulls away, appearing embarrassed. "Do you want a tour of the house? You raised me like your own in this house. So I'm happy to tell you the many memories I have. It might help you remember?"

"I think that might help."

Kyle leads me from the kitchen and gives me a tour of my house, ensuring he tells me at least two memories he associates with each room or area. It's not until we reach a closed door do I begin to remember...

"I won't let you do this!"

But this isn't Misha's choice.

I stumble into his bedroom because there is no other place I wish to be than in here. My stomach churns and my heart begins to race. My body wants me to expel the drugs, but there is no way. As each moment blurs in time, the pain subsides as everything is moving in slow motion.

"Mom, please, no...forgive me."

I collapse face-first onto Misha's bed. His scent engulfs me and wraps me into a tight embrace. I inhale deeply and sigh contently.

The silence is welcomed as I close my eyes and transport myself to happier times—when Misha was alive. I start from the beginning, from when I first held him in my arms.

Moving pictures flicker in and out of focus, cataloging my life with Misha. This is where I want to be forever. I may not have had any control over Misha's death, but I do over mine. And this is what I choose.

"I love you. Please live…live for me."

As I feel the bed dip beside me and Misha's arms wrapping around me, I let go of the sadness and embrace this fate.

Tears are heavy in my eyes as, with my final breath, I whisper, "I love you too."

"You remember," Kyle says, watching me with wide eyes as I return to the now.

Nodding, I clutch on to the memory because I'll never let it go.

Reaching for the door handle, I open the door and what I see has memory after memory collide into me. I see Misha hunched over his desk as he studies for exams. He's then lying on the bed, tossing a football into the air as he talks on the phone to his girlfriend.

Trista…

"I was wondering if I could talk to you about Misha. He was…"

That's what she said to me at Misha's funeral, but I never got to hear what she wanted to say.

"Kyle, do you know Misha's girlfriend? Trista?"

"Yes."

"I need to speak to her immediately!"

I run down the hallway to…my room.

I remember.

Being here is what the remedy is. Not being locked in a place which does more harm than good.

Storming into my walk-in closet, I see beautiful outfits hanging, but I also see empty hangers.

"And why are you wearing my dress? Just because I'm not home doesn't mean you can come and go as you please."

I said those words to Joy when she visited me. I was so angry at her.

"Luna! Please!" Joy pleads, and when she attempts to touch my shoulder, I lunge and bite her hand. "Oh my god!"

She recoils, cradling it to her chest as two orderlies run over to wheel me away.

"Oh, and by the way," I call over my shoulder. "Stay out of my fucking house!"

I've been told she was just trying to help, but helping herself to my clothes when I'm locked away seems a little disrespectful.

Something feels very wrong and I can't help but shake this foreboding feeling that things are about to get so much worse.

I begin to strip off and slip into a pair of jeans and a white knitted sweater. Once my boots are laced, I grab my coat and on instinct, reach into the pocket to feel a movie ticket. I wore this coat when Misha and I went to see a rerun that was playing at the local cinema.

Things are starting to slowly come back and I know that when they do, all hell will break loose.

107

I asked Kyle to organize the meeting between Trista and I, but that I'd like to talk to her alone. The reason being, I think Joy has something to do with all of this.

It can't be a coincidence that she's missing. She's either fled, or her choices have caught up to her.

The untouched coffee sits in front of me as I try to blend in. I don't want to raise any suspicion because I am still a fugitive as such.

I'm thankful to have Kyle on my side as it's nice to have a friend. I know staying at my house is a stupid idea, but it's the only place where I feel safe.

A beautiful young woman enters, her red hair tied back into a high ponytail. She searches the diner and when her eyes land on me, I know this is Trista. She comes rushing over, tears in her green eyes.

I don't even have a chance to stand before she's embracing me in a tight hug. "Oh, Ms. Huxley. It's so good to see you."

I softly rub her back, allowing her to shed her tears because I understand this is a lot for her. We all loved Misha. His death impacted us all.

When her sniffs cease, she lets me go and sits across from me, wiping her red-rimmed eyes. "I didn't think I'd ever see you again. We all heard what happened. I'm so sorry."

All I can do is nod and smile. "Thank you. I wanted to ask you a few questions."

"Of course."

I lean across the table as I don't want anyone overhearing us.

"The day of Misha's...funeral, you wanted to tell me something. Do you remember?"

The moment Trista lowers her eyes, I know that she does. "I don't think—"

"Please, Trista, I need your help. I think Misha was hiding a secret and—"

"He was," she softly interrupts, swallowing past the lump in her throat. "He never wanted you to know, but he started hearing voices quite young and to deal with those voices, he started taking drugs to help silence them. To help feed his addiction, he got into dealing, and as you can imagine, it just got worse."

I feel like an utter failure. How did I not know this? He was my son, and I failed to see his struggles.

"Why didn't he tell me? I would have helped him."

"He was embarrassed. And he didn't want to worry you. He loved you so much. I think it was a struggle he wanted to overcome himself. But he just fell deeper and deeper in. He also told me that a woman he was seeing wouldn't leave him alone.

"It was a mistake," she's quick to add while my mouth falls open. "But he said she knew a secret."

"A secret about him? And who was the woman?"

Trista shrugs, but when she bites her lip, I know there's more. "I think it had to do with his dad."

Images of Jonathan in that hospital bed, shriveled and so... dead is something I wish I could forget. "Is there anything else you can share with me?"

Reaching into her bag, she retrieves a pen and paper and writes something down. She slides it across the table to me. I see it's an address.

"This is where he would go to score his drugs."

My heart breaks. How could I have been so blind? My son was struggling and the one person who should have been there for him, wasn't…because I didn't know.

"You were a good mother, Ms. Huxley." Trista reaches for my hand, squeezing it kindly as she can clearly read my thoughts. "You were Misha's world because he was yours. You were often mistaken for his older sister, something his friends used to tease him about because you were the mom they wanted to—"

Her pause has me smiling because I can fill in the blanks.

A memory smashes into me—it's when Misha was at school. I remember his principle not believing I was his mother because I looked about ten years younger than my age. I still do. When I proved I was in fact Misha's mom, the principle's tune soon changed and he asked me out on a date.

Misha made sure that didn't happen. He was so protective of me. Our bond was so special.

Tears well, but I brush them away. "Thank you for meeting with me. I really appreciate it. Do you think you could keep this between us?"

She places her fingers to her lips and performs a lock and throwing away the key gesture. My secret is safe.

I fold the piece of paper and place it into my pocket. "I've got to go."

Each second being here is a risk.

"Will I see you again?" she asks, and I understand why she seems so sad.

When we lose someone we love, seeing another person who loved them just as much as you did tends to help heal the wounds, if only for a moment. It's a bond that is forever shared.

So I reply as honestly as I can. "I hope so."

I leave the diner and run to Kyle's car where he waits for me. I open the door and jump in because it's still raining.

"My father is expecting us." His dry tone reveals this won't be a happy reunion.

The radio fills the silence as Kyle drives.

I wonder if I should tell him about the address Trista gave me. My gut is telling me to keep it a secret. I don't know why, but I decide to trust it. I'm not even sure what I expect to find if I do go there.

I mean, the damage is done.

Kyle taps the steering wheel as we wait at a red light. It's apparent he's worried about Joy and not overjoyed at seeing his dad.

"I can talk to your dad on my own?" I offer, as I don't want him doing anything he's not comfortable with.

"No, it's okay. I don't trust him alone with you. And besides, Misha would kill me if I didn't go with you." A bittersweet smile plays at his lips. We all miss him—my beautiful boy.

We drive the rest of the way in silence until we approach a stunning house in what appears to be an affluent neighborhood. Kyle drives up the driveway and parks out front. He peers out the windshield, his lip turned up in disgust.

From the house alone, it's safe to assume Kyle's father does okay for himself.

"Let's do this."

We both run from the car to avoid the pelting rain. The front door opens even before we're up the stairs. A woman greets us with a smile, but Kyle grunts in response.

"I'm here to see my father."

The woman steps aside, a little hurt by his rudeness, allowing us entry. "Hi, I'm Sophie."

I shake her hand and assume she is Kyle's stepmom.

"Your father is in his office."

Kyle doesn't bother to reply and walks down the hallway.

"Thank you for having us over," I say to Sophie, not wanting to be rude.

But I soon realize the reason she appears sheepish is because she is the other woman. Being Joy's best friend, she probably believes I hate her.

And maybe I did.

But now, she's the least of my concerns.

Kyle inhales sharply before turning left. I follow and when I enter, I see a man with graying hair look up from his desk. When he sees us, he smiles, but it's strained. He places his gold pen on the paperwork and stands.

On the walls are awards and newspaper clippings revealing his occupation—he's the DA.

Kyle takes a step back, making it clear hugging is out of the question.

"Hi, son. You're looking well."

Kyle snickers. "Dominic."

Kyle's father's name is Dominic. It doesn't ring any bells.

"What can I do for you?"

"Have you seen or spoken to Mom?"

Dominic clears his throat. "No, not in some time. Why?"

"Because she's missing."

Dominic frowns and leans against his desk, crossing his arms and ankles. "For how long?"

"Over a week."

"Have you gone to the police?"

"Are you fucking serious? Of course I have. This is a waste of time."

"Son…"

But Kyle has had enough, it seems.

He charges out of the room while Dominic sighs.

"I'm so sorry about Misha," he says after a few awkward moments.

"Thank you. I don't know if you heard, but I was committed, by Joy, in fact."

"That doesn't surprise me."

His comment catches my attention. "Why do you say that?"

He peers over my shoulder before pushing off the desk and closes the door. "I'm not sure what Joy told you—"

I stop him before he can continue. "I don't remember much. Electric shock therapy does that to you."

His mouth drops open in horror. "That is beyond disgusting. How can I help?"

I'm not here to judge because we've all done things we're not proud of. I know friend code should mean I should be mad at him for what he did to Joy, but I can't help but think Joy isn't innocent.

"Kyle told me you cheated on Joy and excuse me for being so blunt, but was there a reason why?"

Dominic runs a hand through his hair. "Joy has this ability to lure people in and make them feel sorry for her. Good people. I suppose it's in our nature to want to help, but to someone like Joy, she exploited that kindness. I've not told anyone this before, but Kyle…he isn't my son. This put a huge strain on our marriage."

"What?"

"I can't have children, so I know for a fact. But I got a paternity test to be sure. I stayed with Joy for as long as I could, but there comes a point in your life where you have to put yourself first. I fell in love with Sophie, contrary to how Joy may have portrayed it.

"No doubt I was the heartless bastard. But she was the one who cheated and got pregnant by another man while we were married. It doesn't excuse my infidelities, but we were so out of love by then, strangers would be better acquainted than us."

"Did she ever tell you who Kyle's father was?"

"No, she always claimed I was. But science doesn't lie."

There's something else he's hiding. "Please, anything will help."

Dominic appears torn whether to tell me or not. "Her relationship with Misha was…strange."

"Strange how?"

"It went beyond that of a best friend looking after her friend's child."

My stomach suddenly drops. "What does that mean?"

"It means what you think it means. I would see them in town and I know Joy, she was interested in your son how a woman is when she wants a man."

"Did I know?" I ask, horrified.

"I highly doubt that. If you did, I'm sure you and Joy would not be friends. Misha was your world, and you did everything for that boy. Joy was always very competitive with you, but with your lovely nature, you never saw it. You always saw the good in others. I am so sorry this has happened to you, Luna. If I can help, please let me know."

And just like that, I realize that every story has two sides. I no doubt would have taken Joy's side because she was my friend, but she had me committed and then left me there to rot. What sort of friend does that?

"Kyle doesn't know the truth?"

Dominic shakes his head. "No, I would never do that to him. He will always be my son, regardless."

I admire him for his kindness.

"I know Joy would have told you that I wanted half of everything in the divorce and it's true. But I didn't want it for me. I wanted it for Kyle. All the money from the divorce I've put into a trust fund for him, which he will receive when he turns twenty-five. I didn't trust Joy not to blow it all on herself."

Just who is this woman?

Was I a total idiot not to see Joy for the obvious horrible human that she is, or that my son was struggling mentally and therefore turned to drugs?

"Don't beat yourself up over this, Luna," Dominic kindly says, clearly reading my expression. "Joy was a master manipulator. And you are a good person. If you need anything, please don't hesitate to call."

"Thank you. If I was ever awful to you, I'm sorry."

Dominic smiles. "You never were. Take care of yourself."

We bid farewell and I know this won't be the last time I hear from him.

Sophie escorts me to the door with nothing but hospitality. Kyle's hatred toward them is because of Joy who certainly wasn't a victim in this.

What Dominic shared about her and Misha, if that is true, that may play a part in why she's missing. Perhaps she doesn't want me to know the truth.

Kyle is waiting for me in the car.

When I enter, he doesn't speak. He simply speeds off, while I wonder what to do next.

Eight

Dutch

I'll never take a shower for granted ever again.

Even though I'm sitting in a chair designed for the shower, I am so thankful that I can wash my own back after so many weeks of Alanna giving me a sponge bath. Just the thought of her has me reaching for the tap and turning it to cold.

I've not played the piano since the night I responded to her in ways other than with disgust, as I am afraid that it'll happen again.

Music was my escape, but since the transplant, it's been nothing but a burden.

Maybe my music came with an expiration date. I sometimes felt as if my defect of a heart is what made me special, so maybe now that I have a "normal" heart, the music has stopped.

But I know that's not true.

Playing music with Alanna feet away, I felt "it." I've never known what "it" was because that's not how art works. An artist just knows. And I hate how that feeling returned because of Alanna.

I scrub the sponge over my skin, attempting to wash away the disgust which lingers on me. I want to hate what I wrote, but I can't. It's been playing over and over in my head since the moment my fingers touched those keys.

It was something I took for granted because it used to happen every single time I played. But now that I know what it feels like for it to be taken away, I never want to lose it again.

But the question is, what do I have to lose to hear it again?

Switching off the water, I decide to dress and find something to eat.

It's a struggle, but I dry off and change into the torn blue jeans and white tank Alanna gave me. I slip on my silver rings and chains, which is exactly the things I usually wear. She's clearly paid attention as everything is a perfect fit.

Is she wanting things to go back to "normal"?

Surprisingly, this place has running water and the bathroom is functioning.

I've not ventured far in fear of bumping into Alanna. But something is up.

She's left me unbound in my room and not visited as often as I thought. The other bizarre thing, is that Jonathan is still in that damn rocking chair. I thought she would be guarding him with her life. But she seems happy for him to sit with me, trusting that I won't throw him over the railing.

I decide to suck it up and find where she is.

Once my boots are laced, I lean onto the crutches and hobble out of the bathroom, listening for any signs of movement. I suddenly wonder if Alanna has left me alone.

I take each step carefully, as I don't want to break the other leg, and when I finally get to the bottom of the staircase, I take three deep breaths as that took it out of me. I'm still too weak to even contemplate an escape.

As much as I want to play piano, I decide to check out the rest of the house and any possible escape routes. The kitchen is as operational as the bathroom, which again surprises me. The rest of the house is in shambles, however.

I walk through a doorway which leads out into an abandoned greenhouse.

The glass panes are mostly intact, but the windows are so small and barred, there is no way I could squeeze through them even if all the panes were broken. The ground is littered with leaves long fallen from their branches.

Vines wrap around the pillars which appear to be squeezing the life from them. Seems an appropriate analogy for this entire clusterfuck.

My boots echo in the silence and although it's daytime, the green moss on the windows shadows the room in murkiness, tricking the brain into thinking the sun has surrendered to the moon.

There is a door at the end of the room and that door is slightly ajar.

Is this a trick? The classic horror movie script where viewers are screaming for their beloved hero not to go out the door as nothing but danger looms?

I pause with my hand splayed against the splintered wood, wrestling with what I should do.

In the end, curiosity overtakes good sense and I push open

the door.

It's a dreary morning with fog so thick, I can barely see three feet in front of me. It's cold out, but as I commence a slow walk into the grassy field, I forget everything because this is the first time I've been free.

It feels foreign—something which is a basic human right was taken away from me, and now it feels like I'm relearning how to walk, which is in fact true thanks to Alanna breaking my fucking knee.

The crutches catch in the soggy grass, but I persevere.

The white fog is soon dotted with slashes of red and that's because there's a fire burning ahead. It appears contained. I venture toward it and the closer I get, I hear the crackling of the fire, as well as someone's tears.

"Alanna?" I say when I see her standing around a drum of fire.

She peers up, quickly wiping away her tears. "Hi. Glad the clothes fit."

Really?

But I play along.

"What are you doing out here?"

She shrugs, and for the first time ever, she seems... vulnerable. "I was just thinking."

"And you had to do that around a fire in the fucking cold?"

She half smiles but she appears tired. "I know you think I'm crazy. And cruel."

I don't disagree because that's just the tip of the iceberg.

"But I did all of this for him. Love makes you do some crazy things. I know this isn't normal...but I can't stop," she says in a whisper, as if ashamed. "How do I make it stop?"

"Make what stop?"

"The hurting of a broken heart."

I refuse to feel any shred of sympathy for her, but it's hard to see her as a monster when she begins to cry again.

"I know I'm not innocent in any of this, but neither was Joy. Or Jonathan. Or Misha. Or Luna."

My teeth clench at the mention of her.

"Luna has done nothing. She lost her son, her fucking sanity, because of you and Joy."

"She could have told Misha the truth," Alanna replies, but there's no bite to her tone. "She knew how determined he was and that sooner or later, he would find out any way he could."

I don't like what she's implying.

"That doesn't give you the right to play God!" I snap, shaking my head. "You've hurt so many people, and for what?"

Her eyes turn poignant as she smiles. "For love."

Her response has the rage simmering because there are no rules when it comes to love. But what she's done, she's hurt the ones I love. So what's the acceptable punishment all in the name of love?

"How did Jonathan die?" I ask again because I know she was the reason behind it.

She stares into the fire, almost transfixed by it. "Everything you know is true. He played piano. He had a bad heart. He was Misha's father. And he was a philandering bastard who was still in love with Luna. She was the one who got away for him and his entire life, he was searching for that love again. I believed him when he told me he loved me. But what kind of man loves like that? Says he loves one woman while he fucks another?"

"Joy?"

121

She nods, her head bowed. "It was supposed to be her driving, not him."

"What do you mean?"

"It was her car, but he was the one who was driving that night. I didn't mean for it to be him. The engine of a car is so similar to that of the insides of a human being. It didn't take much. A cutting of a single wire can cause so much harm. So, it was poetic justice, really, that that bitch did the same thing to Misha; the person she loved."

Oh my fucking god.

Alanna wanted to eradicate Joy from the picture, but instead, Jonathan was the one behind the wheel, setting the stage for what his son was soon to endure. Alanna used her mistake as a blueprint for Joy.

This shit just gets worse.

"You may have loved Jonathan," I say with a sigh. "But the only person he loved was himself. Both you and Joy were fighting for his love, blaming Luna, but she never wanted his love. Jonathan is the monster because if he loved you, he wouldn't have been fucking Joy. Or pining after a woman who didn't want him."

I can't believe this entire thing all comes down to one thing—love.

Love, in the most twisted, macabre sense, but love nonetheless.

Alanna trembles, her tears robbing her of words and breath.

"So this is why you tried so hard to 'resurrect' him? 'Cause of guilt."

She doesn't need to reply. I know the answer.

"We're all guilty of something, Dutch."

Her statement doesn't carry any blame, merely fact because I too am guilty. I betrayed Luna when I handed her back over to Parkfields, believing she was a monster when I should have listened to my heart.

I did it in the name of love because I thought I was helping her.

But I shake my head firmly because I'm not the same as Alanna.

I'm not.

I think of Joy and the satisfaction I felt when she took her last breath. I also did that in the name of love. I then think about slipping my hands around Alanna's neck and choking the life from her for everything she's done to Luna.

And I do that…in the name of love.

Realization hits me and I grip onto the crutches, afraid of the truth which is staring me straight in the eye.

"I know I can never bring Jonathan back, but it was nice to pretend for a little while," Alanna whispers, reaching for something at her feet. "It was nice because I didn't have to face what I had done. That I was the reason he died. I killed the man I loved and I'll have to live with that on my conscience for the rest of my life."

The thing she reached for is her wedding dress, the dress which she tosses into the fire, stone-faced because she realizes it's over.

I think back to when I first woke and how she said I was the perfect match for Jonathan—and I now see she means that in more ways than one. She couldn't give Jonathan Misha's heart which would have been the perfect match if Jonathan were alive.

But he wasn't.

She gave me that heart because she wanted me, Dutch Atwood, to live.

Reality and fiction have skewed for her as she is obviously unstable, but after losing the love of your life, isn't that expected? I mean, look at what Luna did when she lost Misha.

Love, the crux of it all.

Alanna watches the dress burn, a look of nothingness befalling her. I wonder what she's thinking.

"I don't know what to do now. I've made such a mess of things." She brushes her fingers through her blonde hair and I notice they tremble.

Not in fear, but rather, withdrawal.

"What are you on, Alanna?"

She chokes on a strangled chuckle. "To deal with what, exactly? The voices? The suicidal thoughts? The depression? Take your pick. I never wanted to hurt anyone."

I want to hate her, but in this moment, I don't. I feel sorry for her because I don't sense deceit. And this is what is eating away at me.

I can end this right now. She is vulnerable, and I know she wouldn't put up a fight because it seems like I would be doing her a favor.

If I kill her, does that make me a monster? Do two wrongs make a right? Could I live with that on my conscience for the rest of my life?

Alanna thought she could, but look where she stands right now.

I am caught at a moral crossroad—which way do I choose?

"Did you give me that heart for Jonathan? Or for me?"

I remember her words, but those words were spoken by a delusional, crazy woman. Who I see now doesn't resemble that person at all.

"For you," she replies, reaching into her pocket and offering me a knife. "You'd be doing me a favor. Avenge your lover because I cannot do the same to mine."

Take it…

Misha has been quiet lately, and I know that's because he was never really there. None of this is real—just my subconscious playing tricks on me, akin to that of me believing I couldn't play piano because of my new heart.

But that wasn't true.

I couldn't play because my own fears stopped me. If I didn't have anything "special," which differentiated me from the rest, then how could I create extraordinary music?

"Take it." Alanna nudges her outstretched palm, almost begging I do it.

What is the matter with me?

This is what I wanted…so why can't I move?

"Dutch?"

With a sigh, I do something which I don't understand—I turn around and walk back into the house and do the only thing I'll forever understand.

I sit behind the piano and I begin to play.

Just like it happened the last time I was here, the music comes to me so quickly, I can't keep up. I play like my life depends on it because the louder I play, the softer the voices become until all I hear, all I feel, is the music.

I don't know how long I play, but when I reopen my eyes, I see that it's dark out. And that Alanna sits on the cushioned chair, watching me with nothing but admiration.

And once again, I hate that it seems to be her which stirs this inspiration within.

I stab at the keys one final time, slumping forward and allowing my long hair to shroud my face so I can hide my shame at finding myself here once more.

Alanna doesn't need to fill in the silence with how wonderful my playing is. She just lets what she heard sink in before standing and leaving me alone.

I lower my chin, tempted to slam my head onto the top of the piano, hoping to knock some sense into myself.

What am I doing?

Yes, the music is the best thing I've written in, well…ever, but I hate that Alanna seems to be the reason for it.

My love for music is clearly as unhinged as Alanna's love for Jonathan because I had the opportunity to end it all, but I didn't take it. And I hate myself for it.

But when the music continues humming in my mind just how it once did, I begin to understand Alanna's simple reply of doing all of this for love.

So the question is—what's greater, my love for music? Or my love for Luna?

Once upon a time, the answer would be simple. But I know what it feels like to be without music. The memories linger and the silence threatens to drag me under once again. I can't go back. I won't survive.

Slamming the piano lid down, I grit my teeth in frustration. This shouldn't be hard…but it is.

Tiny footsteps behind me have me pulling my shit together.

"Hey, kiddo," I say, turning around to see Bobby standing

timidly in the doorway. "It's okay. I won't hurt you."

His hair is wet like he just had a bath. I'm thankful Alanna is at least looking after him as he looks showered and fed. I still have to wonder just who he is.

"Are you feeling okay?"

He bites his lip, nodding.

I have no idea how to talk to a little kid. It's been so long since I was one, and even when I was, I hardly fit the stereotype because instead of playing with friends my age, I was BFFs with Mozart and Beethoven. But I won't let Alanna's insanity destroy Bobby's innocence because the shit he's seen, it's enough to mess a kid up for life.

"Do you want to show me your room?"

He quickly casts his eyes downward.

In this moment, I promise myself that I'll be here for Bobby and try my best to be the kind of role model a kid his age needs.

I stand, not wanting to make a big deal of things. "I'm going to check out the rest of the house. Wanna come?"

I don't wait for him to reply, but instead position myself onto the crutches and hobble from the room. When I hear him tiptoeing behind me, I smile in secret because it's nice to have a friend—even if it's a kid.

I have no idea where I'm going, so I venture around downstairs, peering into rooms which are gutted shambles that have seen better days. The farther I venture, the more apparent it is that this was once a squatter's den.

There's faded graffiti on the walls, tags of people who once roamed these empty halls. The faded red carpet is soggy and when I peer upward, I see that a section of the roof has caved in. The fluttering of feathers echoes among the beams as birds take flight from their perches.

The place is filled with squalor and should have been torn down years ago. I wonder how Alanna knew about it and why the hell it's operational.

Lost in the what-ifs, I feel a tug on my arm and peer down to see Bobby with a red ball in his hands.

"You wanna play ball?"

He nods.

"Sure, we can do that. I'll try my best anyway."

He runs down the hallway, ball under his arm, and stops when he is a few feet away. He drops the ball and lines it up before kicking it my way. I hobble toward it and manage to balance on one crutch and use the other to stop the ball.

Using my good leg, I kick it back to Bobby, who runs after it with speed as my aim is off. Sports was never my thing, but Bobby doesn't seem to mind. We continue this back-and-forth game for a while and it's nice to see Bobby smile.

He begins to run backward, indicating that he wants me to go long.

"All right. Are you ready?" I tease, pretending I need a run-up.

He giggles and I realize it's the first time I've heard him laugh. Which is the reason I kick with a little too much enthusiasm and boot the ball into one of the rooms.

He runs after it, but I quickly hobble after him because I don't know if the room is safe.

"Bobby!" I exclaim, trying my best to get there in record time as visions of him dangling from a hole in the floor are too vivid.

Thankfully the room appears to be hole-free, but it's just

as derelict as the rest of the house. The ball is wedged under a fallen roof beam and Bobby is on his hands and knees, trying to yank it out.

"I got it."

I limp over and gently tap Bobby's shoulder, gesturing he's to stand. I don't want him that close to the filth on the floor. I tilt my head and see the ball is wedged quite far in. I use one crutch to try to knock it out, but it's fruitless.

I peer around the back of the beam and see that I can try and push it out that way. I move to the side and am about to use my crutch as a hockey stick, but I see something hidden away in a loose skirting board. I don't know why it catches my eye, but when my heart begins that familiar raced tempo, I know it can't be good.

I forget my injury and drop to half a squat, keeping my injured leg extended out as I reach for what's hidden away. What I find confuses and shocks me at the same time.

In my hand, I hold a thick stack of driver's licenses. All different people, from different states, different ages, with different names. I go through them all, trying to make sense of what this means as this is all too serial killer-ish for my liking.

However, when I see a familiar face, another thought hits me.

This place is a pit of squalor, only fit for those who need somewhere to hide, as they are too ashamed for the world to see them at their weakest.

The license I hold is that of Misha's.

So the question is, why is it here?

Nine

Luna

Kyle is passed out on the couch, exhausted from this entire ordeal, no doubt.

Joy hid so many secrets, ones which I don't think she ever told me because I feel surprised, like the news that Dominic shared was the first time I ever heard it. I wonder why Joy wouldn't tell me. If we were best friends, I would think that's something she'd tell me.

And that has me wondering just who Kyle's biological father is.

I flick the corner of the piece of paper Trista gave me, deep in thought. I don't know why this address of where Misha got his drugs from is so important, but I can't shake the feeling that it conceals a lot more secrets.

Kyle's laptop is open, so I reach for it off the coffee table and type the address into the search bar. I have no expectations, but when I see a run-down mansion, I am a little shocked. It's so… clichéd.

"Pennington Villa," I whisper, not wanting to wake Kyle.

I read about its misfortunate history, wondering if this place was cursed from the moment the foundations were laid. Nothing but horror seemed to follow.

I think of Misha going here late at night, desperate for his next hit. The things he must have done to ensure his habit was fed.

Tears well because my memories are coming back slowly. They may not be lucid, but I remember them. Each day, I remember who I am and the love I felt for my son.

I have to go there.

I don't know why. Morbid curiosity, perhaps?

I just need to see it to believe, I guess.

Quietly closing the laptop, I reach for Kyle's car keys and the old cell he gave me from the coffee table and hold my breath the entire way to his car.

Once inside, I exhale and brush my freshly dyed blonde hair from my face. I found the box of dye under the sink and decided to color my hair to look semi human.

I suddenly feel like this is a mistake…which is exactly the reason I start the car and drive off into the darkness.

The GPS barks directions at me; it's the only thing which fills the silence because I need the quiet to deal with whatever looms ahead. The farther I drive, the grimmer things become—not just my mood, but the neighborhood as well.

It's no surprise a place like Pennington Villa operates in a place like this. The police are no doubt accustomed to bad things happening out here. They probably don't even bother to patrol these streets anymore as the residents are the lawbreakers, so I can't see anyone calling 911 for help.

Misha must have been so desperate to come out here. Or maybe he liked the anonymity?

The GPS directs me down a dead end road and at the end of it, down a long-ass driveway, is Pennington Villa. I can't drive down it, so I park the car a few houses away, worried it won't be here when I return.

This is a bad idea, but I'm here now.

My eyes adjust to the darkness because the bulbs from the streetlights have been smashed. This should set a precedent for what's ahead, but I can't turn back now. I was silly for not arming myself, so I reach for a broken brick by the side of the road and slink into the shadows as I walk up the driveway.

The rusted steel gates are hanging by their hinges, flung wide open and welcoming those brave enough to venture this way to the pits of hell.

Why haven't they torn this place down?

If this Gothic-looking mansion isn't stereotype enough, lightning flashes across the darkened sky, a warning that the heavens are about to open up. I hasten my step because I just want a quick look inside.

All of my senses are warning me to turn around and run, but I can't. It's dark inside, but that doesn't mean no one is home.

The front yard is overgrown, but the foliage is twisted and dead, as if nothing can flourish in this unholy ground. A thunderbolt scares the living shit out of me, but that merely hints at the storm which is brewing.

My breaths grow sharper and quicker. My flight or fight instinct has kicked in.

I decide to venture to the left of the house as I just want to peer through a window and not enter through the front door and when I do, I see a light flickering in one of the rooms.

I'm like a moth to a flame as I walk toward it.

The sky chooses this moment to open up and a heavy downpour begins to fall. I have nothing to shield myself from the punishing weather, so I run toward the window, telling myself just one look, then I leave. My wet hair sticks to my face and I feel like a drowned rat as I slip and slide in the ground which has suddenly turned into sludge.

The pounding rain prohibits me from hearing anything, but the lights grow brighter and it's all the courage I need. Someone is inside and I need to know who.

Did they know Misha?

I don't know why it's so important to me.

I'm careful as I approach the window. It's filthy, but I squat low where a small section is clean. I squint as the rain sticks to my eyelashes, but I press my nose to the glass, hopeful whoever is inside can't see me.

Goose bumps cover me from head to toe, and it has nothing to do with the cold but rather, it feels as if the proverbial saying someone walked over your grave just occurred…and that's because what I see can't be true.

The brick drops from my hand as I can't believe what I'm seeing.

Life isn't full of coincidences—they're signs from the universe, preparing us for the shitshow that looms. But this… this is just too much.

Who I see has me wishing I came with a fucking arsenal because Alanna Norton is mere feet away. So is the little boy,

Bobby, I saw Alanna with in Dutch's room. But it's the man who sits at the dinner table, unrestrained, as he happily sips from a crystal wineglass, which confuses me beyond words.

Why the fuck is Dutch sitting at a dinner table with Alanna, and not stabbing her with the knife? It seems he's too busy cutting through his eight-course meal to worry about revenge.

I suddenly feel so betrayed and so…angry.

What's going on?

When a thunderclap breaks through the darkness, I take that as a sign that there's only one way to find out and for that…I need a fucking shotgun.

Dutch

The urge to stab Alanna in the jugular is so overwhelming, I have to lower my knife and drink my wine instead.

I have no idea why the fuck she thought a "family" dinner was necessary, but here we are. The only good thing about this fiasco is that Bobby seems to be enjoying his meal.

Alanna sits across from me at the large table. I'm surprised this table hasn't been used as firewood. But the good condition of it confirms that it's not been here long.

Misha's driver's license burns a hole in my pocket. He is at the center to all of this, but I doubt he knew how much so. He was at the wrong place, wrong time. The casualty of this entire clusterfuck.

I need to know what this place is. I need to know why Misha's license is here, and most of all, I need to know how Alanna knows about it.

This isn't a coincidence. None of this is.

"You don't like your steak?" Alanna's question snaps me from my thoughts.

Faking a smile, I pat my stomach. "I am stuffed full."

"You hardly ate a thing." Her disappointment is evident. It's also genuine.

I omit the fact that the reason I can't eat much is because the only thing I've eaten for the past God knows how many months has been fed to me through a tube. Eating real food again is like walking—I need to do it slow. But slow is pissing me off.

"My mind has been elsewhere."

Alanna pauses from chewing, indicating she's listening.

"The concert."

"What of it?"

"What happens once it's done? We come back...here?" I gesture to our surroundings in disgust.

"What's wrong with this place? It just needs a new coat of paint and—"

"It needs an exorcism, Alanna." On cue, a scurrying in the corner of the room confirms my claims.

"Why are you like that?"

"Like what?" I ask because she's going to have to be a little more specific.

"Why can't you look at this circumstance as a glass half full? You're always so negative!"

My mouth actually drops open.

I look at Bobby who is biting his lip in fear. "Kiddo, wanna go to my room? We can color in when I'm finished talking?"

He looks at me frightened, but eventually, he nods and runs

from the room.

The moment he's gone, I spit at Alanna, "Are you fucking with me right now? Alanna, I've only just been able to hold my own dick to take a piss. There is no half full. Only fucking insane."

"All I've wanted to do is help you."

"Help me?" I scoff. "How, exactly?"

"Have I hurt you?"

I arch a brow, peering down at my knee.

"Apart from that one time, and you made me angry. All I've ever wanted was to help you."

"For your own gain. Once upon a time, you referred to me as a host to incubate a heart for your dead fiancé! Now you want to play Mother Theresa. I don't think so. Now I have to play to a room full of doctors who are none the wiser that their colleague is Dr. Frankenstein!"

Her chair scrapes along the floor as she stands up abruptly. "I should have let you die!"

"You think?" I mock, shaking my head in awe at her naivety. "I was doing just fine until you came along."

"Fine?" She bursts into laughter. "Because apart from music, you had a budding social life? A circle of friends you could call at any hour and they'd drop anything for you? Or a girlfriend who tolerated being runner-up to your music?"

I clench my jaw because her comments are too close to home. "Fuck you."

"Hate me all you want, but I see it when you play; I inspire you. Every artist needs tragedy to write something heartfelt. All that pain, all that anger, it pours out of you and into the art you create. The best artists are tortured souls who don't need enemies because the biggest enemy to yourself, Dutch…is you. Which is why you won't kill me…even though I know that you want to. Music is your life and I've seen what you're capable of doing without it. Now that you hear it again, are you willing to lose it all?"

Standing, I slam my fists onto the table before leaning forward, ready to tear off Alanna's head. "You don't know me."

The wine bottle spins on the table from the force of my blow and the sound morphs into music. Damn her to hell…

"Yes, I do. I know you better than you think. I bet right now, all you want to do is play."

There's no point fighting back because Alanna has somehow wormed her way into my head and the only way to get her out of it…is to play.

Charging from the room, I don't bother with the crutches and limp toward the piano room. It's lit with candles, but instead of setting a romantic mood, it's a Gothic horror. I kick away the piano stool and begin punishing the keys with every shred of emotion in me.

It comes pouring out of me, like violent lava, needing to escape before it burns me alive. I am so fucking angry because Alanna is right—I've not played like this is so long, I've forgotten what it feels like to…be alive.

This is my drug, and like Misha, I am hooked.

The moment I play the last note, I charge over to where Alanna stands and grip her throat and walk her backward, slamming her up against the wall. I push her so hard, her glasses fall off her face. But the sight of her excited green eyes only summons my demons, and I want more.

"Fuck me," she pants, running her knee over my stirring

cock.

I quickly move out of her reach.

Her suggestion has me gripping her throat even tighter. "I'd rather cut off my dick than touch you."

"You're a…liar." She gasps for air, but she doesn't fight.

The pain—she likes it.

And so do I.

"We're the same."

"We are nothing alike."

"Sure, keep telling yourself that," she barely chokes out as her cheeks turn red. "Kill me, and what happens then? The music stops and you go back to boring little Luna?"

"Shut your fucking mouth!" I squeeze her neck so hard, I feel her throat spasm.

But she smiles.

"You want me. Your words might lie…but your body doesn't." Her eyes flicker as she's on the cusp of passing out, but she's not leaving this conversation without proving me wrong as she reaches down and rubs over my erect cock.

I slam her against the wall again and lower my face to hers so we're inches apart. I don't know what I want to say or do, but it doesn't matter either way, because when I hear her voice, I realize it's too late.

"Dutch?"

Snapping my head to the left, I see a sopping-wet Luna standing in the middle of the room, eyes wide…and it has nothing to do with the well-dressed man who has a gun pressed to her temple with his forearm pressed to her throat.

A winded laugh leaves Alanna, her throat spasming under my grip. "Hi…Daddy."

Ten

Luna

I am so fucking stupid.

I should have turned around when I had the chance, but seeing Dutch with Alanna changed the reason I was here. I came here for answers regarding Misha, but now I'm left with questions about Dutch and why he looked moments away from kissing Alanna.

I was so engrossed in watching him play piano and what seemed like him being inspired by Alanna that I didn't notice a man sneak up behind me before he pressed his gun to my temple and ordered me inside. The moment he led me into the room, I wished he shot me because that would be less painful than watching the man you love with another woman—the woman who ruined your life.

"Luna—"

But it's too late. I saw it, and it's something I will never forget, regardless of how many treatments of electric shock therapy Alanna gives me.

Dutch lets her go.

She coughs frantically, clutching her throat as she attempts to breathe. But she isn't scared. She's excited.

"I found this stowaway spying outside," "Daddy" says.

None of this makes any sense, and I hate that the only people who can explain it are the people I want to throttle with my bare hands.

"You just can't seem to stay out of trouble, can you?"

"You bring out the best in me," I quip, eyeing Alanna something wicked.

I can't look at Dutch.

She laughs, but it's hoarse, thanks to Dutch's grip, but that doesn't make me feel any better.

I may have forgotten some things, but I can recognize when a man wants a woman, and I saw that reflected in Dutch's actions.

I feel sick.

"What are we going to do with her?" Daddy presses the gun deeper into my temple.

"Don't you fucking touch her!" Dutch screams, which only has Daddy tightening the grip on my throat.

I finally meet Dutch's eyes and it's apparent we both have come to the same realization—I'm his Achilles' heel, which is why I'm still alive. And I've willingly walked into the lion's den as prey.

Now that I'm here, they can do with us as they please because they know both Dutch and I will do anything to protect the other.

This is bad. Very bad.

"So you want to keep her?" Daddy asks Alanna like I'm a stray kitten he plucked off the street.

She nods with a sinister grin.

"Okay, sweetheart. I'll take her cell and make sure the car she came in is disposed of. We don't want anyone tracing us back to here. This is dangerous. Are you sure?"

"Yes, Daddy, I am very sure. This is going to be so much fun."

"Yeah, it'll be really fun when I slit your fucking throat, bitch."

Daddy doesn't appreciate me insulting his maybe daughter and pistol-whips me as a result. I instantly feel the warmth of my blood as it trickles down my face. But it only heartens the fire within me.

Daddy lets me go as he knows as well as everyone that I won't run. I won't scream. I won't do anything in fear of the repercussions it may have for Dutch. And possibly Bobby.

"Strip," Alanna orders, wishing to humiliate me.

But it's going to take a lot more than that as I checked my modesty at the door the moment I was tied to that bed in Parkfields and made to use an incontinent pad instead of being able to use the bathroom.

The wet clothes stick to my body, so I am far from graceful, as I take off my sweater and toss it to the floor. I kick off my boots and the jeans soon follow until I'm standing in nothing but my underwear.

Alanna peers at them, hinting those are to be removed also. She won't be satisfied until I'm completely humiliated, it seems.

But I used to be a stripper.

Taking off my clothes is how I made people do what I wanted, and I plan to exploit that as I bend down to slip off my underwear, giving Daddy a glorious view of my ass.

Reaching around, I unhook my bra and let it fall off me before turning around and smiling at Daddy. "Want to show me to my room and read me a bedtime story?" I tease, playing this game he's bound to lose.

His gaze drops to my ample breasts and then lower, where he stares for a little too long to be polite.

Hook, line, and sinker.

"Give her your jacket!" Alanna orders Daddy, suddenly not liking her plan of stripping me bare.

Daddy's gaze soon snaps over my shoulder to Alanna, where he nods and strips out of his jacket, tossing it at me. I make sure he gets a great view of my breasts as I retrieve the jacket and put it on. I draw the lapel to my nose, smelling it and smiling in bliss.

"You smell good, Daddy."

Daddy looks to be in his early fifties. He's dressed in a suit, and I don't think that's because he was somewhere fancy. His gold watch and Italian leather shoes are an indication that he comes from money. And if Alanna is, in fact, his daughter, then that explains why she can get away with the things she does, because money talks.

Daddy grips me by the arm and leads me from the room, but it's not as brutal as it first was.

I don't make eye contact with Dutch because I still don't know how I feel about what I saw. It wasn't innocent.

I know how important music is to him, so if Alanna is his muse, then that means he is also the enemy and like every enemy, he must pay for his sins.

I take in my surroundings as Daddy leads me up a dilapidated staircase and down a hallway. Most rooms are in a state of disorder, but he tosses me into a room which has a bed and matching corpse in a rocking chair.

My fucking ex…

"You seem like a smart girl, so I won't bother restraining you."

"Where's the fun in that?" I quip, turning out my bottom lip dramatically.

Daddy is suddenly out of sorts. He doesn't know what to do with this version of me. I know what he would like to do, however.

Men are fucking stupid. Again, I may not remember many things, but this is something which seems to be self-explanatory. And I plan on exploiting that stupidity to get what I want, and what I want is to bowl Alanna's head down this hallway to strike down her organs that I use as pins.

She has turned me into this monster, so it only seems fitting she experiences the full wrath.

Daddy stands around, dick in hand, appearing to want to say something. But changes his mind at the last minute. He leaves me alone as he makes a hasty exit.

The moment he's gone, I exhale in relief and steady my racing heart. Even though my bravado is fierce, I am terrified inside.

Dutch would have escaped by now if there was a way out, which means we're all prisoners.

I look over at Jonathan and the blanket which covers his lower half. Alanna cares for him which I plan on taking advantage of when the time is right.

The windows have bars over them and from the quick look I had at the other rooms we passed by, there doesn't seem to be any way out other than the door Daddy dragged me through.

As much as I hate it, I need to talk to Dutch and figure out what's going on and what side he is on.

Do I trust him?

No, I don't.

"Luna," and even though his voice makes me want to forgive and forget what I saw, I stand firm because I can only trust myself.

Quashing down nostalgia, I turn around and lock eyes with Dutch.

I wait for him to speak, but his guilt is cemented as he averts his gaze. I don't know where we go from here.

"Is Bobby okay?" I ask because his safety is my only concern right now.

A heavy sigh leaves Dutch before he lifts those blue eyes.

I hate him.

I hate that I respond to him this way when all he's ever been is bad news. He's not good for me; being here proves that. But I can't stop the pull I feel for him, and it has nothing to do with Misha's heart.

A memory crashes into me—when I first heard Dutch's heartbeat. I was drawn to it. I was drawn to him.

Misha's heart may give him life, but I am in love with Dutch. The heart which beats within his chest is a part of me as much as it is a part of him.

In some twisted way, Misha brought us together and I'll be damned if my son's death is in vain.

"He doesn't talk. I don't know where his parents are. I know nothing about him."

"Why does Alanna have him?"

Dutch steps forward; I take two steps back.

The distress on his face is apparent, but it's going to take a lot more than his pretty face to have me forgetting what I saw.

"I think she was afraid of me and was using Bobby as protection, knowing I wouldn't hurt her in front of a child."

I don't fail to notice his use of past tense. "She certainly didn't look afraid downstairs."

"Luna, let me explain."

"What's there to explain? She wasn't rubbing your cock then?"

"Yes, she was, but…I don't understand it. I hate her, but I think I am that fucked up, I am somehow using that hatred to write music. Like a coping mechanism, perhaps? I don't know and I fucking hate it."

"So she's your muse? You need the antichrist in heels to play? Is that what you're telling me? Because I hate to break it to you but your muse is going to meet a tragic ending when I cut off her fucking head!

"Do you know what she did to me? I can't remember anything. I can't remember my son because of her!"

"He knows, Luna."

Enter the bitch in question.

"He knows because he was the one who handed you back over to me once you escaped."

And just like that…it all comes back to me.

I remember the air of freedom.

I taste forbidden kisses.

I feel the sting of being dragged back to Parkfields because Dutch…betrayed me.

"I thought I was doing the right thing," he solemnly says, his regret clear.

But the sting of betrayal is too hard to stomach and I look at him through new eyes—he didn't trust me, and now, I don't trust him.

The only thing that matters is getting out of here…but not before I take from Alanna what she took from me.

Her heart.

"Hurts, doesn't it?"

I don't take the bait, but Alanna gloats because she's won this round.

"Hurts to watch the man you love, want somebody else."

And just like that, I realize the reason Alanna didn't kill me—she wanted her own revenge. She wanted me to feel the pain she felt because Jonathan never loved her. He loved me… and she hates me for it.

And now that Dutch believes he needs her to play, she thinks I will crumble and curse the world for all the atrocities it's delivered. She thinks this will break me.

Yes, it hurts like a bitch, but her actions only confirm that I am the alpha—I always have been.

This all started with Jonathan…so it seems fitting it ends with him.

Dutch watches me closely, and I hate that he knows me better than I know myself.

He lunges for Alanna, restraining her with an arm around her throat, and when he does, I reach for Jonathan's skeletal arm and yank him from his chair.

"No!" Alanna screams and her terror, it's music to my ears.

I drag his corpse ass along the floor with only one thing in mind.

"No, no, no!" Alanna cries over and over as Dutch leads her behind me and forces her to stand and watch.

I stand by the railing, Jonathan's brittle corpse limp as I lift it up, and without thought, I toss him over the balustrade. When I hear a shatter on the concrete floor below, I smile sweetly at Alanna.

"Hurts to watch the man you love want somebody else."

Dutch lets her go.

I know my punishment is coming, but for now, she frantically runs down the stairs and I watch as she begins to gather the broken pieces of Jonathan, sobbing hysterically. But she's going to need a lot more than some glue to piece him back together again.

With his skull in her hands, she peers up at me with nothing but pure hatred.

"It's fucking war, bitch," I spit before turning around and walking back to my room.

Dutch follows, and I sit on the end of the bed in silence. He knows I want answers and I want them now.

He runs his fingers through his long hair as if needing a moment, and I know whatever he's about to tell me is going to be big.

"Joy is dead. Alanna killed her."

I should feel something, but I don't. I think deep down, I knew something bad had happened to her.

So Dutch continues. "She was the one who was driving the car the night Misha…"

I hold back my tears because I can't break down. I need this as fuel to pave my path of revenge.

"But Alanna is the one who was behind it. Joy thought it was you driving. But Alanna wanted Misha's heart for Jonathan."

"Jonathan has been dead for a very long time," I say, hating to state the obvious but what the hell.

"She is a very sick woman and I think she thought she could make amends for taking Jonathan's life by giving him his son's heart."

"So why did she give it to you?"

Dutch walks forward while I grip the edge of the bed to stop myself from slapping his cheek. But what he does next, it has my walls crumbling.

He sits beside me and gently intertwines our fingers. "I'm so sorry, baby. I fucked up. I don't deserve your forgiveness. I hate myself for everything I've done."

I stare at our fingers interlocked. I should pull away, but I can't.

"There's more?"

He squeezes my fingers softly. "Joy was sleeping with Misha. For a very long time."

I inhale sharply but nod, gesturing I want it all.

"Misha was hearing voices, which was why he turned to drugs. He—"

"I know," I interrupt, not wanting to relive the pain of that revelation again. "Joy's son, Kyle, told me. It's why I'm here. This is the house where he would come to get his drugs."

Something passes over Dutch. I don't know what, until he reaches into his pocket, offering me a driver's license.

It's Misha's.

"Where did you find this?"

"Hidden in the walls. Maybe he got high one day and left it behind? Maybe it was security for his dealers in case they needed to find where he lived? Maybe—"

His pause has me wetting my lips nervously. "What?"

"It isn't a coincidence Alanna knew about this place. Did Kyle tell you who his dealer was?"

I shake my head.

Dutch runs his thumb over my inner wrist. "What if Alanna is connected somehow? She has access to drugs and we know she has no conscience. It would explain how she knew who Misha was. Who you are. This isn't a coincidence. We both know that."

This is all too much to fathom. But what I've been through over the past however many months, proves that anything is possible.

"What do you want to do?"

I mull over his question.

There are so many things I want to do, but there is only thing which seems fair. "She took away my baby, so it only seems fair I take away hers."

Dutch gulps because seeing as Alanna doesn't have a child, it would mean she needs to get pregnant and I don't have the genetic makeup to do that.

"I wouldn't ask that of you. And I would never do that to an innocent child. But Alanna must pride herself on her work. You're her—"

"Project?" Dutch fills in the blanks, and he's right.

"What if we showed the world what a true monster she really is?"

149

Dutch nods slowly, and I can see the wheels turning. "She's kept me alive for another reason—to gloat to her colleagues about the transplant. She has organized a concert in a month's time to show the world what a wonderful doctor and person she is. There still must be talk about Parkfields. We had an 'excursion' to prove to the townsfolk that all was well. It was how we escaped."

"And Daddy must be on some medical board to make sure no bad press comes its way?"

"It makes sense. He wouldn't want his reputation tarnished. I mean, it wouldn't look good if the world found out his daughter was a fucking psychopath."

"With Jonathan gone," I say quickly as I know time is running out. "She's going to need another obsession. You. Although, I think she's already hooked."

Dutch appears ashamed of the fact. "I'll do anything you want."

"Anything?" I ask because once he says yes, he can't take it back.

Turning to face me, he cups my face into his hands and lowers his lips to mine until they're a hair's breadth away. "Anything."

His presence warms me. I want him so much, it hurts. So, I seal this union with a lover's kiss.

I press my mouth to his and the moment I do, I remember…

I remember his kisses.

I remember the love he expressed without any words.

I remember that he loved me as much as I loved him.

And it's because of that love that we will win.

Dutch takes control and coaxes my mouth open with his

skillful tongue. I moan as he takes control. He doesn't just kiss; he fucks my mouth with his. He threads his fingers through my hair and moves me so he can fuck my mouth deeper and harder.

He bites my bottom lip softly before sweeping his tongue along it. He then uses that tongue to rob me of any coherent thought as he works me into a heaving mess. His lips are soft, but they aren't gentle because that's not what I want.

Unable to help myself, I climb onto his lap with our mouths still locked in a lover's embrace and gasp when I feel he's hard. Images of Alanna rubbing over his dick has an animalistic possession overtaking me, and I begin to rock.

"Fuck, Luna," he says, breaking our kiss to peer down where my bare sex is rubbing over the bulge in his jeans.

Daddy's jacket is parted open, my breasts on display, so Dutch leans forward and takes one into his mouth. He licks my nipple as he fondles my breast. With the other hand, he places it on my hip, encouraging me to ride him faster.

The friction of his jeans hurts in a good way.

I grip Dutch's long hair and yank his head away. His eyes are wild and confused. His lips wet and swollen.

"Hit me."

"What?" The horror slashes at his angelic face.

"You said anything. So, hit me." I let him go, but his hair is a mess thanks to me tugging on it.

"No," he replies, horrified I would ask this of him. "I would never do that."

"She needs to think you pick her. She thinks what she said has made me hate you."

He stills me from rocking, plagued by his fears. "And has

it?"

"I want to hate you because nothing but tragedy seems to follow us, and the smart thing to do would be to stay away from you." I place my hand over his heart. "But I can't. And it has nothing to do with the heart which beats inside you. I can't stay away from you because I love you. And if you love me too… then, you'll hit me."

It's a bittersweet admission because it's hardly laced with rainbows and flowers.

Dutch swallows down his revulsion at what I am asking. He knows it'll work because I plan on doing to her what she has tried to do to Dutch and me. I'm going to drive a wedge between her and Daddy and use him to get the fuck out of here.

Remember, men are foolish creatures.

Alanna will no doubt inflict the harshest of punishments on me and the person I will go to will be her daddy for comfort. He looks like the type of man who likes to be the hero. He does this to excuse the fact that he is a deplorable human being.

I climb off of Dutch and stand in front of him, pleading he does this because Alanna will be up here soon and when she does, we need to convince her that we hate one another. We can't fight her.

But we can mindfuck her.

"You're a fucking pussy," I belittle with intent, shaking my head. "My son didn't die for nothing! And I'll be damned if that psychotic bitch wins."

I raise my voice, needing to get Alanna's attention.

"Fight me," I beg, knowing how crazy this is.

But Dutch stands firm. "Please don't ask me to do this. I can't."

"So she wins? You're just going to forget what she did?" I scream because I want her to hear this argument. "You're her fucking lap dog! You're pathetic."

Dutch clenches his jaw as he stands slowly. He towers over me, and I love it. I love that this man who could hurt me would rather rip off his own arms than cause me harm.

But right now, his chivalry isn't helping.

"Fine, have it your way then."

Before he can stop me, I slap his cheek—hard—leaving behind a red imprint.

He closes his eyes briefly, composing himself as he knows what I'm doing. "I won't hit you."

Closing the distance between us, I stand on tippy-toes, but he's standing at over six foot, so I don't even reach his chin. "Because you don't want to hurt me? Too late! You already have."

I slap his cheek again.

He cups it, moving his jaw from side to side.

"I can do this all day."

With his reddening cheek and mussed hair, he looks like he's been in the wars. There's just one thing we need to add… blood.

Knowing this may be our last kiss, I slam my mouth over his and kiss him with hunger and anger. He scoops me up into his arms, lifting me up, and I wrap my legs around his tapered waist. I love the feel of him and I commit it to memory before I bite down on his lip so hard, I draw blood.

He hisses as I pull away, eyes alight as I watch blood trickle down his chiseled chin. I want to lick it away, but I can't.

The moment I hear Alanna's frantic footsteps, Dutch lowers

me and reaches for the rocking chair. He gestures with his head that I'm to move. The moment I do, he hurls it at the wall, it shattering into a million pieces.

"I was trying to help!" he screams, nodding his head that I'm to go to the corner where the broken chair is.

We're about to stage a scene, it seems.

I half slump against the wall, gripping my ribs and panting as one would if they were thrown across a room. Alanna runs into the room, stopping and taking in the surroundings. She notices Dutch's disheveled state and then looks at me, where I am faking injuries as I gasp for breath.

She isn't convinced, seeing as Dutch held her back when her beloved did a swan dive over the balustrade. But she can't deny his injuries. And I am a wonderful actress.

I charge for her, ready to claw out her eyes, but Dutch intervenes, just how I knew he would. He pins me to his chest as I fight him wildly.

"I am going to kill you both!" I cry, lunging for Alanna, who actually takes a step back.

Dutch holds me tightly, pretending to be holding me back, but I know if Alanna tries to hurt me, he will have no qualms throwing her off the balcony. If only it was that easy, but now that Daddy is involved, she has reinforcements.

We have to be smart.

Daddy enters, appearing baffled by the commotion he missed by probably dumping Kyle's car off a cliff.

Alanna storms forward, ready to pluck out my eyes, and I feel Dutch tense, but it's Daddy's voice that stops Alanna.

"Enough, Lana!" he orders sternly. "Parkfields is under the microscope as it is. We can't have any more bad press. We use

Luna as a model patient. We show the board the wonderful work we do. Your great-grandfather didn't sacrifice it all for you to ruin it!"

I've wondered why Alanna, a surgeon, would have such close ties to the hospital. It now makes perfect sense. It seems crazy has run in her family for generations.

"But she needs to pay," Alanna says, stomping her foot in anger.

I can't help the laugh which bursts from me. "Temper tantrum much?"

Dutch tightens his hold around me. He's warning me not to poke the bear.

"And she will, but after we get the medical board off our asses. Okay, sweetheart? We get through this concert, Luna will show them that she's cured, and then we can put this all behind us."

"She's not going to help us," Alanna scoffs, knowing me too well.

"She will, won't you, pet?" Daddy says, using that nickname with intent; he wants me to remember my place.

"And if I don't?"

"Then you will go back to Parkfields, and I will ensure you stay there until you're old and gray, wishing Alanna did kill you, as that would be far more merciful than being locked away for the rest of your life. I'm sure the orderlies are missing you dearly."

The threat sends a shiver down my spine as Daddy has found my weakness—I have nothing left to fight for but my freedom. Going back to Parkfields is a death sentence, an everlasting sentence, however, because death would be easy compared to living another day in that place.

I don't reply, but Daddy can see it on my face.

"And, Dutch, you'll do as I say because if you don't, I'll make you watch Luna get tortured in every possible way there is. And I can be very creative. I mean, who do you think Lana learned from?"

He looks at her with love…and then something else as he grips the back of her neck and kisses her passionately, leaving both Dutch and I speechless.

Just when I thought this couldn't get any more messed up…

They kiss how lovers kiss, not how father and daughter should.

Alanna moans into Daddy's mouth as he squeezes her ass. They continue kissing until Daddy pulls away, rubbing his thumb along Alanna's bottom lip.

"Such a good girl," he says while I hold back my vomit. "Daddy is so proud."

Whatever Daddy did seems to calm Alanna as she smiles. "You heard Daddy. Looks like we're all stuck together for a while. Let's make you comfortable then."

Daddy reaches into his pocket and gives Alanna some handcuffs. The thought of being restrained again sends me into a panic, but Dutch discreetly runs his thumb over my hip, hinting it'll be okay.

Dutch walks me over to the bed, but Alanna shakes her head. "Not in here."

She walks out of the room, indicating we're to follow.

Dutch doesn't let me go as he carries me from the room. We enter the bathroom, and when Alanna stands by an old coiled wall heater, it seems she won't be satisfied until she strips me of my dignity as well as my clothes and freedom.

Dutch hesitates, but I wriggle subtly, wanting him to do it.

He places me on the floor, which consists of dirty, broken tiles. My naked state has the sharp edges of those tiles poking into me. And that's the reason Alanna chose this very spot to tie me up like a dog. She handcuffs me with my hands behind my back.

Anxiety tackles me, but I look at Dutch, and those blue eyes quieten the panic. I know he won't let anything happen to me. And when Daddy stands in the doorway, looking at me with obsessive hunger, I know he won't either until he gets what he wants.

In case he changes his mind, I open my legs, giving him a glimpse of what he wants.

He licks his lips in approval.

As I once said, men are stupid…and that stupidity is going to bring this house of horrors to its knees.

Eleven

Dutch

I wake in a cold sweat for two reasons.

The first—I had the worst nightmare; however, it was just my brain reliving the events of yesterday.

And the second is that Alanna stands over my bed, watching me.

"Hello, sleepyhead."

Sleepyhead? I'm pretty sure I've been asleep for five minutes as fatigue finally overtook me. I wanted to go to Luna, but Alanna set up camp outside the bathroom, ensuring no one could go to her as she sees the way Daddy watches her.

"Hey," I croak, sitting up and brushing the hair from my eyes.

It's still dark out. I can't remember the last time I saw the time, and as for what day or month it is, I have no fucking clue.

"Are you hungry? I made breakfast."

I don't have time to answer before Alanna is yanking off the blanket and pulling me out of bed. I'm shirtless and she makes a point of looking at my chest before lingering a little too long on the front of my boxers.

I reach for my jeans and need to sit to put them on because of this damn bandage on my knee.

"I'll change your dressing after we eat."

Hell will freeze over before I thank Alanna, so I simply give her a stiff-upper-lip smile. I don't bother with a shirt as it'll give me an excuse to use the bathroom to shower and see Luna.

I hobble from the room, not needing the crutches, which is a small win for me. But I can't allow Alanna to get wind of my recovery. If she does, Luna won't be the only person tied up.

Alanna purposely avoids the bathroom, and I limp behind her. She has a wheelchair positioned near the stairs. I want to walk, but I sit and allow her to escort me down the stairs. She wheels me into the kitchen.

Bobby is sitting at the table, happily eating his pancakes. No sign of Daddy, however. I don't know his name, and I don't want to know it because it won't make a difference when I rip out his spine and beat him to death with it.

I don't know if he and Alanna are, in fact, related. It would explain why she's so fucked up. But it doesn't excuse her behavior. Nor does it change the fact that I am going to take great pleasure in killing her.

I was fucking insane for ever thinking she inspired my music. What she's done has changed the way I look at life and how I feel, and that's what's inspired me. These feelings of pure hatred I've never felt before because I've never hated anyone in my life until I met Alanna.

Artists need emotion to create—some use heartbreak or love. Me? It seems unadulterated disgust and revulsion is what I need to create the most fucked-up music which I am most proud of. It shouldn't surprise me, however, as I've always gravitated to where the shadows like to hide.

I sit at the table and offer my fist to Bobby. He looks at it before fist-bumping me when Alanna turns her back to us. He too is mindful of her, it seems.

"How do you like your eggs?" she asks, heating up a pan on the small camping stove she has set up on the counter.

I'm about to tell her where she can shove her eggs, but Bobby shakes his head subtly.

"Sunny side up."

"Sunny side up, coming right up," she singsongs while I eye her suspiciously.

Why is she so perky?

She hums under her breath while cooking up a storm.

I massage my temples, in desperate need of sleep and stabbing Alanna in the throat as she butchers Mozart. Music was once my happy place but it's because of the music that I'm here. It would be easier to stop, but I can't.

Music is like air for me.

I know that this is Luna's plan, but I hate it. I can't sit down here and eat breakfast while she's chained to a heater like a fucking dog. I don't know if I have it in me to entertain this charade for another few weeks.

Bobby is watching me closely and rolls a marble to me. I smile, about to roll it back, but he shakes his head, gesturing with his little hand that it's a gift. In this place of horror, his innocence reminds me of why I need to play this game.

I act in haste, and no doubt, he too will suffer the coincidences.

"I hope you're hungry," Alanna says happily, placing a plate in front of me.

It's piled high with food and although it looks and smells great, my stomach gurgles.

"You don't like it?"

She's wringing her hands in front of her, appearing anxious. When did she turn into a Stepford wife?

I suddenly realize why.

She lived to please Jonathan, and now that he is nothing but a pile of dust, she seems to want to please me instead.

This shitshow just gets worse.

"I love it. Thank you." I pick up the plastic fork and don't fail to notice there's no knife.

Smart move on her behalf.

I use the fork to cut through my breakfast, feeling incredibly creeped out as Alanna watches me while I eat. When I can't eat any more, I push the plate away and use the napkin to wipe my mouth.

"That was great. I think I'll take a shower."

Alanna's happiness is soon replaced with annoyance. "I thought you'd want to play piano first?"

Standing, I ruffle Bobby's hair as he listens to the conversation closely. "I will after I shower."

As I make my way to the doorway, Alanna all but shoves the wheelchair my way, hinting showering alone won't be happening.

She still doesn't trust me.

And she shouldn't.

I sit and don't say a word as she drags me up the stairs. She's out of breath by the time we reach the top. She will soon tire of this and she'll either learn to trust me or she won't let me out of my room.

We reach the bathroom, which is lit by candles, but most have burned out, so Luna sits in partial darkness.

When I see her, my heart breaks.

Alanna cuffed her so she can't move. She also can't use the restroom which I am sure she needs.

"Alanna, if Luna is meant to be your get out of jail free card, then may I suggest you treat her with some kindness. She won't last a week like this."

Luna sits as tall as she can, seeing as she's cuffed, refusing to show weakness—my courageous goddess.

I know we're supposed to make Alanna think her plan to put Luna and me against one another worked, but I can't do this. I would rather take our chances at escape than have Luna be subjected to such treatment.

"Still trying to be her knight in shining armor?" she snaps, not appreciating my suggestion.

"I'm quite comfortable where I am, but thanks anyway," Luna quips, her voice hoarse.

"See," Alanna sweetly says. "You're the only one with the issue, it seems."

Luna is the better actor out of us, and I know that's because she won't let anything stand in the way of her revenge. She will endure everything Alanna throws at her in the name of avenging her son.

I don't know why I can't hear Misha anymore. Maybe I never heard him in the first place. Maybe I am fucking crazy after all.

He was the unexpected passenger which I grew accustomed to and answered the questions which plagued me.

"Fine."

Standing, I take off my jeans and even though it's a struggle, I get them off without any help. My boxers soon follow. I don't look at Luna because she does things to my body that I don't want happening in front of Alanna.

I wait for the water to heat, ignoring Alanna leering because I know what she's doing. "I bet you're happy to shower. No doubt you're sick of those sponge baths."

I grunt in response.

I move under the spray, thankful for the hot water as it helps alleviate some of the tension from my shoulders. I hate that Luna can't experience this warmth because she must be cold and sore sitting on that floor.

"Let me help."

Before I can object, she pries the soap from my hands and commences washing my chest. I stand still, refusing to show any sort of emotion because this is all for show. She wants to put ideas in Luna's head, considering she saw Alanna's hand on my cock.

I shiver in disgust, but Alanna mistakes my response as arousal.

She washes me carefully, but when she gets to my dick, I snatch the soap back from her. There's no way I'm allowing her that much control. I wash myself quickly as I am done with this situation.

When she disappears, I meet Luna's eyes in the darkness. I don't even bother drying off and drop to a half squat, cupping her cheeks and kissing her fiercely. She moans, meeting my passion head-on which instantly makes me hard.

Her mouth fits perfectly to mine, and the fire between us only grows. I hold her prisoner with my kisses, never wanting to let her go. But I must.

"Are you okay?" I ask, brushing away the hair from her face.

"I will be when we kill that fucking bitch," she replies, eyes alight.

"I can't leave you like this. I'll think of something."

"The only way she'll let her guard down is if she thinks she's won," Luna wisely says. "She did with you, didn't she?"

Luna is right.

The more I've "let her in," the less she's treated me like a prisoner.

"I won't pretend with her like that. I can't. I know that makes me weak, but—"

"It's far from weak," she interrupts, leaning forward as far as she can and nuzzling into my neck. "I couldn't stand it. I have another idea. Daddy."

I tense because I know she's right. But that doesn't mean I like it an iota.

"If they think they need us, we're safe. I'll do what I have to but please know, it's all just pretend."

"Why can't we just try our luck and kill them both?"

She glances behind her, at her cuffed wrists, then to my bandaged knee. "We only have one chance at this."

"I just can't stand seeing you treated this way."

"I've been through worse...like when I thought you were dead."

The perpetual cloud of sadness just grows heavier. "I'm not going anywhere."

And I mean it.

I place a quick kiss to her lips before standing and commence drying off as I hear Alanna's footsteps approaching. When she enters, I see she holds a stack of clothes.

I hobble from the room and go to my room so I can get dressed in there.

Alanna follows, offering me the clothes.

Again, she has brought things I would usually wear. Before I can slip into the black jeans, however, she gestures to the bed.

"I'll change your bandage."

Alanna conveniently didn't pack any boxers, so I sit down, ensuring the towel stays tucked around my waist so I'm covered. She reaches for her medical bag and retrieves what she needs. As she's cutting through the bandage, I watch her work with interest.

Her hands have helped so many, but they've also destroyed. I hate her for what she's done, but I can't help but feel like her life is such a waste. She could have done so much good in the world, if not for the fact that she's fucking insane.

"You and Daddy look…close," I opt for instead of stating the obvious, which is incestuous.

She doesn't reply, which means this topic is off limits.

She removes the bandage, and I peer down at my knee which is actually better than I expected it to be. "How long will I need the crutches for?"

I know this isn't Alanna's forte, but she seems to be a jack of all medical trades.

"I think you should be able to put some weight on it in a week or so. But you'll have to take it easy. You don't want to overexert yourself before the concert."

"Why is this concert so important to you?"

Alanna rubs some ointment on my knee before unraveling a new bandage and commences wrapping it tightly. I wait for her to reply, but I can see she's stalling.

"Alanna?"

"It's not important to me," she finally replies, eyes still focused on bandaging my knee. "It's important for you to see that no matter what you think of me, I was able to help make history. This concert will change your life because word has spread of your heart transplant and when they witness your talent, you'll be able to play piano at any venue, in any part of the world of your choosing because everyone loves a happy ending.

"Everyone wants the good guy to win."

"I am grateful for what you've done, I just wish you didn't do all the other stuff in between." How can she trust me not to tell anyone? I still don't understand it.

"I don't expect you to overlook everything I've done, but I thought you'd understand my actions because I would do anything for love. Just how I know you'd do anything for Luna. She may not see it, but you did what you thought was best for her."

"I did that not knowing that everything I believed was based on a lie. Let us go, Alanna. We won't tell anyone. Who would believe us, anyway? Two psychiatric escapee patients? Your reputation proceeds ours. Don't you want this over with?"

She finishes bandaging my knee but keeps her hands wrapped around it, as if deep in thought.

Is she contemplating what I said?

"I know you're not a bad person," I say, ignoring the lies

which spill from my mouth. "Yes, you've done some bad things, but you've also done good. Make this wrong a right and let us go."

The air is heavy and I think Alanna is actually mulling over what I said. I need to keep going and say anything to twist her arm.

"What do you want?"

She finally peers up at me. "I want to be happy," she whispers sadly. "My whole life, I just wanted to be loved. When Daddy found me, he promised to take care of me, and he did. He made sure I was fed and schooled. I owe everything to him."

And what did he expect in return because he doesn't seem like the charitable type?

"How old were you?"

"Five," she replies with honesty, looking away. "I was dumped at Saint Agnes when I was a baby. Such a cliché. I was born into this world without love and it's all I ever wanted."

In most stories, there's a villain, but we don't usually get their backstories. They're just the monsters we want to kill. But this explains Alanna's skewed view on life and love. I don't feel sorry for her. But I guess now, it helps me understand why she's so fucked up.

Jonathan's ammo was to prey on women he could manipulate for his own personal gain, but Alanna was something he didn't bargain for. He got what he deserved. She did the world a favor. But killing Alanna, I still can't help but feel like it's such a waste.

I am so fucking torn over this entire thing. I want her dead. But in the next breath, I wonder if maybe she can be helped.

Maybe if she got help, real help and not that of a predator like Daddy, who should be helping his "daughter," and not encouraging her, she could get better.

But after the things she's done, I don't think there is any getting better. And besides, Luna would never let that happen.

"This has to stop, Alanna," I say, reaching down and placing a finger under her chin to coax her to look at me. "You know this is wrong."

Her lower lip trembles.

When I see her humanity, it makes it hard to wish ill harm on her. I'm not that cruel. But every action has a consequence, and this is Alanna's.

"Everything okay, Lana?"

The moment she hears Daddy, she quickly pulls away. "Yes, fine. Just changed Dutch's bandage. I'll take him to practice the piano once he's dressed."

She stands and brushes past Daddy, who stands in the doorway. He grabs her arm so hard that she flinches. "Where's my kiss?"

She smiles, but it's strained. She pecks his cheek and takes off down the hallway, but he doesn't follow. He enters my room instead.

"I know what you're doing," he says, not bothering with pretenses. "It won't work."

"And what exactly am I doing?" I challenge with a smirk.

"Don't insult me, Dutch. You're an intelligent man, which is the reason why you're still alive."

"I beg to differ...the reason I'm still alive is because your daughter wanted to cut out my heart and give it to her very dead fiancé."

Daddy doesn't stir, meaning he knows all about Alanna's plans.

"She has always been an optimist."

"Optimist?" I scoff, standing and squaring off with this dickhead. "She is insane. But it seems the apple doesn't fall from the tree. If you cared about her, you'd have her committed and given the help she needs."

"I can't do that. She'd never be able to practice again."

"And you say that like it's a bad thing. Unless I stuttered, she gave me a heart with the intention of cutting it back out to revive her fiancé to relieve herself of the guilt of killing him. She's dangerous…to everyone around her, and to herself."

"As her…parent—" I don't even know what term to use. "You're supposed to protect her. Not encourage her delusions. If Luna and I are needed to vouch for Parkfields, then you know it's only a matter of time before the truth comes out.

"That place is fucking hell on earth and if it's been in your family for generations, then I hate to think of what happened to the many patients who passed through its doors."

Daddy just listens, stroking his gray mustache like a fucking creep. "You have no fear; it's remarkable."

"I've seen your daughter fuck a corpse, Doc. We're well past fear. I'll play your fucking concert and sing Parkfields's and Alanna's praises, but if something happens to Luna, I will sing like a fucking canary."

"If only Lana did that transplant on a nobody, none of this would be happening. People don't seem to care about the nobodies."

"That's fucking deplorable, you self-entitled fuck," I spit, shaking my head. "Who made you judge, jury, and executioner to decide such a thing? No one's life is more important."

I remember the guilt I felt on the way to the hospital. For

me to live, someone just died, someone who didn't deserve that fate.

"That is noble but unrealistic in this world."

Alanna suddenly appears to be the lesser of two evils when compared to this asshole.

I'm about to give him an earful when the foundations of the mansion rock—literally.

It takes about three seconds before Daddy and I are scrambling out the door, hell-bent on getting to what sounds like Wrestlemania taking place down the hallway. But Wrestlemania is child's play compared to what we see.

Luna has Alanna in a headlock and is ramming her face into what's left of a wall. The plaster shatters around her, but that doesn't stop Luna. She spins around and drives Alanna's head into the opposite wall—over and over again.

Alanna tries to fight her off, but she doesn't stand a chance.

Daddy runs for Luna, but I launch forward, tackling him to the floor. I pin him down with my weight, but the fucker is strong, and I'm wounded, something which he takes advantage of as he reaches around with his free arm and punches me in the back of my knee.

It hurts like a motherfucker, but I breathe past the pain and use all my weight to keep him down. He flails like a wild animal, but I am running on rage and pure adrenaline—this is a fight he's going to lose.

I place my forearm against his throat, arching his head back so I choke the life out of this asshole. He desperately claws at my arm, but I only press down harder. He gasps for air, and I suddenly realize that I have no qualms killing this asshole.

If that makes me a monster, then so be it.

The fight in him dies, but when I peer up and see a syringe pressed into Luna's throat, I freeze.

"Let him go," Alanna says, spitting out a mouthful of blood. She stands behind Luna who uses her eyes as cues; she'd rather die than surrender.

"What's in the syringe?"

"That's for me to know and you to find out. Will you take the risk? Can you live with that on your conscience?"

"Don't listen to her!" Luna screams, begging I finish Daddy off, who wheezes for air. "She's nothing without him. You can show the world what monsters they both are."

So much for our plans to fly under the radar. But both Luna and I are fighters; we don't submit like dogs.

I don't fail to notice Alanna use the term you as she knows there is no we if I do this. I kill Daddy, and as a result, Alanna kills Luna. I don't know what's in the syringe. It's Russian roulette but with Luna's life.

I can't do that. I could never live with myself.

"Dutch!" Luna cries, but I can't.

I loosen my hold on Daddy's throat and roll off him as he gasps for breath. I stand, pleading Luna forgives me for being weak. She's not angry, but we both know we will pay dearly for our rebellion.

The ruse is up.

Once Daddy is able to breathe without sounding like a winded hyena, he comes to a shaky stand and I know what's coming and embrace the first punch with a smile on my face. He punches my stomach, my ribs, back to my face.

All the while, I laugh with blood trickling from my mouth and nose. It only angers him further, and when he is about to kick my knee, Alanna screams.

"Enough! He needs to be able to play. You said it, we need them both."

I'm half standing, wavering on the spot and seeing double as I clutch my bruised ribs, but I refuse to drop. Instead, I laugh like a raving lunatic.

"You're both fucking dead."

Alanna shoves Luna toward me, and I lunge forward to catch her. But she's the one who ends up supporting me as I almost fall onto my ass. She clutches onto me, coaxing me to rest my weight on her.

It's apparent this little family gathering is over, so she walks me toward the bedroom as Alanna and Daddy know we're not going anywhere.

"You stubborn man," Luna says under her breath as we hobble down the hallway. "You could have ended it all."

"Without you, there's no life to live." My words are slurred and my vision is spotted, but I need her to know that she is my world.

I don't know where we go from here, but we're together and that's all I care about for now.

She helps me to the bed, where I slump onto it, attempting to sit upright. I then realize I almost killed a man wearing a fucking towel. I burst into laughter once again.

"I think you're concussed," Luna says with concern as she examines my injuries. "Let me find something to clean you up."

I don't argue and pass out the moment she leaves the room.

I wake sometime later, unsure how long I've been out. But

that's the least of my concerns because of who I wake up to.

Luna.

She's asleep in my arms, her hair damp and smelling like strawberries from the shower she must have taken. Her skin is warm and her breath tickles my chest as she's snuggled in close. We're both naked underneath the blanket.

Why aren't we both tied up? I don't understand it.

If they didn't need us, I know we'd both be dead. I guess being "famous" has helped. And they need Luna as she's the only sane person inside Parkfields. If they were to use any of the other patients, their ruse would surely be up.

That's the only reason we're not dead.

Maybe they believe we will cooperate if we're together because we sure as hell didn't being apart. Alanna is the reason I'm alive. Daddy couldn't give a fuck. But she has a small shred of humanity inside of her when it comes to me.

"Stop thinking so loud," Luna groans, snuggling closer into me.

I can't help but chuckle.

I trace my fingers up and down her back, which instantly kisses her skin with goose bumps. "Sorry, go back to sleep."

"I'm awake now." Her croaky voice hints she needs more sleep.

"Why aren't we gagged and tied to the bed?"

She sighs and her breasts pressed to me instantly has me wishing I used another phrase. "I think they've given up fighting us. They know we won't give in. But there's no way out of this fucking place. So we're trapped. I figure they think if they let us do what we want, we will do what they want and then they let us go? And we all win."

"I think you're right. The moment we're not needed, we become disposable. So we have to keep reminding them how useful we are."

"She has to die," Luna says, pulling out of my arms to look into my eyes. "I'm sorry I didn't stick to the plan. The moment she uncuffed me, I had to hurt her and all rational thought was forgotten."

The room is pitch black, only the moonlight providing some silver light to steal the darkness.

I kiss the tip of Luna's nose. "And she will. But we have to behave somewhat until we do what they want. I won't lose you again. I fucked up once, and I'll spend the rest of my life making it up to you."

Luna is silent as she places her palm to my chest. My scar has long healed, but when she touches it, like always, it aches.

"He doesn't talk to you anymore, does he?"

"I'm not sure that he ever did," I reply. "Is your memory coming back?"

She nods slowly. "Every day, every minute, I remember more and more. I remember Jonathan. He was a horrible man. I tried to protect Misha from him, but I didn't realize he needed him. I was wrong not to tell him the truth."

"You did what you thought was right."

"I know, but I can't help but think all of this is my fault." Her voice breaks. "Misha might still be alive—"

"Don't think that," I say, quickly defusing that thought. "The thing about hindsight is that it's fucking useless. You tried to protect your boy, as every mother should. There's nothing for you to feel guilty about."

"How did we get here?" It's a rhetorical question. "This is

so crazy."

"Yeah, it really is. There is no silver lining in this situation, but I don't regret meeting you. I just wish both of us could be here. It's because of Misha that I'm alive and for that, I am thankful to him, and to you. I know you might resent me for the fact, but I would have happily given up my life if it meant he could live."

The moon decides to go into hiding, veiling the room in darkness. But I don't need to see Luna to witness her tears.

Luna and I have been more apart than together, but our love has survived, and that means something. To feel this way about her, this is real. We fight harder for each other's safety than we do our own, and if that's not true love, then I don't know what love is.

"Luna, I—"

But she doesn't let me finish.

She closes the space between us, pressing her lips to mine. The moment we kiss, I forget everything but the way she tastes and feels. I get lost in the emotion because this is more than a physical connection; this is fate.

I draw her closer so we're pressed chest to chest, our hearts beating in unison which is tragically beautiful. Threading my fingers through her long hair, I take control, fucking her mouth with my tongue. She moans, as I know she likes it rough.

My dick is instantly hard, pressed against her, and I want nothing more than to slip inside her and forget this nightmare we call our reality.

With our mouths still locked, Luna reaches down and begins jerking me off.

It's now my turn to moan as her touch sets me on fire.

MONICA JAMES

We continue kissing as she works me into a fucking mess. She can do whatever she wants to me. I am hers.

She breaks our kiss, only to continue those kisses down my throat and over my chest. I roll onto my back, surrendering myself to this woman whom I love more than anyone in this world. She scores her fingernails down my stomach as she rests between my legs.

The moment she takes my dick into her mouth, I close my eyes and die a thousand fucking deaths. She uses her hand to stroke me as her mouth and tongue work me in ways I never thought possible. Reaching down, I gently place my hand on the back of her head, but she interlaces her fingers through mine, coaxing me to mouth fuck her.

When I hit the back of her throat, she gags, but instead of pulling away, she recovers, only to continue giving me the blow job of my life. But this relationship is a two-way street, so I yank her up, spin her so she's lying on my chest and I can eat her pussy as my dick slides back into her hot mouth.

Her shapely ass is in my face and I want to eat that too, so I grip her hips and position her so I can slide my tongue between her pussy and ass. She whimpers around my dick but doesn't stop. I tongue fuck her ass, while I play with her pussy, and she is so damn wet, all I want to do is feel her as she's riding my cock.

She rocks against my tongue and mouth; she wants to come.

So I lift her up and turn her so she's facing me. I don't need words; our bodies speak for us.

She positions herself as she grips my cock, before sliding down onto me. Her whimpers have my dick only growing harder.

The moment I'm fully sheathed, a sated moan leaves her, and then, then she begins to move.

She places her hands on my chest, rocking her hips as she fucks me—slow at first, before picking up the pace.

This is her show; I am here for her. I want her to take everything from me. I just want to make her feel good.

Her pussy feels fucking incredible, and it takes all my willpower not to come. I want this to last forever. She picks up the pace. Her breathless exhalations mixed with mine is an aphrodisiac within itself because you can't fake this chemistry.

It's like every cell in my body is alive.

I grip her hips and move with her as she picks up the pace, her rhythm robbing me of air because she consumes every single part of me. She lifts her hips, only to slam back down onto me. She moves up and down, back and forth, setting my world on fire.

Sex with Luna is something out of this world because of the connection we share. Each time I enter her, I feel my love for her growing tenfold, so much so, my heart threatens to explode from my chest. She places her hand over my heart, as if reading my mind.

We will be connected eternally, and for that, she is my forever and a day.

She rolls her hips and I swear to fuck, she is tracing the alphabet on my cock with her pussy.

One hand still gripping her waist, with the other, I reach down and commence rubbing over her clit. She is so hot and wet, the perfect combination. I encourage her to ride me faster because I want her to come before I do.

"I love you," she pants, and my heart swells.

"Say it again."

"I love you."

With a growl, I grip the back of her neck and pull her toward my mouth so I can kiss the ever-living fuck out of her as I meet her thrust for thrust. She whimpers, allowing me to dominate her so we can both finish in a fucking mess.

I can be a gentle lover, but with Luna, I have no control. I want to consume every part of her. Our lips are still locked as I guide her to fuck me hard and fast. When she tires, I take over and flip her onto her back so I can fuck her.

Being over her this way is fucking perfection and I lift her leg so I can deepen the angle. She cries into my mouth, gripping my biceps as if needing to hold on. But I don't give her a reprieve. I continue sinking into her over and over and grasp her hip so she can bounce on my cock.

We are joined in the most intimate way, but it's still not close enough and that's because I love her with every beat of my heart…and she needs to know that. I don't deserve her love, but for some reason, she loves me and that makes me the luckiest son of a bitch alive.

Dropping her leg, I grip both hips and fuck her until she's screaming my name, and when she spasms around me, I confess, "And I love you."

She comes hard, her body trembling and the feel of her pussy clenching around me has me pulling out and coming on her stomach with a sated roar. I collapse on top of her, kissing her face as I cup her cheeks.

She is perfect.

Our hearts sprint in unison and when they slow, I roll off of Luna, but reach for her hand. Our breaths are lulled, both of us sated beyond words. I suddenly realize I don't hear music… but I'm not panicked because my love for Luna precedes any love I know.

"Where are they?" she asks, her voice hoarse from screaming my name, something which makes me happy.

"Who knows? I have no idea where we go from here," I confess, because anything is possible. "Daddy is more dangerous than Alanna. He's the one we have to watch."

"So we're supposed to, what? Co-exist until the concert, and then what?"

"They need us. We wouldn't be alive if they didn't."

"I know, but what are they going to do to ensure we don't forget they're the ones in control?"

She's right.

This isn't a partnership. We are still their prisoners, and they will remind us of that fact every chance they get. But Alanna is suddenly not the mamma monster. Daddy is the one I'm most concerned about.

Luna huddles close as she, too, knows that this is only the beginning.

Twelve

Dutch

I wake a little while later, thankful Luna is still in my arms. Not so thankful, however, when I open my eyes and see Daddy sitting in a chair at the foot of our bed. The chair once Jonathan inhabited.

It pleases me to see his neck is chafed raw, thanks to me almost choking the life from him. Too bad I didn't succeed.

Slipping out of bed quietly, I make sure the blanket covers Luna because I don't want this asshole looking at her. I put on some jeans and leave the room, assuming he'll follow. When I hear his footsteps, I take the stairs carefully because, thanks to Daddy punching me in the knee, I'm hobbling like an invalid.

When I get to the kitchen, I see there's a fresh pot of coffee, but Alanna isn't anywhere to be seen. I don't know where she is, but it's clear Daddy is the one calling the shots. I pour myself some coffee and wait for him to speak.

"Lana isn't a bad person. She's just…always had a creative imagination."

"I suppose it takes a special kind of person to want to perform a transplant on a dead person," I sarcastically say. "I don't want to know about you or Alanna. I don't care. I'm here because I have no choice. Luna and I will do what you want, but so help me God, if you fuck us over, I will kill you both."

Daddy laughs, appearing surprised by my candidness. "Shame that we need one another alive then because it seems we're thinking the same thing. Do what you're told, and we won't have any problems."

It's on the tip of my tongue to tell him to go fuck himself, but I nod in response.

"Do I need to remind you of what happens if you don't?"

"Listen, asshole," I spit, eyeing him something wicked. "I don't take too kindly to threats. If you piss me off, I'll have no issues finishing what I started. We good?"

Daddy's jaw clenches, but he knows I'm not playing. "I really wish she killed you."

"Me too, grandpa." I finish my coffee and leave the room because this conversation is done.

I decide to play some piano, seeing as our survival fucking depends on it. Candles flicker, lighting the room in a Gothic glimmer. It's the perfect scenery to play. I hate that this has become my norm as I sit at the piano and the music flows from me with ease.

This is what it was like before the operation, where music came to me without thought because it was a feeling I transformed into song. The piece of music I'll play for the musical board will be a fucking masterpiece because it may well be the last thing I ever play.

Luna has made clear it's do or die, and I am all in.

Once I play the final note, I realize that Luna stands a few feet away, watching me.

She's wearing my white T-shirt which sits just above her knees. Her hair sits in a tangled mess and I remember what we did for it to get that way. My cock instantly stirs.

"That was beautiful," she says in awe.

"There's something a lot more beautiful than that," I reply, smiling at her.

She walks over as I shuffle backward so she can sit on my lap. The moment she does, I gently bite her shoulder which is exposed, thanks to my T-shirt hanging off her.

"Music is an extension of you," she states, clearly being able to see the close connection I share with it when I played. "No wonder you would have done anything to hear it again."

"Almost anything," I correct, because I need her to know that I would never do anything with Alanna for the sake of my music. Been there, done that, and it was a fucking nightmare.

Luna leans back into my chest with a sigh. "I was thinking about what you said, about Misha's license being here. It makes sense that Alanna might have been his dealer."

I wrap my arms around her waist. "This is so fucked up. She has destroyed so many lives."

"She has, and we have to sit back and play nice. I can't do it."

"Luna—"

"No, I don't care about the repercussions. As long as that bitch dies, I will happily accept whatever fate I deserve."

"I know, baby, but all in good time. I know it feels like we're doing nothing, but we're at a disadvantage now."

Luna is quiet, which is never a good thing. "Why has she done this? All of this?"

I mull over her question and answer the only way I know how. "I think because she's lonely."

Luna waits for more, but there is no more. Alanna wants to be loved and will find that love any way she can. It doesn't make sense to us, but we're not mentally unhinged.

"She's love sick," she mutters under her breath, as if deep in thought. "Well, we're going to give her so much fucking love, she's going to choke on it."

"What do you mean?" I ask as I am so confused.

"I have another plan, one which will be a lot easier to stick to. How about some reverse psychology? We've been fighting with hate. How about we fight with love?"

"How?"

Before Luna can answer, Alanna enters. Luna doesn't shift off my lap. She only leans back farther into me.

"I'm pleased the music is coming back to you, Dutch," Alanna says, ignoring Luna and focusing on me.

"He's wonderful." Luna doesn't care that Alanna is giving her the silent treatment. "I didn't realize how much so. No wonder you wanted to save his life."

And here we go…

"Pieces of my memory are coming back, and I remember Jonathan."

Alanna's lips pull into a tight line.

"I remember how he could manipulate someone into doing things they wouldn't normally do. I mean, look what he did with Joy…that bitch. I know what she did with Misha. She took advantage of him when he was weak and needed help. She's the monster. And as far as I'm concerned, she got what she deserved."

Alanna watches Luna closely, looking for any signs of deceit. But Luna's ploy is impenetrable.

"Jonathan loved me," Alanna says, like a fucking broken record.

"Of course he did," Luna agrees calmly. "You wouldn't have done all of this if he didn't. All you wanted was your happily ever after with your man. What woman doesn't want that? We have a lot more in common than you think. Joy ruined both our lives. We're fighting for the same thing—love. I don't want to be your friend. But I understand why you've done the things that you have."

Luna is so convincing, I almost believe her.

"Misha is dead, but Dutch is alive because of him…and because of you. I can't forget that. I won't fight you anymore. I just want my happily ever after. Don't you?"

Alanna's eyes soften and I remember when she first unveiled her wedding gown. I was so fucking creeped out at the time, but looking back, I see how utterly sad this entire thing is. And Luna is playing on that.

She carefully stands and walks over to Alanna. When she offers her hand, Alanna peers down at it like it's a grenade. But Luna doesn't waver.

"This will be a lot easier on us all if we just co-exist. We all need something from one another. So let's just learn to get along."

There is no way Alanna is going to fall for this.

But she does.

Alanna doesn't realize she just signed her own death

warrant the moment she places her hand into Luna's. Luna smiles as she too can see the reality that she's won.

"Excellent. First things first. We need clothes and toiletries if we're expected to stay here."

Alanna nods, removing her hand from Luna's. "Okay, I'll go into town and grab some things. In the meantime, might be worthwhile thinking about what you're going to tell the medical board. You're a model patient, after all."

"I am?"

"Yes, you and Dutch are the only patients in Parkfields's history to ever escape, only to be returned and rehabilitated. Everyone is eager to hear your story."

Alanna smiles broadly, believing her bullshit. She is broken beyond repair. I can't help but compare her character to Constance Blackwood in the novel penned by Shirley Jackson. Always smiling, it seems she never saw things for what they truly were as a coping mechanism.

Constance refused to accept the things she did, and also the things she knew.

Alanna is the same.

She's living in a fantasy world because in that world, she doesn't have to accept what she's done.

She leaves us alone, and the moment she does, Luna wipes her hand on her T-shirt as if needing to rub Alanna's touch away. She turns to look at me with a smirk.

"There's someone else who needs to pay for their role in this."

I wait for her to share who.

"Noah," she says, and her smirk is replaced with a scowl. "I intend to expose Parkfields for the hell on earth that it is, but not before Noah gets what he deserves."

"That motherfucker," I say, clenching my jaw because it's apparent something else has happened.

Luna averts her gaze, and an anger overtakes me, robbing me of breath. My heart clenches and I purge my fury the only way I know how—I play. I play so damn long, my fingers cramp and my body aches, but the pain only fuels what's to come.

Luna colors in with Bobby, while I fruitlessly look for a way out.

The door in the greenhouse is now locked, which confirms that Daddy and Alanna have left. They have their lives to live, as they don't want to stir any suspicion. I'm half tempted to break down the door, but if I do that, we go to the police with what proof?

Our tale is so fantastic no one would believe it as the truth. And Daddy and Alanna are well aware of that. They're upstanding citizens, while Luna and I are merely the "crazy people" who got a second chance.

Luna has been trying all day to get any information out of Bobby. But so far, she's failed.

She doesn't press, and it's apparent what a wonderful mother she was. I can see and hear her sadness because, without a doubt, she's thinking of Misha when with Bobby.

I decide to check out the rest of the house and leave Luna with Bobby because I am seconds away from exploding. This is no life for either of them to live, and I feel a failure for not doing more.

My leg is getting better and I can stand for longer, so I

venture up the stairs. This house is barely standing, but in some ways, it adds to the charm of it. I look into each room, hoping to see something new, hoping to see a way out.

I don't, however…that is until I get to the end of the hallway and notice a patch of frayed carpet wetter than the rest of the hallway. I peer up at the ceiling, and what I see has me kicking myself.

An attic.

The hatch is ajar, and I jump up, pulling on the cord. I can't believe when a ladder folds outward, appearing untouched unlike the rest of the house. I climb it and ascend into darkness.

Boosting myself up, I stand on the wooden floor, which seems solid, so I walk on it, searching for some sort of light. I bump blindly into random things, but as my eyes adjust, I find a small camping gas lantern. I switch it on and see something I wasn't expecting to—this attic is in good condition.

It looks as if this is someone's room.

Holding the lantern out in front of me, I examine each corner and am sickened when I see old rusted chains and cuffs attached to a wall. Near it is a single stained mattress. There are drawings on the wall which are done in crayon.

I walk toward this creepy-as-fuck scene and take a closer look at the scribbles, which, judging by the faded appearance, were done a while ago. It's a scene that contrasts my current surroundings. It's bright and colorful, thanks to the sun and rainbow which shine brightly in the blue sky.

There's a small girl playing with a dog near a lake, and in the background sits a mansion on a hill. It's drawn in black. As I lean forward and strain my eyes, a chill comes over me when I see the red blob near the house has arms and legs.

It also had a head…which now sits a few feet away.

I guess this drawing was done by a child who either has a very morbid imagination or drew this from memory. I wonder who the child is, and if he or she called this place their bedroom?

I take a look around but don't see anything else which strikes me as odd.

The rest of this house is in shambles, and the one place which should be a mess is kept in immaculate condition. Something isn't right.

I decide to leave the lantern behind as I don't want Alanna or Daddy to know I was here. I descend the ladder and leave the hatch ajar, how I found it.

It surprises me when I see that it's dark outside. I didn't think I was gone for that long. This place is like a fucking black hole.

After being in the attic, I want to shower. It's ridiculous, but I feel like I am covered in filth. Whatever happened up there isn't good.

I wait for the water to warm up as I strip off. Hopefully Alanna brings us some clothes, unless she fancies us walking around naked.

This is beyond frustrating being reliant on others as your freedom has been stolen.

Standing under the spray, I hang my head low, the warm water kneading out the knots in my back. I feel a hundred years old. I clutch the crucifix at my throat, asking an invisible god for help. I don't think he's listening, however, because the sins I've committed have doomed my soul to hell.

I feel helpless and I hate it.

Suddenly, a warmth soothes the helplessness, and that's

because Luna stands behind me.

She loops her arms under mine and begins washing my chest with the bar of soap. Her front is pressed to my back. She tends to me with such care, I close my eyes and lose myself in the woman who has changed my world.

I hate that we're here. But our history has been paved with sadness and bloodshed since the moment we met. Is this our normal? Is that what our future holds because once this is finally over, can we forget all that we've done?

Will Luna forever look at me and be reminded of a past we both want to forget?

The thought has me gripping her wrist, with the intent to stop her because I don't deserve her kindness.

But she gently pries her hand away.

Before I can speak, she stands in front of me. No words are spoken, but her beautiful face says it all. We connect without talking, something we learned to do when locked up against our will.

I run my thumb along her hot mouth, wiping the fallen droplets away. She peers up at me with those beautiful eyes and leaves me a mess as always. We know that our future is uncertain, but we've both lived like each day is our last, and that's because they may have been.

She stands on her toes and begins kissing my neck softly. I arch my head back, threading my fingers through her hair as she tongues over my throbbing pulse. She continues to kiss down my throat and over my collarbones, using her tongue to lick away the water which trickles down my skin.

I watch as she kisses and licks my chest. My cock is hard.

Luna gently bites my nipple before taking my dick into her

hand and commences stroking my shaft.

A groan explodes from me because whenever she touches me, my body goes into overdrive. It is never enough.

Her mouth and hand move in unison. I try and coax her to kiss me. But she stubbornly stands her ground and I know why that is when she drops to her knees and takes my cock into her mouth.

"Fuck," I curse, thrusting forward and hitting the back of her throat.

I quickly try and pull back because that wasn't intentional, but Luna grips my hips and encourages me to fuck her mouth. I can't stop because I want this as much as her. I take her face into my hands and pump my hips.

She gags and pulls away…only to take me back into her mouth and continues giving me the best damn blow job of my life.

She sucks and tongues the underside of my cock while clutching my thighs. She's all wet, her flesh pink and soft, and I am so fucking turned on, I'm seconds away from coming in her mouth.

She is relentless and doesn't stop, and when I peer down and see her touching herself, I almost explode…but when I do, it'll be inside her.

Lifting her up, I slam my mouth to hers, kissing her fiercely. She doesn't have time to recover before I spin her around and press her against the tiled wall. She arches her back and spreads her legs and that's all the invitation I need to sink into her pussy.

We both moan the moment I am in deep, but I can't wait to savor the moment. I begin fucking her hard, gripping her hip and encouraging her to bow her back further so she can bounce on my dick. She does exactly this and the sight and sounds are just too much.

Her pussy clenches around me, and I slam my fist against the tiles, groaning loudly. "Again."

She does as I order, moving her lithe body as she anchors herself by splaying her palms against the wall and taking everything I give as she rides me hard. I grip her hips, controlling the rhythm and wanting to hold on to Luna because the floor is slippery and I am not holding back.

The water sloshes around us and her ass is like a delectable peach. I smack it—hard.

I've always been an ass guy and when an ass such as Luna's is within reach, all I want to do is eat it and…fuck it. I know she likes ass play as she's not shied away from it. I continue fucking her and run my thumb along the pleat of her ass.

The water acts as some lubrication, but it's going to take a lot more than that if I want to take her there. I instead circle her ass with my thumb until she loosens up and opens to me like a flower in bloom. As I fuck her, I gently work my thumb into her ass until I sink in deep.

She gasps, and just as I'm about to retreat, she clenches and sucks me back in.

I fuck her with my cock and thumb, spreading her ass wide, deepening the angle of both penetrations. The sight is so glorious, I never want it to end, but I know Luna wants to come.

I hold one hip while spreading her ass wide with the other hand, so I fuck her harder and faster because I've got her. I want her to milk every last drop of pleasure from me because I won't come until she does.

She turns over her shoulder to look at me and my fuck,

I want to mark this woman as mine. It's so barbaric, but she belongs to me and I want everyone to know that she does.

She watches me fuck her and doesn't hide the fact that she approves of what she sees as she tongues that sexy upper lip.

I want to die.

I smack her ass one more time as I pull out and slam back into her pussy. She gasps as her eyes close and she comes in a wild frenzy. I watch the mess I made with pride and the moment she stops convulsing around my cock, I'm about to pull out, but Luna reaches around, holding me to her.

"Come inside of me."

I don't need to be asked twice and do as she says with fucking pleasure. I come so hard, I see stars, but this is the only way to experience sex.

When I'm done, I collapse onto her back, supporting her by wrapping my arm under her stomach. We're both panting, catching our breaths because it only gets better.

I gently spin Luna around and kiss her softly. "I lose all control with you," I mumble against her mouth.

"Good."

Reaching behind her, I switch off the water and reach for a towel. She is sleepy on her feet, and I love the look on her. I dry her off before wrapping the towel around her. I grab the other towel and do my thing, unable to take my eyes off Luna and her flushed skin.

I brush my fingers through my wet hair, realizing how long it is.

Luna is watching every movement and when her chest begins to rise and fall rapidly, my dick is instantly hard again. She smirks and reaches down, rubbing my cock through the towel.

"I always get my man hard again," she whispers, eyes locked with mine as I forget to breathe. "Because the second time is always better."

First, second, third...I'm not complaining because being with Luna is always fucking perfection.

Thirteen

Luna

I'm dressed in the simple white dress that was left for me in the kitchen. Clothes, supplies, and food were also left, which makes me think we won't be seeing much of Alanna or Daddy unless we have to.

I hope they're running scared because Dutch and I have proven that we're not going to be victims. We will do what they want…only to watch their kingdom crumble around them when we burn it to the ground.

It seems strange to me that they don't just kill us and claim it to be a horrible accident. But I believe it's because of Alanna's affection for Dutch that we're still alive. As for Daddy, he clearly wants the bad press gone.

Dutch is playing piano, and I know he takes his frustrations out while doing so. It's apparent music is his outlet and I believe he's used it as a wall to hide behind. Music has always been

there for him and been his true love since he was small.

I'll never forget what I saw between him and Alanna, but I guess if music was involved, Dutch was torn. I know he would never hurt me, but I don't know if push comes to shove that he would be able to do what I want to Alanna.

I don't care if her past is tragic. Or that her childhood was disturbed. We all have a choice in life, and Alanna chose to hurt so many others for her own selfish gain. And it's because of this that I don't intend on telling Dutch what I plan on doing.

I don't have a plan per se, other than Alanna being dead at the end of it.

However, I'm afraid that Dutch may have a change of heart at the last minute, wanting to help Alanna because I know him; his heart is big and kind. There's no way he has Misha's heart without remnants of Misha remaining.

Misha would do the same thing.

But there is no fucking way I am letting her live. And I'll do anything, even fight Dutch until the death if I have to, to make sure she dies, and dies by my hand.

If what Dutch says is true and she has been starved of love, then I will lure her in that way. I can't fight with hate. But I can with love.

Bobby enters the kitchen, dressed in his overalls and shoes with laces he tied on his own. I still haven't been able to find out anything about him, but it's clear he's not had the best start in life. I hate that he's here.

He deserves to be playing in the sunshine. Not hidden in the shadows.

"Are you hungry?"

He nods and climbs onto the seat at the counter.

I decide to make pancakes from the measly supplies that were left for us. And what kid doesn't like pancakes?

As I combine the ingredients, a memory crashes into me of when I was in my kitchen at home, making pancakes for Misha.

His big blue eyes would widen in excitement when I put his pancakes in front of him. They were always shaped differently which was more fun than eating them. I can still hear his excitement when asking what his pancakes would be.

Tears sting my eyes because now, my son is merely a memory, memories which were stolen away. But they're returning, and I don't intend to ever forget again.

Brushing away my tears, I place the Mickey Mouse ears-shaped pancakes on a paper plate and present them to Bobby with a smile. His little face lights up when he sees them. I give him a plastic fork, which he happily accepts before sawing off Mickey's left ear and stuffing his little mouth full.

I have zero appetite, but cook the rest of the mix as I know Dutch will eat what I don't.

Once I am done cleaning up, I see Bobby playing with two cars, using the counter as a raceway. I wonder if Alanna actually cares for him. Or if she's just using him as a pawn in her sick game. If she wasn't a doctor, I could pretend he was hurt or sick, and needed to go to the hospital and use that as an excuse to get out of here.

But she would only send people here to examine him.

We truly are their prisoners in every sense of the word.

"Hey, baby." Dutch wraps his arms around my middle, kissing the top of my head. It's amazing how natural things feel with him in this far-from-natural situation.

"How'd it go?" I ask, leaning into him.

"Great. I don't think I've ever played music as I do now. I suppose it's the circumstances we find ourselves in."

He steals a pancake and I laugh, turning around in his arms. I can't help but admire him as he is shirtless and those V-muscles I like so very much are pronounced. His eyes are exceptionally blue, just as they always are when he finishes playing.

He is like a walking Instagram filter. He's beyond good-looking. He's a work of art—mind, body, and soul. His blond hair is getting long and I run my fingers through it.

"You need a haircut."

He allows me to fuss over him, chewing his pancakes with a smirk. I want to kiss that smirk from his face, but don't because Bobby is watching us. However, I do want him to see what "normal" interactions are because God knows the horrors he's been exposed to.

"You both need a haircut," I say, smiling at Bobby, who continues banging his cars into one another.

I can see something is on Dutch's mind, but he doesn't want to say what it is with Bobby in the room. He reaches for a piece of paper and red crayon and begins to write something down. Once he's done, he offers me the paper.

I read over it and look at him, confused, as what he wrote makes no sense. He said he found what appears to be a child's room in the attic. The room is equipped with chains and a single mattress as a bed.

"What is this place?" I whisper, shaking my head.

It's not Bobby's room. Well, I don't think that it is. But Dutch is certain it's untouched, unlike the rest of the house which is barely standing.

This place deserves to be burned to the ground as nothing but horror lives here. And that's just confirmed when I hear my name being called from outside the front door.

Dutch pauses from chewing, and when my name is shouted once more, he quickly grabs the cooling frying pan as a weapon. "Stay here."

I scoff in response and instead, snatch the flashlight off the counter.

"Kiddo, I need you to go to your room and cover your ears, okay? Wait for me to come get you," Dutch says to Bobby, trying to stay calm. "It's going to be all right. We won't leave you."

Bobby jumps down from the stool and surprises us both as he hugs Dutch's legs.

Dutch ruffles Bobby's hair, but it's evident he's as moved as I am. "Go."

Bobby does as he is told, his little legs almost too fast for his small body as he runs from the room.

"Luna! Are you in there?"

That voice…I know who it is.

"Kyle?"

"Who the fuck is Kyle?"

"Joy's son," I explain, running to the front door. "Kyle!"

The door is locked, so I race to the closest window and see him standing on the porch, cupping his hands to peer into another window.

"Kyle!" I scream, banging on the window.

"Luna?"

A relieved sigh escapes me when he runs over to where I am.

"Open the door," he says while Dutch scoffs.

"Is this kid for real?"

I ignore Dutch's wisecrack. "I can't. We're locked in."

"What do you mean? You lost your keys?"

"Oh my fucking god," Dutch says with a cynical laugh. "If he's here to rescue us, I think we need a backup plan."

"Kyle, you need to go to the police. Tell them we're being held against our will by Dr. Alanna Norton." It's a long shot, but at least it'll draw some attention to the place, and a thought hits me—we have Bobby.

He can vouch for us because he will talk if it means saving Dutch. It's clear his love for Dutch is deep and if that love is threatened, I know Bobby will talk.

"Kyle!" I scream because him standing around is not helping. "Go!"

I know this is a lot to take in, but he can go into shock after he goes to the police. Maybe I am just so desensitized to this, I've lost my humanity.

"We're kinda in a hurry, buddy," Dutch says from behind me.

His unimpressed tone snaps Kyle into action, and he nods. "I'll be back."

He takes one last look at me, and I hold my breath because this might be it—we might actually get out of here alive.

He sprints from the house, and Dutch and I watch until his figure gets smaller and smaller. My stomach twists in knots, and only when he disappears from sight do I turn around and exhale in relief.

But that's all in vain.

"Fuck!" Dutch curses, banging on the window. "No, you fuck! Don't talk to him!"

Spinning back around, I see Kyle has returned, but not with the police—he's with Noah.

Panic and fear overwhelm me, and I want to be sick. But I don't have time for that.

I watch as Noah walks Kyle back to the porch who animatedly points to the house while talking incessantly. I can't hear what he's saying but bless him for thinking Noah is one of the good guys.

"For fuck's sake," Dutch spits, moving away from the window. "Luna, it's fucking time. Do or die, baby."

He lunges for me, kissing me with a heightened passion, because we know things are about to get messy. But no matter what happens, we see this through to the end.

We break apart, and Dutch hides in the piano room, frying pan in hand, while I stand in the doorway, waiting for Noah to enter. When the lock clicks open, I place my hands behind my back, gripping the flashlight.

I have no idea why Noah has keys to this place, but I can question that later.

"She said a Dr. Alanna Norton is holding her against her will," Kyle says frantically as the door squeaks open.

The daylight hurts my eyes because I've been locked in hell for endless days and nights, but my vision has never been clearer. The moment Noah sees me, I smile.

Kyle is talking, but I have no idea what he's saying because all I can focus on is ripping off Noah's head.

"Miss me?" I mock while Noah smirks, locking the door behind him.

He does something that confuses me—he suddenly tosses his keys out the window.

Dutch is about to charge out from the room, but life doesn't want to cut us a break it seems when Noah reaches into his pocket and pulls out a gun. He places it at the back of Kyle's head.

"I did miss you," he replies, while Kyle's eyes widen.

"What's going on?"

"Where is he?" Noah asks as he knows I wouldn't be anywhere without Dutch.

I make no eye contact with Dutch, hoping we still have a chance to catch Noah unawares.

"I'm not playing!" Noah shouts, shoving the gun into Kyle's head, who squeaks in fear.

Every part of me wants to fight, but I can't. I won't drag Kyle into this mess. But I'm afraid it's already too late.

"I'm sorry, Luna," he says, his horror evident. "There was a signal from the GPS on my car which was traced back to here. I just wanted to help."

"It's okay, Kyle," I assure him because this isn't his fault.

"No, Kyle, it's really not okay," Noah mocks, cocking the gun. "Because in about three seconds, we're going to see what the inside of your head looks like."

I know the things Noah is capable of. His threat isn't empty.

"It's me you want. Let him go, and I won't fight you. You can do whatever you want to me. Just let him go."

Noah ponders over my offer, but we both know he's merely humoring me.

"Whatever I want?" he says, moving his lips from side to side in contemplation. "That's a very dangerous offer. I mean, what I want right now is for you to get on your knees and beg."

"Beg for what?" I ask, unable to keep the disgust from my

tone.

"Beg that I don't blow this kid's head off. Beg for forgiveness for breaking my nose. But most of all, I want you to beg me to fuck you."

Men like Noah get off on power, and I've never surrendered. However, given the circumstances, I'm not sure if I have a choice.

I don't need to look at Dutch to know he is pleading I don't do this. But as I see it, this might work in our favor.

With Noah distracted, Dutch may be able to catch him off guard.

As far as plans go, this is a clusterfuck waiting to happen, but what other choice do I have?

Noah has a gun. I have a flashlight. The odds are not in my favor.

"Fine, you win," I say, slowly revealing what I have in my hands as I drop the flashlight at my feet.

Noah smirks. "Cheeky little sweetheart. What else are you hiding?"

Dutch is biding his time because we both know Kyle won't be able to fight Noah. So this is all on me.

"Let him go, and I'll show you," I reply, ensuring my confidence shines.

Noah won't fall for a doe-eyed act, so the only angle I can play is me doing this because I have no other choice, which is what he wants.

"Come here, and I'll let him go."

This won't end well; I just hope it won't end well for him.

I walk toward Noah, wishing I could give facial cues to Kyle to stomp on Noah's foot, or rear back and connect with his nose. Anything that'll give us an advantage.

But the fear in Kyle's eyes reveals how desensitized I really am.

"Stop," Noah orders.

I do.

"Take off your dress."

Again, another way for him to humiliate me. But has he forgotten I took my clothes off for a living and exploited men's stupidity for my gain?

If I waver, Dutch will think I'm scared and swoop in to rescue me. So without a second thought, I slip my dress off over my head. I toss it to the floor, daring Noah to do better.

Kyle turns his cheek as best he can with a gun pointed at the back of his head to protect my modesty. I appreciate the gesture, but things will get a lot worse before they get better.

I only have on underwear. But that's still too much for Noah.

"Those too."

He won't be satisfied until I'm entirely degraded. But again, I hold my head high and take off the white cotton underwear. I don't shy away or cover my nakedness. I stand proud, daring Noah to do his best.

"Touch yourself."

I exhale slowly, needing a moment because this man is beyond vile.

"Why me? From the very beginning, you showed an interest in me. Why?"

Noah smirks, and I realize it's because he knew me. And it's not just from the dirty magazines my pictures were in. This is personal.

"I don't think I gave you permission to talk."

I know Dutch is about two seconds away from ripping off Noah's head, but I can't let that happen. If I give Noah what he wants and distract him for long enough, it might give Dutch the window he needs to take him down.

There's no room for error, which is why I lock eyes with Noah and commence touching my breasts slowly. I circle my areola with my pointer, ensuring the strokes are deliberate to hypnotize Noah in a sense.

Kyle is still looking away, but I have Noah's full attention.

I know how to seduce men. I did it for a living. But Noah isn't a man; he's a little boy with a god complex.

I use everything he's done to me as fuel to lure him into this trap which he set for himself. Like Dutch once told me, he tunes into the universe to hear music.

So I do the same thing.

I move my body in sync with the howling wind outside as the music flows through me. I use myself as an instrument and play Noah, who is utterly engrossed as I slither my hands down my body. I never break eye contact with him and make him believe this is all for him.

Swaying my hips, I allow Dutch's music to steer me as I close my eyes and remember the way he looked behind the piano. His fingers moved with ease as his silver rings caught the candlelight. His dirty blond hair shielding his downturned face. The muscles in his upper body taut and defined. And my most favorite thing of all—the top button of his jeans undone, revealing the soft hairs from his navel, leading downward.

I know how they feel when I run my fingernails through them. As well as when I lick his stomach, leading down to his dick.

This show is for no one else but Dutch because I love him with every echo of my heart, and with that, I rub two fingers over my sex, not surprised to feel I'm wet. I only have to think about him to get turned on.

This has never happened with anyone else before and I know if we get out of this unscathed, I want him to be my forever. I can't remember life without him, and I only want to make new memories which don't involve death or getting myself off in a room full of people.

My nipples tighten when I relive the memory of Dutch and me being utterly lost in each other. The way he touches me, kisses me, I know he loves me too. Through hate, we've found love, and that is rather incredible.

I remember the way his mouth dominates mine. The way his touches set me on fire. I wish my fingers were his, but I pretend that they are. I rub over my aching center, surprised I am this aroused. But I know it's common for feelings of anxiety or fear to be overcome with feelings of pleasure.

It's the perfect balance.

And right now, I would rather come than deal with what's ahead.

I hear a muffle, then a thud, like someone dropping to the floor. I don't open my eyes, however.

I continue chasing my orgasm as I think about Dutch and those impossibly blue eyes softening as he tells me he loves me.

Hands grip my upper arms roughly, tossing me to the floor.

I still don't open my eyes.

Desperate lips lick and suck at my neck before leading across to my mouth, molesting me with a frantic tongue.

205

I don't focus on this reality, but rather, I am lost in a world where it's just Dutch and me. A world where there's no pain, only love.

I know this is killing Dutch, watching and not being able to help. But he knows I can handle myself and that we only have one shot to get this right.

"You're right, I took an interest in you because I knew your…son. Who do you think sold him his drugs? Who do you think he worked for to feed his habit?" Noah whispers into my ear as he pins me with his weight.

"He thought he was better than all of us, but your boy was nothing but a junkie. And a self-entitled little shit, thanks to his momma spoiling him. He owes me a lot of money, so I figure you can pay off his debts…but not before I finally fuck this little cunt of yours, and you're going to love it. You can thank your son for all this."

The question of who Misha's dealer was has been answered. Makes sense why Noah knew where to come. Nothing in this entire affair has been a coincidence. But Dutch and I are caught up in a mess we never wanted to create.

As I see it, Noah is, in part, responsible for Misha's, therefore…he must die.

I can feel his erection digging into me, so I reach down and begin touching him over his jeans. He moans into my mouth as he assaults my mouth and the moment he plunges his tongue down my throat, I bite down—hard.

I'm about to twist off his dick, but a loud thwack ends my fantasy, and I'm dragged back to reality when I open my eyes and see Dutch standing above me, frying pan in hand. The usual blue to his eyes is now consumed in black.

I've never seen him this angry before.

He glares at a semi-conscious Noah, who moans on the floor beside me. The blood trickling from the corner of his forehead confirms what I thought—Dutch smacked him in the head with the frying pan.

He is about to hit him again, but I calmly say, "No, he deserves to be awake for this."

Dutch wrestles with his desire to maim and kill, but he eventually concedes. He offers me my dress, which I accept and slip on. Once dressed, he picks me up and crushes me into his chest.

"That was the hardest thing I ever had to do. Please don't ask that of me ever again."

"I promise," I whisper into his neck, his smell comforting me.

Looking over his shoulder, I see Kyle slumped on the floor. I assume Noah knocked him out so he could give in to temptation—silly little lamb because he's about to pay the price for his arrogance.

"He was Misha's dealer," I reveal, looking at the son of a bitch who I want to punish in every possible way.

Dutch lets me go and I see something pass over him.

"What is it?"

"It explains why Old Timer was giving him the drugs he stole from the hospital." When I look at Dutch, confused, he explains further. "Old Timer helped me out in exchange that I was to give him my meds. I saw him give Noah the drugs, and I wondered why he wanted them. I now know."

"Oh my god," I gasp, sickened. "That hospital is nothing but evil. This is all connected for a reason. It was never a coincidence. Joy. Alanna. Jonathan. Misha. Me. You. This was all a fucked-up cosmic kiss of the universe which fated us to hell.

"Jonathan is the reason for all this. I wish that bastard wasn't dead because I would kill him a thousand times over for what he's done."

Dutch sighs before planting a kiss to my forehead.

He looks over at Kyle, and I wonder what he's doing as he checks his pockets. "No cell," he explains. "He probably left it in the car."

"I saw his dad before I came here," I share. "Kyle isn't his son. He doesn't know who the father is."

Dutch pales as his thoughts are suddenly on the same path as mine. "His father couldn't be?"

"At this stage, anything is possible. Joy was sleeping with Jonathan and seemed to have a strong connection with Misha. Could it be because Misha was Kyle's half-brother?"

Vomit rises because that is beyond horrifying. But Joy was hardly one to grapple with her morals. Look what she did to my son.

"Either way, I can't let anything happen to Kyle. Blood or not, he will always be Misha's brother. He's family, and I protect my family."

Dutch nods and carefully picks him up. "I'll put him in the bedroom. Noah knocked him out pretty hard. I don't think he'll be awake anytime soon."

"Good."

Dutch doesn't ask questions as he leaves the room with Kyle over his shoulder.

The moment I'm alone with Noah, I inhale sharply as what

he revealed sinks in. How can one person destroy the lives of so many? Especially someone as…regular as Noah.

Misha could have changed the world. But he never got the chance because this asshole played a part in his demise. I'm not blaming Noah because in the end, Misha's choices were his alone. Just how Noah chooses to do horrible things.

Every choice has a consequence—and I am Noah's.

Gripping both his ankles, I drag him into the kitchen, taking great satisfaction in every sharp shred of debris that sticks into him. He groans but is too out of it to fight back. I drop his legs and peer around the room for something to tie him with.

Dutch appears, old rope in hand like he read my mind. "The attic," he explains, and it doesn't surprise me.

He walks over to Noah and yanks him up by the front of his T-shirt. Noah hangs like a raggedy doll as Dutch displays his strength and throws him into a rickety wooden chair. His anger is apparent, and I won't lie. The alpha in him turns me on.

He jerks Noah's arms behind his back and commences tying him up. This won't hold Noah for long, so I have to ensure he's far too incapacitated to move. Once Dutch is done, he takes a step back, and without hesitation, slaps Noah across the face to wake him up.

I'm surprised he didn't knock him out with the force, but Noah eventually comes to.

"Wha—" he slurs, his brain slowly playing catch-up when he tugs at the rope around his wrists.

"Hi, sweetheart," I mock as he's done to me many times.

"Untie me," he demands, eyeing me something vicious.

I laugh in response. "How does it feel?"

He took great pleasure in binding me to that hospital bed,

ensuring I was humiliated in every possible way. It's now his turn.

"My memory is coming back," I reveal. "I remember all the disgusting things that you've done. And I remember that you liked it."

"Fuck you," he spits, his bravado shining strong. That will change very soon.

"What happened to you for you to be this way? Didn't your mommy hug you enough?"

Dutch chuckles, enjoying the show.

"Just so you know, your little boy did anything, and I mean anything, to score." His demented smile is innuendo enough.

"I can't change the past, but I can the present…one which you won't be existing in."

I reach for a packet of matches off the dirty counter, which is broken in half, and light a match. The flame is hypnotic as I brush a finger through it.

"Tell me what you did to Misha," I say, lighting a few candles which have blown out. "How did you meet him?"

The warm hum of the candlelight dancing in the wind is the only sound which fills the room.

"What do you want to know?"

"Everything."

"Your son was as crazy as you," Noah replies. "On the outside, he appeared to have his shit together, playing ball, dating the popular girl, but he was messed up. And the way he dealt with that was to get fucked up.

"But like every junkie, one taste had them craving more. And when more wasn't enough, he was willing to do anything to quiet the noise in his head. They're all the same. Coming to me saying it's the last time, but we all know it's bullshit.

"Don't shoot the messenger. It's not my fault he was damaged. I suspect that's the case because he didn't want to disappoint you. He turned to drugs instead of his mother… which doesn't say much about your parenting skills."

Noah is saying this to throw me off course. But his words only make things sharper.

"What else?"

Noah's smug smile falls off his face as that clearly wasn't the reaction he was expecting.

"Don't hold back," I quip, blowing out the flame on the match right before it burns out.

"He would come here and get fucked up, crying in the corner of the room about his daddy. Felt sorry for the kid."

"So to help him, you offered him a job?" Dutch snarls, his anger palpable. "You are a motherfucker."

"You should be thanking me…you can live because of his dead heart."

Dutch advances forward and punches him in the jaw.

Noah's head snaps back with a satisfying crack. He spits out a mouthful of blood, eyes filled with rage.

"Alanna met him at the hospital," he says with spite. "He was looking to score. That day condemned his fate. She found out who he was and whose son he was. We're all connected because of that day. She asked me to introduce them and got to know him. I don't know much else about that…you'll have to ask her. But she took a shining to him."

I failed as a parent. All of this is my fault. I never understood any of this, but now that the pieces are falling into place, I realize that Misha is the epicenter—just like his heart—to this all.

It was one chance meeting which triggered this nightmare.

"So you worked at Parkfields to get free drugs which you sold and made money from?"

"Guess so, and not to mention, there's something about crazy chicks. Money can be made everywhere. You just need to know where to look. I'm an entrepreneur."

Dutch scoffs, not at all humored.

"How long did Misha deal for?"

Noah purses his lips in thought. "I don't know. Two years or so."

Now this is a shock. How could I not see it?

I think back and try and remember any signs—but I didn't see any. He was always my beautiful boy. He could do no wrong. But there was so much wrong and now he's dead because I was too blind to see the truth.

"He was a functioning junkie, Luna," Noah says, as my poker face has slipped. "Happens all the time. With that smile, he was my best dealer. Could sell to anyone, and the more he sold, the more he got high."

Noah is happy to share these details because he thinks he has the upper hand, that he somehow is the one in control. But I've heard enough.

Lighting another match, I walk behind the counter and reach for a plastic spoon left on the bench. I use the flame to mold it into what I want. The action is somewhat cathartic because this will be over soon.

"We're all to blame for something. I will never forgive myself for not being able to help Misha. But unlike you, he was more than a messed-up kid. He was loved. And his memory will always live…unlike you."

I use the rough edge of the counter to shape the burned-down spoon into something other than a spoon.

"We all make choices in our lives and although Misha didn't make the right ones, he never hurt anyone other than himself. You, on the other hand…"

A small droplet of blood forms on the end of my thumb the moment I press it into the sharpened tip of my homemade shiv.

I lock eyes with Dutch, who nods.

He knows what I have to do and he won't judge me for it.

When I step out from behind the counter and Noah sees the shiv in my hand, his arrogance soon turns to panic. "I can help you."

"I highly doubt that."

"You want to bring Parkfields and Alanna down, right? I'm the character witness you need. I will tell the police everything. You kill me, and who will corroborate your story?"

He's right…but that's a risk I'm willing to take.

"What do you think?" I ask Dutch.

He walks toward me and gently places a kiss on the tip of my nose. I am instantly reassured. "I think you kill that motherfucker."

Such words coupled with kindness make me smile because, finally, Dutch and I can take back what was stolen from us.

"What? No," Noah says, fighting frantically to get free. "Please don't kill me."

I could drag this affair out, but honestly, Noah is an oxygen thief, and he has taken breaths that Misha will never take and for that, I calmly walk over to him and slash his throat open.

Blood spurts from the wound, coating my face, my dress, but I stand tall, watching Noah gasp for air as he struggles to breathe. Bloody air bubbles form at the wound on his throat, which pop as he continues to fight for life.

But this is the end.

Music suddenly drowns out his gurgling.

Dutch commences playing the most beautiful yet haunting piece of music. It begins to pick up speed the louder Noah gasps. It feels as though Dutch wishes to provide some beauty in something so grotesque.

I watch with utter satisfaction as his eyes lock on mine, no doubt cursing my name. I'll see him in hell, I suppose, because I, too, am a sinner.

The blood trickles down his neck, and the candlelight only seems to draw out the vibrant color. This macabre sight warms my heart, and before long, Noah's chest stops rising and falling. And just like that, he's dead.

I thought I would feel something, but I don't.

I feel nothing at all as the shiv drops to the floor.

Leaving behind the scene of madness, I follow the music in a trancelike state. When I see Dutch playing, a rush of desire overcomes me, and I revel in the madness as I slip off my bloodstained dress. I walk over to him and run my fingers through his hair.

He doesn't stop playing. In fact, the tempo increases, as does the urgency of the song. It feels as though he is encapsulating everything we just experienced into music.

From his hair, I work my fingers down his cheek, caressing over the stubble, before scratching down the side of his throat. The rhythm of his heartbeat pounds strongly, and I lean down and bite over his pulse.

He allows me to take what I need because the reality of

what I did crashes into me.

I killed a man, and I'll happily do it again.

Does that make me a monster?

Gripping Dutch's hair, I yank his head to the side, biting his neck harder. I don't know why I need to do it; I just take comfort in feeling his heart beat against my lips.

He doesn't stop playing. The music is beautiful.

I continue softly biting him—over his shoulder, down his back; I want to eat him alive.

I wait for the guilt to set in, but it doesn't. All I feel is the satisfaction of avenging my son and the excitement of delivering the same fate to others who have played a part in hurting Misha.

I kiss, then bite, then suck every inch of Dutch's slick skin. I want him inside me to fill the void which grows hungrier and hungrier as each second passes. I'm far from gentle, but we both need the fire to help remind us that we're still alive.

The notes end mid song as Dutch turns over his shoulder and loops his hand behind my head, dragging my mouth to his. We kiss like it's the last day on earth because it may well be.

He pulls my hair, angling my head so he can mouth fuck me with that tongue which has licked every part of me. I want him so bad, it hurts. This is a different kind of need and I know it's because of what I just did.

My body trembles, adrenaline coursing through me. I need a release, and I need it now.

I don't need to ask Dutch; he knows what I want as he stands and spins me so I'm bent over the piano. He takes advantage of me being naked and drops to his knees behind me, where he spreads my legs and begins eating me out from behind.

I arch my back and stand on tippy-toes as I want him to

215

devour every single inch of me.

He grips the backs of my thighs and angles his mouth so he's working between my ass and my sex. He is destroying me with every stroke of his tongue. I grip the edge of the piano, needing the support because he is leaving me a legless mess.

"Fuck me," I order because I need him inside me. I need the closeness that only he can provide.

With one last stroke of his tongue, he stands and I hear the frantic sound of his zipper being yanked down, followed by his jeans coming off. He grips my hips and positions his dick at my sex, rubbing me how I like.

He doesn't waver. He enters me in one swift stroke and we both groan because it feels incredible.

He commences moving, far from slow and gentle. It's what I need. The feel of him punishing me this way has me opening my legs wider, surrendering myself to him.

He spreads one ass cheek wide and sinks into me hard and fast. The cool surface of the piano only adds to the heightened sensation of being fucked this way. Even though this is carnal, it's also filled with love. Sex comes in many forms, but at the root of it, we share nothing but love.

"You bent over this piano as I fuck you is the hottest thing I've ever seen," Dutch pants, slapping my ass as he pulls out before slamming back in.

He is an animal, but I want more, and I hint at what more I want as I raise my hips, shaking my ass. We've dabbled in ass play before, but I want him to break me in half. It doesn't make sense, but in some ways, I need to be punished for what I did to Noah because I have no guilt.

"Baby—" Dutch says, out of breath. "Are you sure?"

I don't reply. I shift my hips so he pulls out and position my ass for his taking. I know this is going to hurt, and that's why I want it. I need the pain.

He uses the pad of his thumb to rub over my back entrance before gently sliding the tip in and out. While doing this, he sinks two fingers into my sex and commences fucking me with his fingers, back and front. I rock my hips, never having felt this full.

As his skillful fingers play me in a quivering mess, he works his thumb deeper and deeper into my ass. When he is all the way in, he slowly moves back and forth and around and around. It stings, but I know he's only preparing me for what's to come.

I focus on his breath. I can hear he is holding back in fear of hurting me.

I know it takes a lot of prepping for anal sex. The things you read about in books is all nonsense. It's not easy. It takes time and a careful lover to ensure it feels good.

And my lover is very skilled and knows how to make everything feel good.

He pulls out his thumb and spits in his hand. It's carnal and turns me on.

When I feel the thick head of his cock nudging my back entrance, I breathe slowly and on the exhale, Dutch slowly works his dick into me.

Instantly, the burn I feel is uncomfortable, and on instinct, I tense up. But Dutch leans down and commences kissing the side of my throat.

His fingers are still inside my sex and his lips on my throat. It's sensory overload, so I focus on this moment and let go. When I do, Dutch sinks into my ass very slowly. I feel like I am

217

being torn down the middle at how deep he is, but when he begins sliding in and out, the pain gives way to pleasure and he begins to fuck me.

He removes his fingers and steadies me by gripping my hips. He fucks me long and slow, his strokes measured.

"You okay?" he asks with a hoarse breath.

"Yes."

He begins to move faster, pulling all the way out, before sinking back in.

He does this over and over, allowing my body to adjust to this delicious intrusion and before long, I am meeting him thrust for thrust. It hurts, but it's a good pain. It's the sort of pain that reminds us we're alive.

When he reads my pleasure, he picks up the pace and fucks me harder. I can feel every single inch of him—his ample size brings tears to my eyes.

I reach around to my sex and begin playing with myself. I am so needy, every part of me wants to explode.

Dutch spreads my ass wide, the angle deepening. I cry out because this is surrender in its purest form.

"I love you," he pants, the sound of our flesh slapping music to my ears and heart.

"I love you." My orgasm is so close, I can taste it like sweetened honey. I want it, and I want it now.

I rub over my clit, bouncing back on Dutch's dick and as he pulls out all the way, only to slam back into me so hard, I jolt up the piano and come with a guttural moan. I lose all train of thought and lose myself in this moment that I'll never forget.

Dutch comes inside me with a roar.

When we're both spent, he pulls out, only to spin me around

and kiss me fiercely. I mold my body to his, never wanting to let go.

Once we catch our breaths, Dutch reaches for my hands and I see that they're bloody. I didn't even realize they were. The fact that we experienced such pleasure covered in blood seals our future wrapped forever in a bloodstained kiss.

Fourteen

Dutch

Peering at Noah's dead body should make me feel something, but all I can think is, did this motherfucker have to make such a mess?

I'm standing in front of his corpse, wondering where the fuck I am to put him. I don't want Bobby or Luna seeing him when they wake up. But I can't go outside to bury him. I can't even chop him up into tiny pieces.

When did my life turn to this?

I have Noah's gun tucked into my jeans at the small of my back. I checked his pockets for a cell, but nothing. The gun is a small win for us.

I don't want Daddy or Alanna knowing we have it, which is why I need to get rid of Noah.

He tossed his keys out the window which I'm guessing he did in case he ever ended up where he currently is. If not, I assume he'd wait for Alanna to come.

Or, maybe, there's a secret way out?

I've searched every corner of this house, and found nothing. Maybe I've overlooked something. It's a long shot, but I am fresh out of ideas.

Noah isn't going anywhere, so I decide to search every inch of this house in case I missed something vital. My leg is better, so I can finally walk without any pain. I start with the kitchen, looking under every bit of debris, but come up empty.

There isn't much in the way of secret passages, so I continue on to the next room and then the next, but nothing. I'm frustrated because I can't help but think I'm missing something.

But what?

The house is ransacked, and most of the rooms are filled with turnover furniture or garbage. But something niggles at me.

Why did Noah toss his keys out the window with confidence? There has to be a way out without a key.

I walk into the piano room and stare into the fire which burns softly in the fireplace. This room always provides me warmth; both literally and metaphorically. It's always the warmest room in this place...

"You fucking idiot," I curse myself as I run up the stairs to my bedroom where Luna sleeps.

Kyle is in another room where I assume he's still coming to.

I don't want to wake either of them, but if my hunch is right, then we can get the fuck out of here right now.

I stare at the same fireplace which is in the piano room, however, the one in here is never lit. I never paid any attention to it, but now, I pray that it's our way out.

Walking over to it, I examine it closely, looking for anything that's out of place. I run my fingers over the bricks, feeling for anything that shouldn't be there. There is a wooden mantel above the fireplace and it's the small hole at the end of it which interests me.

I bend low and peer into it, but I can't see anything. Why it interests me is because I don't know what its purpose is.

I quickly run downstairs and into the piano room, and as expected, there is no hole in the mantel above the fireplace. I tear at the cross around my neck and charge back upstairs.

"Dutch?" Luna sleepily asks as she sits up in bed, brushing the hair from her face.

I don't have time to explain, however, as I wedge the corner of my crucifix into the hole and wiggle it carefully. "C'mon, you asshole," I mumble under my breath because I know I'm right.

I don't feel anything give under the force, but I persevere.

"Dutch, what are you doing?"

I continue moving the crucifix, realizing this hole is, in fact, a lock and I won't give up until I feel…

"Oh my god," Luna gasps when there's a click before the brick wall of the fireplace slides across, revealing a secret passageway.

I crouch low, peering into the dark void, unsure where this leads. But I'll be damned if I don't find out.

Slipping the crucifix back on, I turn to Luna who is standing behind me, eyes wide as she too looks at the hole in the wall.

"Stay here," I say, knowing how this will go down.

"No way. I'm going with you."

Standing, I cup her cheeks, begging she does what she's told—for once. "Luna, please. We don't know what's down there."

"Which is all the more reason to come with you," she interrupts. "Bad things tend to happen when we're apart."

Which is true. But not this time.

"What happens to Bobby and Kyle if something happens to us both? All of this would have been for nothing."

"Please don't ask this of me."

"I'm not. In the end, it's your choice. But after everything we've been through, I'm guessing what's behind door number two isn't good. If I'm worrying about you, I won't be focused. And vice versa. I'll be back in no time. In the meantime—" I offer her the gun, but she shakes her head.

"You need it more than me. Besides, I can take of myself."

"I know you can, baby." Noah's corpse is proof of that.

We both know this is a horrible idea, but what other choice is there?

I've never been one for goodbyes, so I grip the back of her head and plant a quick kiss to Luna's forehead. I don't want to leave her. But I'll be back.

I don't look back as I snatch a candle from the mantel and crouch low and walk through the small doorway. It takes a while for my eyes to adjust, but then they do, I see that I'm inside the walls of the house.

I was expecting a room, but this leads out into a crossroads of walls. I turn left, leading toward the piano room and walk slowly, wishing to mask my steps. The walls are covered in cobwebs and insects and mice scatter when they see me approaching.

Creepiness levels just amped up to ten thousand because I hate to think who's been inside these walls, watching, unbeknown to the occupants.

A thought suddenly occurs to me. What if Alanna and Daddy never really left and have been watching us the entire time, watching and studying us like mice in a maze?

I shield the candle with my hand as there is a slight breeze. This narrow passageway is no coincidence—this was constructed with intent. My senses are sharpened and I anticipate anything and everything.

I continue walking until I see a small doorway at the end of the hallway.

"Motherfucker," I curse under my breath because I was right.

The moment I get to it, I crouch low and turn the old brass knob and open the unlocked door.

Wind and rain lash me because the door opens out to the roof. I peer out carefully and see the steep drop if one were to take one wrong step outside this doorway. The roof tiles look slippery, thanks to the rain and the moss growing on them.

I look to the left, however, and see there is some piping which leads to a long drainpipe. Far from ideal, but it can be done. If I can scale across this and climb down the pipe, then I can go to the front door where Noah's keys are.

There's no question as to what needs to be done.

I place the candle onto the floor, which has blown out thanks to the howling wind, and carefully grip the edge of the doorway and place my bare foot onto the piping to see if it'll hold my weight. Instantly, my foot slips, but I hold on to the doorway firmly.

Rubbing my foot onto the pant leg of my jeans to dry it off, I try again. I turn my body so I'm facing the roof and begin

carefully scaling the pipe. I hold on to the tiles and take slow, steady steps because I can't rush this.

The torrents of rain blind me as my wet hair sticks to my face, but I persevere. I don't look down, only focusing on how far I have to go. Thunder echoes loudly, followed by lightning. It feels as though the heavens are punishing me for my sins because the atmosphere is one of utter darkness and dread.

Each step I take only gets harder because the rain is punishing and the wind picks up speed. My fingers grip the jagged tiles because one wrong move and it's a long way down. I measure each step and the rain sounding against the roof reminds me of a high-hat sounding.

I zero in on the sounds the universe throws at me and hum along to the rhythm in my head. The chaos soon becomes music and I envision each sound a note I can play on the piano.

Music, as always, helps me, and I use it now to push past the reality of falling to my death. Each step is transformed into music and I hum along to the song inside my head. I know I use music as a coping mechanism; I always have.

But it's how I'm wired, and when I step onto the small ledge around the drainpipe, I embrace my strangeness because it's saved my ass time and time again. I latch on to the pipe and slide down it with ease, thanks to it being slick because of the rain.

When my feet touch the ground, only then do I peer up and see how far up I really was.

The earth is sludge beneath me, so I take big steps as I run toward the front door. A flash of lightning bounces off Noah's keys on the porch.

Snatching them, I race to the front door and fumble with

the keys. I try two, they don't fit in the lock. But the third, it clicks and I shove open the door. It slams shut behind me because the wind now resembles a hurricane.

I run up the stairs and down the hallway to the bedroom. "Let's go!" I shout, but the moment I enter the room, I stop dead in my tracks because Luna was right. Bad things tend to happen when we're apart.

Luna is where I left her, but Daddy is now with her—holding the shiv she made to kill Noah to her throat.

"Here he is," he quips with a large smile. "You're really too smart for your own good."

The gun at the small of my back is my only saving grace, so I need to play it smart. "So you have been watching us this entire time then?"

"Not the entire time."

"But enough to appear at the right times? Don't fucking insult me."

Daddy chuckles. "If you just listened, none of this would have happened. Lana is sweet on you, but I should have just killed you both and been done with it."

"Go on then," I challenge, calling his bluff.

If he wanted us dead, we would be already. It has nothing to do with Alanna. He needs us because of his precious reputation and that of Parkfields.

To a man like Daddy, his reputation is everything to him. His efforts to "help" those who need it are no doubt celebrated among his peers. To have that reputation tarnished would be a punishment worse than death.

But he knows he can't bet on Luna and me.

We're not going to roll over. So now, he needs to get creative.

"I don't need you both, so you choose…who lives and who dies."

"What?" Luna gasps, eyes wide.

"That's easy," I calmly reply. "You know I won't stop until one of us is dead."

"I know. But your death will have a far bigger impact because of who you are. And my colleagues are excited to see you perform."

"I won't be paraded like a prized poodle."

"I'm pretty sure you'll do anything I say to save the one you love."

Luna has always been my Achilles' heel. That's why she's still alive. I know she believes she's the reason for all this, but the truth is, I am.

"You know I won't do what you ask," I state firmly, subtly making eye contact with Luna.

We need a window where she is out of harm's way so I can shoot this fucker between the eyes.

"I saw the attic," I reveal, hoping to distract him. "Nice setup you have up there."

"You just can't mind your own business, can you?"

"Whose room was it? Yours?"

This house has been in Daddy's family for generations. The horrors these walls have seen would be ghastly.

"Shut up," he snarls, pressing the makeshift blade into Luna's throat. A droplet of blood trickles down her neck.

"How about you fight like a man, Big Daddy, and stop hiding behind women? Alanna has bigger balls than you do. What's your damage? Your momma didn't tuck you in at night? Or maybe she tucked you in too tight," I add, seeing as incest doesn't seem to be a big deal in this family.

On the outside, Daddy looks like a respectable, law-abiding citizen with his well-cut suit and dazzling smile. But it's men like him that are the most dangerous. Everyone suspects the bad guys to be monsters, but it's the "good guys" who are far worse.

"You're going to let us go and be thankful we're not going to report your asses to the cops. I don't care if they believe us or not. I'll take my chances." I'm talking up a big game because letting us go isn't an option.

But I need to bide my time until I can take this fucker down.

Daddy ponders over my threat and sighs. "I suppose it would be easier if we came to some sort of an agreement, as this arrangement isn't working."

"No shit," I counter.

Daddy takes his time while I look at Luna, hoping she can read my facial cues.

She can.

"Fine, you can go…but I want one thing in return."

"What?"

There's a pregnant pause before Daddy says, "This."

In one swift motion, he cuts across Luna's throat, her blood coating his fingers as she gasps for air.

And just like that, Daddy wins…

"No!" I scream, my world crumbling as he shoves her to the floor like she is nothing but garbage.

My heart breaks into a thousand irreparable pieces and although I don't hear Misha anymore, I know that he speaks to me via his heart.

He always will.

I run to where Luna is, bleeding out on the floor.

Dropping to my knees, I place my hands over her throat to stop the bleeding. "It's going to be okay. You're going to be okay."

She coughs, spittle and blood trickling down her chin. Tears are in her wide eyes because she's dying, and she knows it.

She didn't get a chance to live.

She doesn't deserve this fate.

Her eyes suddenly roll back into her head, and I lift her limp body into my arms. "Stay with me!" I cry, putting pressure over the deep wound.

I feel muscle and flesh beneath my fingers.

She opens her mouth, but nothing comes out. Her floppy hand finds the strength to attempt to pry my fingers away from her throat. She is asking I let her go, let her go to a place where there will be no more pain.

"No!" I scream. "I'm not about to let you die. Fucking no!"

But there's just so much blood.

I feel the life draining from Luna's body with every labored breath she takes. But it can't end like this.

"Don't leave me," I sob, blood and tears intermingled at this life which only seems to take. "You hear me! You fight!"

I suddenly understand how Alanna felt, watching the love of her life die and being helpless to stop it. Her preserving Jonathan and wishing to resurrect him doesn't seem so crazy now that I'm faced with the same fate because I would do anything to save Luna's life.

Her breaths slow, and her eyes slip shut. She's leaving me with each pained breath she takes.

I hear a trigger being cocked before the cool metal of a gun barrel is pressed to my temple. But this is a small mercy because I don't want to live in a world where Luna doesn't exist.

I brace for death as I embrace my love in my arms; if I'm to die, then I want to leave this earth with Luna by my side.

But an ear-shattering boom reveals this life isn't done with me just yet.

Peering up, I see Alanna standing a few feet away, smoking gun in her shaky hand, the gun she just shot Daddy with.

I don't know what's going on other than the fact that Daddy is dead because Alanna shot him straight through the heart. But why?

He's lying in a twisted heap, his body turned at a grotesque angle. It gives me no pleasure seeing him dead because he died too easily.

But that can wait.

"Alanna!" I scream, Luna's broken body in my arms. "Please help me."

She shot Daddy because she saw I was in danger. In her own fucked-up way, Alanna loves me. I doubt she would have done that if Luna was the one in danger, but she has saved me time and time again.

It's hard to see someone as the villain when they keep trying to save you.

Alanna continues staring at Daddy, appearing to be in shock at what she did. "He was going to hurt you," she says in a monotone.

"Yes, he was. You saved me. Thank you. But I need your help. Luna is hurt. Please help her."

She's a doctor, for fuck's sake.

Luna's pulse grows shallower and shallower, and I know it's

only a matter of time.

A thought suddenly occurs to me…

"Give her my heart! We know it's a match."

"What?" Alanna gasps, shaking her head. "No. I will not."

"She's dying, Alanna. She doesn't deserve this. Please help her. Help me. If you don't, then I will do it for you."

I rip the gun out from my back and place it over my heart.

"No!" she screams, shaking her head violently.

Alanna grapples with what to do because Luna dying benefits her. But her feelings for me are stopping her from walking away.

Another idea occurs to me…one where Luna and I both get to live. Not that I give a shit about my life. But I need to live to know that Luna survived.

"I will do anything you want," I beg, brushing away my tears with the back of my bloody hand. "I'll…love you and never leave you. I promise."

That's all Alanna's ever wanted—to be loved and never have someone leave.

And she knows I mean every single word because I will do anything to save Luna's life, just how she did with Jonathan.

"Promise?" she asks, her lower lip quivering.

"I promise."

She looks at Luna, who is cradled against my chest, and I know she wishes to have someone love her as much as I do Luna.

"Carry her into the kitchen," she orders before running out of the room.

I don't ask questions and sprint through the house, taking the stairs two at a time. I gently place Luna onto the kitchen counter, and when Alanna enters with her black doctor's bag, a small shred of hope raps at my heart.

She hurriedly searches through her bag, producing a vial and syringe. "It's so she doesn't feel any pain," she assures me.

At this point, I have to trust her.

Once she's injected Luna, she rips open packets of sterilized medical tools. "She's lost a lot of blood."

I stand back, watching as Alanna slips on gloves and examines Luna's wound. It's deep, but Luna is a fighter. Alanna looks at her gold wristwatch, and I assume she's waiting for the meds to kick in.

But there's no time.

"Just do it," I beg, hoping the pain of Alanna sewing Luna up will be enough to knock her out.

"It's not enough time."

"We don't have time!"

She knows I'm right and commences covering the wound with a brown solution. It smells like iodine. "I need to cut away some flesh."

"Do what you have to."

She nods, and when she reaches for the scalpel, I hope I made the right choice. I'm trusting the woman who is the reason why we're here.

She inhales, and on her exhale, she carefully cuts away the hanging skin at Luna's throat. Luna begins to convulse, a strangled moan trapped in her chest.

I rush over to her and grip her cold hand. "I'm here, baby. It's okay."

Alanna continues cutting the serrated wound with precision, her hand never wavering. Once the wound is cleaned up, she begins to stitch it up with care. I never let go of Luna's hand. I never leave her side and once Alanna is done, I realize I've just tied Alanna to us forever.

Something which I think Luna will never forgive me for.

"She needs blood," Alanna says, snapping off her bloody gloves and hunting through her bag. "We know you're a match."

I don't argue and offer my arm to Alanna who stabs it with a needle and feeds my blood into Luna. I watch the red life source flow from my veins into the clear tube and into Luna.

It's beautiful but macabre to watch.

Alanna cleans up, and every so often, checks the blood transfusion to ensure everything is going okay. She offers me some candy, knowing I'm feeling a little dizzy.

"Is she going to be okay?" I ask, sucking on the sickly sweet candy.

"I think so."

"She needs to go to the hospital."

Alanna purses her lips. "I can't do that. I do that and then questions will be asked. How do we explain what happened?"

She's right, because this is one big fucking mess. "Why did you shoot him?"

This is the only time Alanna's hand trembles. "Because he was going to hurt you."

"What happens now?"

Alanna peers over her shoulder at a very dead Noah. "We clean up our mess first."

She gently removes the needle from my arm, placing a bandage over it. She does the same to Luna before disposing of the medical waste like she would in a hospital.

I'm still a little dizzy, but when I walk over to Noah, I snap the fuck into action. "We bury him?"

She nods.

I grip the back of the chair and drag his ass through the house toward the greenhouse. Alanna unlocks the door and we trek through the torrential rain and winds toward the wooded area.

Dragging a corpse tied to a chair in the pitch black and through mud is as fun as it sounds, but when we get far enough, I drop the chair onto the ground.

Alanna turned back around while I was walking and I see why when she returns with a shovel in hand. She offers it to me, and I begin digging a grave.

Digging a grave isn't as quick or easy a task as they make it seem in the movies. But I continue because it's two graves I'll be digging.

"How did Noah know about this house? He told me he dealt to Misha. If this house has been in your family, then why did he have access to it?"

"He helped Daddy."

"Helped him how?" I hate to think of what his help entailed because I remember what he did to that poor girl in the tunnels.

Everything begins to make sense.

Daddy was the one calling the shots and I wonder if maybe Bobby is somehow connected to him.

"This world is full of monsters, Dutch. You think I'm one of them, but I'm not."

I don't ask any more questions because I can join the dots. I always wondered why Alanna didn't fire Noah's ass, but it seems she wasn't the one pulling the strings.

I suddenly remember the attic and the childlike drawings

on the wall. "Did Daddy lock you in the attic?"

I can read her discomfort instantly.

I then wonder if that is where she still sleeps, as I've not seen "her" room.

"That motherfucker." No wonder she's so fucked up.

I continue digging two graves, and we don't speak another word.

Fifteen

Dutch

Daddy and Noah are buried in shallow graves out back. It should be over. But it's far from.

Kyle is a witness and Alanna knows that if she lets him go, he'll go to the police. So he's upstairs, playing with Bobby.

Luna still hasn't woken. She lies in bed, asleep. And I've not left her side.

Alanna has brought some medical supplies over and hooked her up to an IV. I know she's doing this because we made a promise and I don't intend to go back on my word.

Alanna is checking Luna's vitals, and I hate that I don't look at her with utter contempt.

I can't.

She saved Luna's life.

That doesn't erase all the shitty things she's done, but it's hard to see her as a monster when she saved the life of the person I love.

I'm beyond exhausted, but I can't sleep.

The concert is not far away and even though Luna will probably never talk to me again, I plan on playing it. I will honor my promise to Alanna. I will show her love, and by that, I mean getting her the help she needs.

It's hard to hate someone who continues helping you.

I can't tell Alanna this, of course. But I will use the concert as an opportunity to hopefully talk to someone who can help me. It's a long shot, but Alanna needs help, and I can only hope that when she gets it, she might be able to live a normal life.

As for me, I doubt normal is on the cards for me ever again.

Once upon a time, music was the only thing that mattered to me, but life has changed so much. I needed to experience it to understand it and realize I was using music to hide behind.

The only thing that matters to me now is Luna waking up.

I run my thumb along the back of her knuckles, thankful she's a little warmer.

The pain I feel is indescribable. I've never felt it before. Not even when I thought I could never play music again. I thought that was torturing, but this is far worse.

I just need her to open her eyes…

My head is bowed when I hear a soft moan.

I lift my chin and see that my prayers have been answered. "Luna?"

Her eyes flutter open but keep slipping shut.

"It's okay, baby. You're safe." I lean forward in my chair, gripping her hand in mine. "Take your time."

And when her eyes open and remain open, it's as though

my heart begins to beat once again.

She turns her cheek to look at me, and when I meet her eyes, she does something which kills me—she smiles.

She wets her lips, and I quickly reach for the glass of water. I carefully place the straw to her lips and encourage her to take a small sip. When she does, she coughs and makes a pained face.

"I know it hurts," I say, placing the glass on the floor so I can retake her hand. "Do you remember what happened?"

She mulls over my comment before she weakly reaches up and feels over the bandage on her throat. She tries to speak, but nothing comes out.

"Don't push yourself."

But her eyes widen, hinting she wants to know what's going on.

Here goes nothing…

"Alanna helped you," I reveal, holding her hand tighter. "She shot Daddy because he was about to kill me. I asked that she helped you, and she did. You would have died if she didn't."

Luna yanks her hand from mine.

"Luna, I had no choice. What did you expect me to do? Let you die?"

She nods.

"No, and you would have done the same. I know you hate me, but that's the price I'm willing to pay."

Luna sighs and stubbornly opens her mouth because even though her vocal cords were almost severed, she won't let that stop her.

"What?" she barely whispers.

I know what she's asking—what did I promise in exchange for her life?

"To never leave her…and to love her."

Luna closes her eyes, disgusted.

"Luna—"

But she turns her cheek, angered I would strike a deal with the devil.

I knew it was coming, but I don't regret my decision. And I would make it again if faced with the same choice.

I give Luna some space and leave the room in search of Alanna.

I feel like someone other than me—every part of me aches. My heart is always heavy and I wonder if my body is rejecting the organ which changed every aspect of my life.

Alanna is on her laptop in the greenhouse. She always seems to be in here. I wonder why.

"Hi," she says, looking up at me over the rims of her black-framed glasses.

"Luna is awake."

Alanna sighs but eventually gives me a half smile. "That's good news. I'll give her some supplements in her IV to help nourish her back to health quicker."

This conversation is beyond weird. Once upon a time, she tried to kill Luna multiple times, and now, she's helping her get stronger.

"I was just reading an email from the medical board about the concert. They'd like you to speak briefly about your transplant. They know about the heart memory transfer, so I think they are interested in your experience regarding this."

I look at Alanna with wide eyes. "You're fucking joking. I will play the piano and play the best fucking piece of my life, but talking about the transplant? Alanna, that's insane."

"I know, but like I mentioned, you're a medical miracle. There are people from around the world attending."

I shake my head because she failed to mention all this.

"You promised," she says softly, and there isn't a trace of blackmail in her tone.

And I did.

I know what this will do for Alanna's career. Her name will never be forgotten.

But this makes my plan of getting her help nigh impossible.

"If I do this, do you promise that Luna and I can leave here freely? I will honor my promise to you, but I won't do that a prisoner."

"I promise."

I don't know how this will work, but I will figure it out once I get this concert out of the way and Luna and I are free.

"Okay, fine."

She claps happily, and a genuine smile passes over her face.

This is fucking crazy.

"Luna, you shouldn't be out of bed!" Alanna says, springing from her seat.

When I turn over my shoulder, I see the betrayal reflected in Luna's eyes.

Alanna is digging through her bag, but Luna shakes her head, hinting she'd rather die than have her help again.

She points to the bandage on her throat, asking how long will her injuries last.

"Your voice will come back in a few days. The scar, however, will take longer to heal. I will change the bandages for you."

In response, Luna flips her off.

Goes without saying Luna is not interested in any truce

with Alanna.

Alanna doesn't say anything but instead offers me a vial and syringe.

Luna has ripped out the IV, however, so I'm not sure what I'm supposed to do.

"I'm going to check on Bobby." Alanna gives us some time alone, which most would consider polite, but Luna glares at Alanna like she is about to tackle her to the floor.

Once she's gone, Luna snatches a red crayon and a piece of paper from the counter and frantically scribbles something down. She walks over to me and slams the piece of paper into my chest.

I read what she wrote: She will die regardless of whatever deal you made to save my life.

I sigh, frustrated by her stubbornness. "She could have let you die."

Luna raises her hand as if to say she should have.

"Luna, please, no more blood. If we kill her, we're just as bad as she is."

Luna almost rips the piece of paper in my hands as she writes something else.

She killed my son.

"I know, but—"

Luna points her finger at me, demanding I stop talking. She writes more.

You don't have to do anything, but if you try to stop me...

"You'll what?" I ask when I read what she wrote, but stopped because she doesn't have the guts to say it. "You'll kill me too?"

She doesn't reply, but it's written all over her face.

"I'm playing this concert. I'm sorry if you hate me, but she saved your life. She needs help, and I'm going to try and get it for her."

In response, Luna slaps my cheek, putting an end to this conversation.

And the ones after it.

I'm sitting at the piano, brushing my fingers over the keys as I hear the music in my head while Bobby watches me with intrigue. Alanna is sitting on the floor cross-legged as she reads over some files.

This is all so normal when, in fact, nothing about this fucking is.

Luna hasn't acknowledged me all day, and I've decided to give her some space. I know she hates me, but I hope she will understand why I did what I did.

Bobby bounces over to Alanna and offers her a marble from his pocket. She happily accepts with a smile, which makes hating her even more impossible.

I would be the monster if I didn't show her mercy, wouldn't I?

At this point, I don't know anything anymore.

Something doesn't sit right. I don't know what it is…but it's suddenly too quiet…until I hear a noise in the walls.

I don't cause a scene when I get up and excuse myself to use the bathroom. The moment I'm out in the foyer, I run up the stairs and into my bedroom because, as suspected, Luna isn't here, and the fireplace door is open.

"Fuck," I curse and quickly enter through the door.

I can't call out to her, so I mute my footsteps and hope I'm not too late. Luna isn't strong enough to be climbing on any roofs. I barely made it across unscathed.

With my heart in my throat, I quicken my steps because I can see light at the end of the corridor, which means Luna has found the door.

The closer I get, I see her standing in front of the doorway, peering down at the long drop.

"Luna!" I whisper-yell.

She turns over her shoulder, and when she sees me, she stubbornly attempts to climb out. In her haste, she loses her footing and slips.

"No!" I cry out, lunging for her and clutching onto her arm to stop her from falling to her death.

She fights me, but I wrap my arms around her and drag her back inside.

I keep her back pinned to my chest as she wriggles frantically. But I won't let her go.

"Please, stop. I'm not the enemy. I love you. Please understand why I did it." I'm tired, so tired, and it must show because Luna stops wriggling.

I kiss the top of her head gently, wishing she'd stop and see why I did this. But I understand she feels nothing but betrayal.

"She'll let us go. Just let me play this concert and then we're free. This benefits her career. She'll get all the love she wants after this from others."

Luna's breaths slow and she calms.

I slowly release her, half expecting her to throw me out the window.

But she doesn't.

She just looks at me with nothing but betrayal. In her eyes,

243

she'd rather have died than me save her life and "owe" Alanna anything.

"This is where we will agree to disagree," I state. "I would have sold my soul to the devil to save you."

Luna wets her lips before she says two rough words which has me realizing we will never be okay. "You did."

Sixteen

Luna

I've not spoken to Dutch for days. And that's not because my voice hasn't returned.

It's by choice.

Every time I look at him, all I can see is his betrayal.

How could he make a deal with Alanna? Has he forgotten what she's done? One good thing doesn't erase all the other horrible shit she's done.

And just in case he's forgotten, she is responsible for Misha's death.

There's no coming back from this for any of us.

If Dutch isn't with me, then he's against me. I wish it were different, but my freedom means nothing if Alanna doesn't suffer for what she's done.

I have decided to go along with this charade of a concert because, what better way to humiliate her than a public execution? I'm still doubtful she will allow me to attend, which is why I need her on my side.

She knows I am hardly the reliable witness for Parkfields, but maybe she thinks my freedom is more important than my revenge?

Regardless, I have a plan, one which will go against all my convictions, but I have no other choice. Kyle is aware of it, and he has my back.

Dutch is in the dark because his hero complex is sure to kick in and ruin everything.

I'm sitting with Bobby in the kitchen who is drawing a picture quietly. I've been so intent on formulating my plans of revenge that I haven't even paid any attention to his art. However, when I look at it, I blanch because no little child should be drawing something so horrible.

There is a boy who is holding a woman's hand. Both appear to be looking at a body lying on the ground. The red around the body hints that something unfortunate happened.

"Is this you?" I ask him softly, as my voice is still very hoarse.

He nods.

"Me?" I point to the lady.

He shakes his head.

"Mommy?"

Again, he shakes his head.

The person has long hair and is wearing a dress, which is why I assume it's a female. Surely it can't be Alanna.

I reach for the blue crayon and write Alanna's name near the woman.

Bobby nods.

This throws me for a loop because why is he holding her

hand? And why does it feel like this picture appears like she saved him?

I don't even want to fathom her as anything but the monster who tortured me just because my ex was her beau.

Groaning, I massage the back of my neck because my body aches all over. I just need this to be done.

"I brought you some things to wear." Alanna enters with a few flashy garments strewn over her forearm.

I doubt this is for me to traipse around in this filth, so I assume it's for her night of nights where she can brag to her friends what an amazing humanitarian she is.

I want to slam her face against the wall until her teeth break in her mouth, but I smile instead.

"Your voice still hasn't returned?"

I shake my head.

"This is normal," she assures me. "There are some dresses here. And some scarves. I thought you might want to cover your neck."

I don't sense any malice in her words. I don't like it. But I nod in gratitude.

How can she be so calm after killing her "father"? She is a sociopath with no conscience, that's why. But I can't help but think about Bobby's picture.

Why is she depicted as a savior and not as a sinner?

"Do you want to go outside for some fresh air?"

I look at her, eyes narrowed, wondering if she plans on burying me alongside the two dead men who are rotting in the ground.

Curiosity gets the better of me, however. I stand and gesture for her to lead the way.

Bobby smiles at Alanna when she gives him a granola bar.

I don't want to see any kindness from her, so I walk ahead, feeling out of sorts because I need to keep my head in the game. She unlocks the door to the greenhouse and walks outside. I half expect this to be a trick, but when I step out and see nothing but an open field, I follow her.

I have no idea why we need air, but here we are.

"I know this is weird," she starts with while I try not to scoff. "I know you can never forgive me for what I've done. I just loved Jonathan so much. And I was blinded by that love. I wanted to do anything for him and when he died, I just…went a little crazy."

A little? Try fucking diabolical.

"I'm trying to right my wrongs. Killing Daddy was the right thing to do. I know I can't bring Misha back—"

The moment she says his name, I turn around and slap her cheek.

She cups her face, surprised I would shit on her apology. But nothing she ever says will excuse her actions. But I need to remember the greater good.

"I deserved that."

I nod and continue walking before I slap her other cheek.

"I promise that if you vouch for Parkfields, I'll let you go. Joy signed over your money and possessions to me," she reveals while I try not to curse. "But I'll sign it back over to you…once you do what I ask. You'll never have to see me again."

I want to ask why, but I know; she wants Dutch. She believes if she turns over this new leaf, he will fall for her bullshit, and she will get the love she always craved.

I understand her messed-up childhood shaped her into the

psychopath that she is, but that doesn't excuse her actions. And nothing she ever says or does will change my mind.

I come to a stop by a drum and see burned-out debris in the bottom. Is Alanna trying to burn her past in hopes for a brighter future?

"Misha was a really lovely young man."

I clench my fists, calming myself down.

"I only spoke to him a couple of times. He was quiet, but I could see intelligence behind those blue eyes. I would have done so many things differently," she confesses, covering her face with her hands.

I cannot believe we are standing out here, talking about Misha like we're best friends. I had a best friend who fucked my son and killed him because Alanna gave her false information. Both can rot in hell.

"In every book, every reader wants to know why…why did the villain do what they did? They want to know their backstory to why they're the bad guy. I know I'm the villain in your story, Luna, and I'm sorry.

"I'm trying to make amends. I know I need help. I don't expect you to forgive me, but I will let you go after the concert. I will clear you as being medically fit and you can live a normal life. Joy, Noah, Daddy, they've all paid for their sins.

"You'll never have to see me again. But I…love Dutch too. I've never hurt him."

Is she really bargaining with me?

We both know that she won't let Dutch go. She once called him Jonathan in her delirium, so it's safe to say she would be more than happy for him to take Jonathan's place.

Is this her trying to call a truce so we can…share?

Something suddenly occurs to me, something which will turn my stomach, but I will do anything to make this bitch suffer in ways unimaginable.

Nodding, I make clear I still hate her guts, but I'll think over what she said.

Having enough fresh air for the day, I head back toward the house. Ironic, I know, that I prefer being in the house of horrors than out here with Alanna.

Dutch is playing piano and by the melancholy tune, it's safe to assume he is saddened with the silent treatment.

I skipped dinner and showered instead because what I'm about to do, I feel I need to be cleansed. This is the worst idea ever, but it came to me when Alanna mentioned her love for Dutch.

Her desperation is disgusting. But I will use it in my favor. Alanna wants love so badly, so I intend to show her love…only to take it away from her as she took away mine.

She isn't stupid. She knows I won't forgive her. I need to win her trust, and what better way than by earning that trust by love-bombing this bitch until she chokes.

I look at my face in the shattered mirror, my jagged reflection a perfect example of how I'm feeling within. Kyle is with Bobby. I gave him the choice to flee through the secret door. But he said he would stay and help me with my plan.

I know he's doing this for Misha. I can't tell him about Joy because no matter what she did, I don't want to hurt Kyle that way.

Sometimes arrogance really is bliss.

It's darker than usual, the moon in hiding, maybe too afraid of what it's about to witness. I have on an oversized T-shirt, but nothing else. My hair is still wet.

I walk down the stairs, psyching myself up for what I have planned. Dutch's music is always magical, it has the ability to transport any listener to another world. I cling on to that when I walk into the room and see Alanna sitting on the bench seat by the window, watching Dutch play.

I take a calming breath before walking over to him.

Alanna watches me closely as I wrap my arms around him from behind and cuddle into him. He doesn't stop playing, but the melancholy tempo picks up speed. I kiss the side of his throat, savoring him because I've missed this closeness between us.

He stops playing suddenly and turns over his shoulder to kiss me passionately. I kiss him back because regardless of the fact that I'm mad at him, I've missed him.

He doesn't keep it PG and devours me as he would if we were alone.

When I hear Alanna's footsteps, I reach out and grip her wrist, stopping her from leaving. I pull away from Dutch who looks at me with utter confusion, but that soon turns to horror when I lean forward and press my lips to Alanna's.

Alanna freezes, unsure of what's going on. But when I nudge her mouth open with my tongue, she concedes and kisses me back with passion. I don't let go of Dutch and continue kissing Alanna.

She moans into my mouth while I stop myself from biting off her tongue. This just isn't about revenge. It's about destroying Alanna in every possible way.

I want her to feel safe, loved, wanted, only to take it away in the most cruelest of ways.

My plan is to do what she wishes at this concert. I will behave, allowing her to experience the love and praise she is so desperate for…before killing her in front of her peers. I know there are a million other ways to deal with this, but this is the only way I see fitting for what she's done.

I don't want private. I want the entire world to witness her death, and done by my hand, as I want her to be shamed by the people she clearly thinks so highly of. I want to do this so everyone knows who Misha was.

He isn't just a name.

He was my son, a son Alanna murdered.

Kyle is to use the secret door to escape and get him and Bobby to safety. I know his dad can assure that.

I understand the repercussions—I just don't care.

I brush over Alanna's breasts, the thin material of her fitted blouse allowing me to feel her hardened nipples. I cup her ample breast which elicits a moan from her. I then sever our kiss, only to kiss Dutch's gaping mouth.

When he tries to speak, I tangle my tongue with his.

Alanna begins to stroke over my hair, my back, as I kiss Dutch slowly. He isn't partaking, however, and pulls away, glaring at me as he wipes his mouth.

He doesn't appreciate being treated like a pawn because he understands the game I'm playing.

In that case, he can watch.

I grip Alanna by the back of the head and kiss her once again. She is supple and lax, allowing me total control. I run my fingers up her leg before reaching under her skirt and rubbing over the front of her lace underwear.

She's wet.

I should feel shame for exploiting her weakness this way, but I don't. All I can think is how much harder the fall for her will be. And to add to that break, I slip my fingers inside her underwear.

I touch over her slick sex before sinking in a finger and begin playing with her.

She writhes and moans into my mouth as she spreads her legs, wanting more as she rides my hand. I add another finger and begin fucking her with my fingers.

She pants into my mouth, surrendering herself to me. I can't believe it's this easy.

As I'm fingering her, I rip open her blouse and yank down her bra so I can fondle one breast. I circle her nipple before flicking it with my thumb.

Her sex is hungry and so wet, and I am punishing her cruelly. But Alanna seems to be enjoying the brutality of it.

With two fingers still working her into a legless mess, I circle her clit with my thumb. I am all over her and when I bite her mouth hard enough to draw blood, she climaxes around my fingers, her sex sucking me into her vile abyss.

I don't even wait for her to stop convulsing.

I sever contact and with my fingers that are coated in her arousal, I rub them across Dutch's lips in spite. He pulls back furiously, gripping my wrist as he stands and drags me from the room.

A smile is on my face, regardless of the repercussions I'm about to face.

He hauls me up the stairs and tosses me into the shower. He

turns the faucet on and drenches us in cold water. I try to fight him, but he grips my throat and slams my back against the wall.

"What the fuck was that?"

I smirk in response.

"I know you can talk. You're just choosing not to. But what you did down there, that was cruel. You're playing on her weaknesses, only to what? Shatter them until she's completely destroyed?"

I hate that he knows me better than I thought.

"This isn't you, Luna!" he screams, his grip on my throat tightening. "I know you're angry, and you have every right to be. But this isn't right. She has said she'll let us go. Isn't that enough for you?"

I simply shiver under the cold water, refusing to speak.

"Fuck!" he roars, slamming his palm against the tiles inches from my head. "We have a chance at freedom, at living a normal life together! Why are you doing this? Talk to me, goddammit!"

Fine, he wants me to talk. I hope he chokes on my words.

"I hate you," I spit with hatred. "You're a fucking traitor."

He loosens his hold on my neck, which gives me the window to lift my knee. Sadly, he reads my intention and turns at the last minute so I connect with his thigh.

His fury is amped to a billion volts, and he does something which angers but turns me on in the same breath—he spins me, slams my face into the wall, and yanks up my T-shirt. I hear his zipper almost being torn off with urgency and before I can tell him to fuck off, he thrusts into me, robbing me of words and air.

He doesn't allow me to adjust to his length and begins fucking me hard.

He fucks me so hard my body slides up and down the wall violently, but I want it.

I need it.

I want him out of control because this emotion can't be faked. I may hate him for not agreeing with me, but I love him so much more, for I know when this is over and done with, I just may lose my mind.

He is trying to save me the pain, just how he always has.

All I want is revenge, but the demons which come with that will destroy me because I'm not a monster. And neither is Alanna at the root of it.

How can I condemn someone who is trying to do better, because wouldn't that mean I was a monster too?

I allow that thought to drift down the drain and focus on my man fucking me hard and fast.

I arch my back so he sinks in deep because I need to feel him. I need him to make me feel alive because maybe I'm dead inside. After everything that's happened, maybe I've reached the point of no return.

"I will fight for you," Dutch says, and I know he means my soul, my sanity.

There's no coming back from taking a person's life. I took Noah's and say I didn't feel a thing, but late at night, straddling sleep, I see his tortured face, I hear his pained screams. He's dead because of me.

And now I want to instill the same fate on Alanna.

What has happened to me?

Dutch grips my hips and rears down, biting the side of my throat. I scream and climax around his pulsating dick. This is dirty and primeval, and this is love.

255

No matter what happens, I know that I will love Dutch until the last beat of my broken heart. But I will kill him if he stands in my way.

Seventeen

Dutch

It seems the medical board went all out with this grand affair because only the elite fill this amphitheater downtown, and with security tight, I wonder just who exactly is on the guest list.

I'm in the dressing room, looking at my reflection in the mirror, wondering how the fuck I ended up here.

I'm dressed in a suit and bow tie. My shoes are polished. My hair is tied back, but the stubborn strands fall around my face.

Alanna ensured Luna and I rode with her and hasn't let us out of her sight. Bobby and Kyle remain in hell, which makes me suspect Luna is up to something.

Alanna's guard has lowered because of what happened between Luna and her the other night, which was a smart move on Luna's part, playing on Alanna's weaknesses to gain the upper hand.

What she did, showed me that Luna will do anything for vengeance, and although I understand, I can't let her condemn herself that way. I know Luna, and when all is said and done, she won't be able to live with what she's done.

And not to mention the fact of her going to jail for the rest of her life.

I want to save her that pain, but to do so, I know she's going to hate me more than she already does. I have a plan, a plan which Luna will never forgive me for.

There's a knock on the door before Alanna enters. She looks beautiful in a champagne-colored dress. Her hair is twisted into some elaborate bun, and her makeup is natural, accenting her beauty.

She smiles when she sees me. "You look wonderful."

"So do you," I reply, trying to amp myself up. It's hard to, however, when I know what looms.

"If anyone asks about Daddy, just agree when I tell them he had to tend to a family emergency overseas."

That's a can of worms I don't want to be getting involved in, so I nod.

It surprises me she's so blasé about his death. Maybe she's relieved? I suspect the room in the attic was hers once upon a time. It would explain why she's so messed up.

There are no winners in this story—only fucking tragedy.

Two men appear in the doorway, their bleached teeth ten shades too white as they smile my way. "It is an absolute honor to meet you, Dutch Atwood," one says, entering and shaking my hand with a little too much zest.

"Where have you been hiding?" the other asks, winking

like we're in some secret club.

"Just recovering," I reply politely. "Getting a heart transplant is tiring work."

Both men look at one another before bursting into laughter. I want to punch them in their faces.

Alanna smiles at me, her relief that I'm playing showing. "Dutch has been practicing tirelessly for tonight. His first performance since the transplant is a big deal."

"That's all thanks to you, Alanna. Your dedication to your patients and work is unmatched. We can't wait to hear about the journey which led to now."

The men leave while I exhale because I still have no idea what to say. Playing the piano is fine, it's the talking and the lying I have an issue with.

But all of that can wait when I see a face I'd almost forgotten, because it feels like a lifetime ago since I last saw it.

"Oh, Dutch," my mom sobs, running into the room and hugging me.

My father trails behind, always a man of few words. I nod at him over my mom's shoulder. She won't let me go.

"Alanna said you can come home. That you're better. We wanted to see you, but thought it would be better for you to heal on your own. I'm so proud of you, playing in front of so many people. My baby boy can show the world what I've always known—that you're special."

I wish I could return her emotion, but I think I am dead inside. I'm not resentful at them for having me committed. They thought they were doing the right thing. And if they hadn't, then I would have never met Luna.

But I'm a different person now. I guess Parkfields did

change me.

"Alanna, it's almost time for everyone to take their seats," a redheaded woman appears, a headset in place.

My parents wish me farewell, thinking a bright new future is ahead. But truth be told, I don't know what's on the cards for me.

What I do know, however, is that I'll be damned if all of this was for nothing because when Luna appears, I refuse to accept anything but a life fully lived for her.

She looks breathtaking in a red silk dress. Alanna no doubt has ensured she looks this way as she can't have her star witness look anything but perfect.

Luna smiles when she catches me staring at her like a lovestruck fool. "Break a leg."

Her innuendo has Alanna paling because it hits a little too close to home, which is exactly the reason Luna said it.

She loops her arm through Alanna's. "Shall we?"

Alanna grins, appearing genuinely happy. I can't help but feel sorry for her.

Luna doesn't, however, and both women leave the room.

This is a clusterfuck waiting to happen.

I hear a microphone tapping and the sounds of an excited audience quietening.

It's showtime.

Some man does a boring introductory speech, trying to be funny and dropping terrible medical puns throughout. I stretch my fingers, and that's as far as a warm-up goes.

The redhead reappears, talking into her headset and gesturing that I'm to follow her.

I walk behind her, suddenly feeling agoraphobic. I've been

cooped up in Parkfields, tied to a bed in wherever I was after the hospital, and then locked inside a haunted mansion. Being out here in the open is suddenly too much.

"Are you all right?" I vaguely hear the redhead ask because her voice soon morphs into a thousand snarling dogs.

This isn't my normal anymore. I've not been around people in so long, I feel as though I've forgotten how to be human.

"Shit." That's what I hear, and hands touching my forehead because I've slid down the wall and on the floor.

The redhead is barking orders, but I block out the chaos and focus on the one anchor which has always been present.

His heart…

Funny, I accepted it as mine, but now I feel I should acknowledge that it's because of Misha that I'm still alive.

The poor kid was caught in a web of deceit and greed, but his death wasn't in vain. I'm proof of that. There's no silver lining in this circumstance because Luna lost her son, but I will do this for him.

"I'm fine," I say, coming to a stand.

The redhead touches the headset in relief. "Keep him talking. Two minutes."

I focus on the sounds around me and the strong beating of my heart. The universe speaks to me, and I plan on speaking back.

We walk down the corridor and then up three steps, where the redhead peeks out through the part in the curtain, awaiting our cue.

This amphitheater is beautiful. It's been a dream of mine to play here. I just never imagined my dream to be a fucking nightmare.

"Please put your hands together in welcoming to the stage, Dutch Atwood!"

The redhead shoves me toward the curtain, shooing me onto the stage. Once I step out, I see just how many people are really here. I didn't ask Alanna for details because I never thought I would play as I figured she or Daddy would kill me first.

But here I am.

I see Luna sitting in the first row. She is the only muse I need.

The white Steinway grand piano with its red inner lid sits in the middle of the stage. It's every pianist's dream to play, not only because it's beautiful, but because it sounds almost unholy. The room is so quiet, you can hear my shoes on the stage floor.

I take a seat on the red stool and place my fingers on the smooth keys. That familiar ache burns in my belly. This is coming home to a familiar friend. I'm not nervous. I never am when I play. I'm not being arrogant. What I mean is that playing music for me is far more comfortable than conversing because song is my voice.

And now, I need this audience to hear what I have to say.

I skim my fingers against the keys, starting the piece off with memories of the moment I knew piano was my true love. I close my eyes and lose myself to the music which is gentle and slow. This time in my life was one of simplicity.

I then lead into when I knew my heart wasn't as strong as I wished it to be. The rhythm is melancholy because I can still remember the dull beating in my chest. Of course this was my mind playing tricks on me, but it made me tackle life differently.

Instead of embracing life, I ran from it, too afraid of finding forever, only for it to be snatched out from under me. I found solace in music, and if it wasn't for piano, I don't think I'd be here today; and that has nothing to do with my defective heart.

This part is sorrow laden, and I've done that with intent because when I reach the next section of music, I slam my fingers on the key, a contrast to what I just played and that's because I play with the memory in mind of when I woke with an alien heart inside my chest.

I could hear "his" heart the moment I opened my eyes. I think back to it and The Raven by Allan Edgar Poe is the perfect analogy to how I felt because all I could hear was someone rapping at my chamber door.

It drove me crazy. So much so, I tried to cut out the infernal bastard with my bare hands. That's what led me to Parkfields— unlike Disneyland, this was the unhappiest place on earth.

I punish the keys with an almost lunatic rhythm as I encapsulate every single emotion I felt in that place.

The desperation.

The desolation.

The fear of dying alone.

My hair has come free, and it falls around my face, but that's what I want; I wish to hide from the horrors which shaped me into someone other than me.

My heart squeezes because it's painful to tap into these memories. They are ones which remained forgotten for a while. This section goes on for seconds, minutes, hours, I don't know.

Music isn't about keeping score.

It's about touching someone with your pain.

And what better pain is there than falling in love?

My muse.

My Luna.

The music changes direction; there are highs and lows, just how my relationship is with Luna. Every single emotion I feel for her is thrown against the keys and expels from me in a rainbow of notes.

I put into song the moment we met, and everything that followed. Our life together is far from conventional, but to survive this, our love knows no bounds. It has survived in the bowels of hell and yet, here we are, still hopeful for something… more.

Which is why I can't let her throw it all away.

And that leads to the last interlude of music, the person who this story has always been about because without him, none of this would be possible.

Misha.

I put his story into notes; the man I've never met but changed my life and helped me live. And to honor him, I can't let anything happen to Luna. She's going to hate me, but I know that she cannot come up here and lie to these good people about Parkfields.

I know she will do everything to expose Parkfields for the hell on earth that it is, publicly of course, because she will want to shame Alanna in front of her peers, and once she's done that, she will tear out Alanna's heart, just how Alanna did to her.

Consequences be damned. She will happily go to prison or be re-institutionalized if it meant Alanna paid for her sins.

But I can't stand back and watch her destroy her life that way. I hope she will understand why I've done what I have.

The guilt, the betrayal, it's all put to music and when I play the final note, I hear him one last time.

Thank you.

Misha's voice is the closing note, which seems fitting as this started with him, and now it ends with him.

My hair falls around me, so I can't see a thing, but when the room erupts into thunderous applause, I smile. Music has the capability to change the fucking world.

I stand awkwardly, hoping the redhead ushers me off stage. But she doesn't.

Alanna instead appears on stage.

She is clapping zealously, tears in her eyes.

In some ways, she got her wish—I am her Frankenstein project. She gave me a heart and lived to tell the tale through song.

I know this will do wonders for her career. Her name will go down in history, and I hate that I've been a part of her victory.

The redhead rushes onto the stage and passes a microphone to Alanna, who gestures I'm to stand near her. I do as she says.

The crowd is still applauding, even Luna. I smile at her, memorizing her face because the next few minutes are about to change everything.

"I think we can do better than that!" Alanna says into the microphone, riling the audience up further.

She gestures her hand to the crowd, then over to me as she wants me to see all of this is for me. But this is for her.

I bow, which only incites them even more.

This is the greatest musical experience of my career, and it's all because of Alanna wanting to cut out my heart.

"Ladies and gentlemen, Dutch Atwood!"

The clapping continues when I see some men in suits discreetly walk down the aisle to where Luna is. She doesn't know what's coming…

Forgive me.

Alanna passes me the microphone which I accept. I wait for the crowd to settle before I speak. "You're too kind."

Chuckles echo off the ornate white walls.

"It's an honor to play for you tonight. It's also a miracle that I'm still alive."

The mood soon calms because who doesn't love a good sob story with a happy ending.

"As you may or may not know, I received a heart transplant. I was told I would die without one. Every day was a miracle. But I was okay with dying. If that was my fate, then I was going to live like every day was my last. The only regret I had was I wouldn't be able to leave behind a small piece of myself through music. But you all changed that by being here tonight, and that's possible because of Dr. Alanna Norton."

The applause starts up once again as Alanna shyly brushes the hair off her brow.

"Alanna never gave up. All she wanted was to help me, even when I didn't want to help myself. The transplant was hard on me and I ended up needing help, something which no one should be ashamed of asking for.

"Parkfields was the best place for me. I got the help I needed to get better. I heard voices and I now know that's a phenomenon called heart memory transfer. Something which Alanna will happily write about in her book."

There are astonished gasps because this was a curveball no one saw, including Luna.

"I am here to say that Parkfields shaped me into the man I am today, and that's all thanks to Alanna…the woman I love."

I lock eyes with Luna, begging she forgives me. But there's no forgiveness here. She simply appears as if she's been told Misha died all over again.

Unable to stand her pain, I reach for Alanna and bring her in for a kiss.

The crowd is silent before they explode in a riotous noise, which is what I wanted because the two men in suits are orderlies from Parkfields who have been instructed to bring Luna to Parkfields.

They have been told to make it discreet and to give Luna a sedative so it appears they're helping her out as opposed to her kicking and screaming. I make sure our kiss lasts long enough for them to escort her out.

When I break our kiss, I see her seat is as empty as is my heart.

We leave the stage, hand in hand, while Alanna looks happier than I've ever seen her before. Her happiness is at the expense of Luna's, but I hope she understands why I did what I did.

We're to mingle with the guests, which we do for what seems like a hundred torturous hours, but I promised Alanna that I would love her…and I never break my promises.

"Did you see Dr. Fueller's face?" Alanna says with a giggle in the back seat of our rented limo. "She was adamant to tarnish my reputation so her hospital could receive all the government funding. But you ensured that'll never happen ever again. I knew you'd change the world, Dutch Atwood." She snuggles into my side.

The night has turned ugly, but I've always found solace in the darkness, so much so now.

It's a still night. The moon in hiding, and when we approach the gates of Parkfields, it seems fitting the night is somber too.

"I know you're worried, but you did the right thing," Alanna says, assuring me. "She belongs where she can get help, not a prison cell."

How I struck this deal with Alanna was easy—I used Luna's tactics and love-bombed Alanna. I told her that Luna was unstable and not a suitable character witness for Parkfields.

But I was.

I would dazzle her peers and ensure Parkfields's reputation was safe.

They would believe me because after my performance, I'm sure I could have convinced them Santa Claus is real.

I also told Alanna I feared Luna would hurt her and that I didn't want Luna to suffer that way. That she needed help, help only Alanna could give her. And Alanna trusted me because I gave her what she's always wanted—love.

I told her I intended to keep my promise to protect her from Luna, and protect Luna from herself because I loved them both. Alanna trusted me because this plan is foolproof. But it's at the expense of Luna.

But I want to help her…and there's only one way I can. And in one place.

The limo pulls up at this forbidding-looking hospital which houses nothing but pain. We step out into the cold night. I remove my suit jacket and place it over Alanna's shoulders.

She smiles, her eyes alight with love and life.

She uses her swipe card, and we enter the place I never

wanted to step foot in again. I hate that Luna is here, but I didn't know what else to do. I couldn't stand back and watch her destroy her life.

She'll understand why I did what I did…in time, she will. It needed to be done here.

Alanna slips off her heels so they don't echo on the floor, it's her calling card as such, but she's changed. We all have.

I've done things I never thought I was capable of. But love, fuck, love makes you do some crazy things.

We walk down the hallway which is lined with broken hospital beds and wheelchairs missing wheels.

Red, white, and blue streamers limply hang from the ceiling—a Fourth of July memory captured in time. A red telephone booth with a black phone is randomly pressed up against one wall and across from it, a faded poster of Marilyn Monroe.

Above the doorway at the end of the corridor are the words Acta, non verba, which is Latin for "deeds, not words."

Alanna opens the door and all I can smell is death…

And I know that, because I've been here before. I've been here because Alanna brought me down here.

The corridors are dark, but Alanna knows the way. There's a leaky pipe somewhere. The buzzing of the fluorescents feel like a jolt of electricity coursing through my veins.

We pass rooms which are inhabitable.

This place is hell.

Alanna continues walking, humming a tune under her breath. She walks past a bathroom which is an immaculate white.

A single white tub sits in the middle of the room.

I suddenly can't breathe because it's so cold…and that's because I was once in that bathtub. And Alanna is to blame.

"Everything okay?" she asks when she sees I've stopped in front of the bathroom doorway.

But no, everything is far from okay because the holes in my memory are soon filled with color, so bright I can see what Alanna did.

"You can't behave that way. I'm trying to help you. I'm trying to make you better so you can play music again. I know that if you can do that again, everything will be all right. We'll be all right again. I love you, Jonathan. Please come back to me."

I blink away the memory, not wanting to alert Alanna and smile. "Yes, fine. It's just hard being here."

"I understand." She rubs my arm. "Let's say our quick goodbyes and then go home."

This was all part of the deal, I remind myself.

Alanna opens a door and when we enter, I see it's just as sterile as the bathroom. The walls are white tiles. There are medical tools on a silver trolley.

But the centerpiece is a silver gurney in the middle of the room, and strapped to it is Luna. She's wearing a white gown, the same one we once both wore.

But here I am in a suit and bow tie.

The leather straps are around her chest and legs, so she can't move. It pains me to see her this way.

"Luna," I say, the betrayal in my voice clear.

I can't help but think back to the time when I thought I was helping her by sending her back here.

She doesn't reply.

But her silence speaks volumes.

"We just want to help you," Alanna says sweetly, and why wouldn't she?

She's won.

"Can you give us a minute?" I ask her, and she nods, trusting me completely.

She kisses me on the mouth, rubbing salt in Luna's open wounds. She leaves, humming happily.

When she's gone, I guiltily walk toward Luna so she can see me. But she won't look at me. I didn't expect her to.

"I didn't know what else to do," I explain, needing her to understand. "People like us don't win. It's people like Alanna that everyone roots for. I knew you would humiliate and kill her on that stage. Tell me I'm wrong."

Luna can't turn her head because a leather strap is across her forehead. "I would have done that and enjoyed every second of it," she replies with contempt.

"And throw your life away?" I cry, not regretting my decision, but regretful it's ended this way. "I couldn't stand by and watch that. What do you think would happen? You'd have your revenge and then spend the rest of your life in jail? No. That's no life to live."

"Why did I go then? If this was your grand plan, why did I need to be there? Why did I need to see you profess your undying love? I know you're wholesome and want to see the good in everyone, but this is fucking ridiculous."

"I needed you to see that all of this is for you."

She scoffs. "You're a fucking coward. Don't you realize I would rather die than be locked up here? We could have tried to make people believe us."

"Who's going to believe us? We're just two people who

are…insane."

And maybe that's what we are.

But we all go a little crazy sometimes…

"I promised to protect you, and this is the only way I know how."

She finally looks at me, and her eyes are on fire as she says, "Go to hell…because I'm already there."

And that's her parting words to me.

With a sigh, I bend down and kiss her cheek before whispering, "Save me a seat, baby."

I pull away with a smirk…because she didn't really think this was the end.

Alanna enters the room. "Shall we go? The doctors will be here soon."

Luna's eyes widen, not understanding what's going on, and she couldn't, because I needed both her and Alanna blind.

Standing, I turn to Alanna, smiling sweetly. "Yes. Let's go home."

Alanna is none the wiser when I reach into my pocket and then extend my hand. She accepts, which is her downfall because in a split second, I inject the syringe which I had hidden in my pocket into her neck.

She gasps, totally surprised, before collapsing into my arms. I catch her and gently place her on the floor.

All the while, Luna looks on, completely stunned. "What's going on?"

"You didn't think it was done, did you?"

Luna is speechless as I begin unfastening the straps around her. When she's free, I help her off the table, only for her to slap my cheek.

I deserved that.

"Let me make it up to you," I say, bending down and picking up Alanna and placing her on the table.

"What did you give her?"

"Something to knock her out for a little while and make her hallucinate like she's on the best LSD." I should know. She once gave it to me. It was her error telling me what drugs did what.

"So what is this?" Luna asks, needing answers.

"This is plan B," I reply, strapping Alanna to the table. "There was no way I would be standing back and watching you ruin your life. No one would believe us. This place, Alanna, they're fucking bulletproof. We wouldn't win doing it your way. But we will my way."

"And what is your way?"

I smirk, ensuring Alanna is strapped in tight. "We both gave Alanna what she so desperately wanted—love. And that love earned her trust. As I see it, we take that away from her… and we make sure it hurts, really, really bad."

Luna's mouth parts when I walk over to the cart with medical tools and reach for a scalpel.

"What about Parkfields? We can't leave them here."

"And we won't. What's a little arson to cover a crime?"

The entire time, I had a plan, and that plan was to give Alanna what she wanted—love.

I promised her the world, only to take it from her. I professed my love for her because Luna's will is still in her name, and with no next of kin, the state, or rather, Parkfields would reap the rewards.

My very PDA is enough for those to believe Alanna left everything to me and not question it when I say she died in the

273

fire, trying to save the place she so loved. Daddy's body will also be among the dead.

"Alanna may go down a hero, but no one believes the bad guys. No one believes the people who they deem crazy. They think we're crazy, then let's show them crazy."

"Why didn't you tell me this? This entire time, I thought you didn't...love me."

"Baby"—I cup the back of her head and draw her forehead to mine—"I've done all of this because I love you...with every beat of my heart. If I told you, would you have agreed to it?"

She shakes her head slowly.

"I've got you, baby. Always. I just want to make sure you're okay with this. There's no turning back."

Luna sighs softly. "She took away my heart...so it only seems fitting...that I take away hers."

Her bloodlust gets me hard, and I realize that Luna and I are one of the same. You can't survive what we have and not be a little bruised around the edges.

But that's half the fun.

Maybe we should just embrace our darkness because being normal is so fucking...boring.

Luna reaches for the scalpel in my hand, running her fingernails across my knuckles. There is something almost carnal about this.

Alanna groans, which has Luna lifting her chin to the ceiling and smiling happily. Once she's composed, she walks to where Alanna is strapped down. The satisfaction Luna feels is evident. She is finally in control.

My heart skips in happiness, and I like to think Misha is happy too. He will never be forgotten. His mother will protect him to the very end.

"What's going on?" Alanna asks, frantically tugging at the straps around her wrists.

When she sees Luna standing by her side, she searches for me. "Dutch? What's happening? Untie me."

"Sorry, Doc, no can do. It's time you know how it feels to be the patient."

Her fear is palpable, and I almost feel sorry for her until Luna walks to a machine in the corner of the room.

"You used this on me...twice. Electric shock therapy to help me," Luna scoffs, tonguing her cheek. "You didn't want to help anyone but yourself."

"This isn't happening. It's just the drugs," Alanna says, squeezing her eyes shut, hoping this is just a bad trip.

If only...

"It is happening here. Let me show you." Luna slashes Alanna's cheek with the scalpel.

A stripe of blood bubbles to the surface, contrasting the pale skin of Alanna, who opens her mouth and begins to scream. "Help!"

"Tsk tsk," Luna quips, peering at the bloody scalpel. "You should know no one can hear you scream down here. Isn't that why you brought me, Dutch, and God knows how many others down here to torture because you're one fucking crazy bitch!"

Luna violently slashes at Alanna's other cheek this time, blood splatter coating her face.

Alanna struggles again, but it's futile—her time is done.

"I'll give you anything," she pleads, looking between Luna and me.

"Anything?" Luna asks, humoring her.

"Yes! Anything. Why are you doing this? I thought I was forgiven for what I did. I said I was sorry!" she screams. "Everyone deserves a second chance!"

Luna giggles, and my fuck, it's the hottest thing I've ever heard. "No, some people really don't. You played a part in my son's death. You knew who I was. I didn't stand a chance. I was subjected to your cruel games when I never wanted to play. You are pathetic. You had to keep the corpse of my ex because no living, breathing man could ever love you."

Ouch.

Even I flinch because that's gotta hurt.

Alanna's lower lip quivers. "You promised to love me. You promised to protect me."

I walk toward Alanna and peer down at her—how the tables have turned. "And I intend to keep that promise. You will be celebrated by your peers because of tonight. They will forever think you were loved. And I will protect you by not exposing what a fucking psychopath you are.

"The small mercy is that we don't allow the world to see what a monster you truly are because everyone seems to feel sorry for the bad guys—Ted Bundy. Richard Ramirez. Jeffrey Dahmer. They all have someone making excuses for why they were the way they were. And with your childhood, you're an HBO documentary's fucking dream.

"But some people…they're just born fucking bad."

Someone like Alanna would get sympathy—she's pretty, smart, and has a shitty backstory. The sympathizers would crown her a martyr. She'd be excused on some technicality, and before we knew it, she'd be Oprah's BFF.

Besides, this is her karma because every action has a

consequence, and she deserves everything that's coming her way.

"My Misha would have changed the world…but he never got the chance. It was stolen from him. I loved him with every piece of my heart. Do you know what that feels like? To have your world ripped out from under you?"

A tear slips from Alanna's eye. "Yes. More than you know. You've both broken my heart."

Luna bursts into laughter. "No, we haven't…not yet anyway."

"I saved your life."

"That was your mistake then. You deserve every single thing you're about to get."

Before Alanna can plead her case, Luna mounts the table, her primitive goddess taking the reins. She unbuckles the strap around Alanna's chest and when Alanna rises up, Luna punches her in the face. Alanna struggles as Luna pounces on her, pinning her down.

This is Luna's show, and I watch, utterly aroused as she rips open the front of Alanna's dress. I've seen this before, and I know this is going to leave a mess.

"No, please, Luna, no! Don't do this. You're not a killer. You're a good person. I'll confess to everything. I'll tell them what I did and the treatment of the patients. No more blood. No one else needs to suffer."

Luna uses her weight to keep Alanna down as she ponders on Alanna's offer of redemption. "What do you think?"

I shrug, unimpressed. "I think she can do better."

"You promised to never leave m-me," Alanna sobs, which is what Luna wants.

She wants to break her down and ensure she leaves this

earth with nothing but pain. "And he won't. Your heart will always be with him."

She leans down and presses a kiss to Alanna's mouth—the final goodbye.

Alanna sobs, terrified and alone.

I should feel something. But she conceived us—we are her creation, and it's time we showed our creator what exactly she reared into his world.

"P-please." It's her final plea. "Don't kill me."

Luna suddenly goes quiet, and I wonder if maybe she has a change of heart...but it's because of her heart and what was done to it that we're here.

"Oh, sweetie...you can't kill what's already dead."

Luna suddenly springs up and raises her arms above her head before bringing them back down and slamming the scalpel into Alanna's chest. She doesn't think twice as she begins dragging the blade downward, carving Alanna open like a turkey on Thanksgiving.

Alanna's wheezes become winded breaths as her body goes into shock. I wonder how it feels. She did the same thing to Joy, so it seems fitting the same is done unto her.

Luna's white gown is slathered in blood and the deeper she cuts, the louder I hear Alanna's heart beating.

It's music—a macabre beat that both Luna and I dance to.

Luna hums a song, 'Heroes' by David Bowie as she smashes down onto Alanna's rib cage with a tool which resembles a hammer. I understand the significance of this song.

This is dedicated to Misha.

Once Luna has opened Alanna up, I slowly walk over, and the gory, bloody mess is far from the precise incision Alanna performed on Joy.

But this, now this is a masterpiece.

I see Alanna's heart is still beating when Luna slashes through the top of the aorta and cuts through tissue and arteries so she can reach into Alanna's chest cavity and rip out her heart.

She holds it in her bloody hands, head hung in victory because this is how our story should end.

Alanna is dead...and my Luna...she's never looked more alive.

She turns to me, heart in her hands, and she has two blood teardrops smudged down her cheeks.

Even though she killed without remorse, her blood is mixed with tears because we're not complete monsters.

Only just...

I search the cupboards, and as expected, I find highly flammable fluids, which I commence drenching the floors and walls with.

"Baby, we have to go."

Luna nods, but I know she wishes she could kill Alanna a hundred times more.

She jumps down from the table and unstraps Alanna before tipping the table onto its side. She can't be found strapped down.

Her missing heart may be an issue, but with Parkfields's reputation, no doubt the townsfolk will conjure up a story that it was eaten by the patients.

Luna places Alanna's heart into the pocket of her gown for safekeeping. "I made a promise to burn this place to the ground. But not with innocent people at risk."

I reach for her bloody hands. "I just watched you slice through someone's chest and rip out her heart, and you're worried about the safety of others?"

Her lips twitch. "They don't deserve to suffer."

And this is why I love her.

"Up to no good again?"

Both Luna and I turn around to see Old Timer standing in the doorway. I hate reunions, but I am fucking happy to see this bastard.

"Snooping around again?"

Old Timer cackles but then looks over our shoulders and to Alanna's corpse.

Luna and I wait with bated breath for his response. "Nice dress."

Luna bursts into maniacal laughter. "Ready to burn this place to the ground? I promised you."

Old Timer digs into his pocket and produces a lighter. It doesn't surprise me. He offers it to Luna.

"Go gather everyone and make sure they're safe."

If anyone can do this, it's Old Timer.

He nods, and he knows this is goodbye. "Can I ask one thing of you?"

"Of course," I say.

"My grandson hasn't come to see me. Do you think you could keep an eye out for him?" Old Timer reaches into his pocket of tricks and shows me a picture of his grandson, as well as a marble. "His name is Bobby. Dr. Norton used to talk often to him when he visited."

"He took a real shining to her."

Luna gasps while I see how things have come full circle.

"I will do my best."

I'll tell him the full story once this is over with.

Old Timer grins a crooked smile. "I knew you were both trouble the moment I met you."

Luna gives him a hug, and he leaves with the important role of all.

Once he's gone, I look at Luna, who reaches for my hand. "Do you hear the music?" she asks while I smile.

"Always."

"I love you, Bowie."

"I love you, Misha."

I toss the lighter into the fluid which ignites the room into blistering flames. We stand hand in hand, watching it engulf the room—no more pain. No more sorrow.

Bowie and Misha are no more.

Hell has finally come home.

Epilogue

Luna

I'm always nervous.

I don't know why. He always plays like an angel. With that dirty blond hair falling over that chiseled face, shielding those bright blue eyes, he is a vision from above.

The way his ringed fingers touch over the keys like a lover's caress lulls the audience into the palms of his hands.

The night Parkfields burned to the ground was the beginning of our new lives.

Old Timer was able to save the people, but Parkfields thankfully didn't foresee the same fate.

The townsfolk didn't help douse the flames—they watched it burn, the eyesore they never wanted finally dead and buried where it belonged.

Dutch and I were thrown a curveball, one which saved us—Dominic traced Kyle's phone, which was outside the house of horrors. Kyle told him everything, and that's when the DA swooped in and saved the day.

He knew what we had done, and I was ready to be punished for my crimes. But it seems fate smiled on me that night because when Dutch told Dominic of our plan, he said he could make this go away. It was the least he could do because we protected his son.

We could expose Alanna, but he was worried the police would dig and if they dug too deep, our crimes would be found. Because Dutch and I are far from innocent in this story.

There are so many players in this intricate tale, but they're all dead. All that remains is us.

We survived.

They didn't.

The end.

And that was enough for Dutch and me because sometimes, life gives you a miracle when you least expect it.

"Daddy," says the blond bundle of joy in my lap as he points his chubby little finger toward the stage.

"Yes, that's right, Bowie. Daddy is about to play."

Our son was born from nothing but love, regardless of the circumstances in which he was conceived. He is our miracle… as is Bobby, who we've adopted. We have Old Timer and his daughter, Katerina's blessing.

My family was taken away in a heartbeat…only to be reborn within another.

I will always love Misha. He is the reason for this all. And his memory will never be forgotten. Dutch made sure of that when he penned a book in honor of him.

Simply titled Heart Sick, Dutch details the heart memory

transfer phenomenon which was an instant bestseller. Medical boards from all over the world wanted to study Dutch because of how rare he is, but he made clear he is no one's lab rat—well, not ever again.

Misha is never forgotten because people from all over the world have read his story through Dutch's eyes.

Dutch kept his word to Alanna and protected her even in death. No one knows what she did. What would it matter anyway? What repercussions can the dead get?

Her body was found, and Dominic smoothed the scandal over. With Parkfields no more, the patients were moved to a hospital that cared for them how they deserved. I know because I volunteer there. I never want anyone to suffer the way I did.

I may not have exposed the secrets of Parkfields, but I'll be damned if I stand back and allow it to happen again.

If anyone knew our story, I know they would see us as the villains as well as the heroes.

But I don't want either.

I just want to be me. I just want to live a normal life, in a normal neighborhood, with my normal family.

But when the lights dim and Dutch walks out on stage, I know normal was never fated for us.

We found love in darkness.

Dutch doesn't judge me for my sins. What we experienced warranted a little crazy.

And when the single stage light illuminates Dutch as he sits behind the grand piano in the concert hall filled with adoring fans, I know that that crazy will always run through our veins… and with every beat of our hearts.

Sitting in a glass case on top of Dutch's piano is a heart…at first, it was seen as grotesque. But when Dutch told his story, it was accepted and celebrated. It was because of a new heart that he is now a renowned pianist worldwide.

Everyone thought it was fitting his "old" heart was a part of his performance.

Dutch runs his fingers over the keys, just as he always does before he entrances the entire audience with his music. I love watching him play, but I have a secret I will never tell him.

I sit in the audience time and time again to look at that heart, in that glass case, as it's a reminder of everything I've done. Of everything I've experienced to be here and to be fucking alive because…it's not his heart inside that glass case.

It reminds me that my son was once a part of this world, and in some ways, he still is.

Inside that glass case sits Alanna's heart because Dutch kept true to his word—he protects Alanna's heart…with every beat of his.

Subscribe to my Newsletter:
https://landing.mailerlite.com/webforms/landing/b4j1v6

Heart Sick Playlist:
https://tinyurl.com/ahshfb59

About the Author

Monica James spent her youth devouring the works of Anne Rice, William Shakespeare, and Emily Dickinson.

When she is not writing, Monica is busy running her own business, but she always finds a balance between the two. She enjoys writing honest, heartfelt, and turbulent stories, hoping to leave an imprint on her readers. She draws her inspiration from life.

She is a bestselling author in the U.S.A., Australia, Canada, France, Germany, Israel, and The U.K.

Monica James resides in Melbourne, Australia, with her wonderful family, and menagerie of animals. She is slightly obsessed with cats, chucks, and lip gloss, and secretly wishes she was a ninja on the weekends.

Connect with Monica James

Facebook: facebook.com/authormonicajames
Twitter: twitter.com/monicajames81
Goodreads: goodreads.com/MonicaJames
Instagram: instagram.com/authormonicajames
Website: authormonicajames.com
TikTok: @authormonicajames
BookBub: bookbub.com/authors/monica-james
Amazon: https://amzn.to/2EWZSyS
Join my Reader Group: http://bit.ly/2nUaRyi

www.ingramcontent.com/pod-product-compliance
Lightning Source LLC
Chambersburg PA
CBHW070113120726
47909CB00002B/588